MANSLAVE

The Eunuchs held me in that freshly debasing posture, my feet in the air and on either side of me. I felt so helpless, not knowing what would come now.

Karif snapped, 'Keep still, slave. We have more work to do.' He had something in his hand, a smooth wooden implement like a small rod with a smooth conical end to it. He looked warningly at me from the end of the slab. 'Do not move. I shall not hurt you . . . unless you squirm.'

He stooped low over my ravaged and thrusting hindquarters, his bald head disappearing somewhere between my feet. My Mistress watched impassively. And I felt something nudge into the very sump of my forbidden passage, pressure coming at once to it.

Oh, celestial Heavens take me now and make me a spirit free from earthly misery!

MANSLAVE

J D Jensen

This book is a work of fiction.
In real life, make sure you practise safe, sane and
consensual sex.

First published in 2006 by
Nexus
Thames Wharf Studios
Rainville Road
London W6 9HA

www.nexus-books.co.uk

Typeset by TW Typesetting, Plymouth, Devon
Printed and bound in Great Britain by Clays Ltd, Elcograf S.p.A.

ISBN 0 352 34040 1
ISBN 9 780352 34040 5

Proem

After these many years, the Grand Lady has allowed me to grow back my hair now, and it is almost white. But only my own dear Mistress saw its straw-gold lustre when I was in my prime – and that was when my skull and my body were shaven to glistening nakedness.

I have known three Grand Ladies in all my humble lifespan in the Pavilion of the Divine Orchid Ladies, but I have only ever had one Mistress. And her beauty was a thousand times greater than the bloom of any orchid. Her grace was that of a goddess and, even in her advanced age, her benevolent wisdom flowed as fast as the Great River of Abundance. I, in comparison, had the brain of a feeble goat.

Oh, forgive me, Honourable Mistress, for saying this not to your gracious face, wherever it may be in that Celestial Heaven. But sometimes her sweet temperament could become like the spring sun rushing suddenly behind a capricious cloud. I can marvel now at the way her demeanour was at once the glorious sweetness of honeysuckle, and then in a trice the withering contempt

1

of the Black Moon. And only then would I see that dark glint of thunder in her eyes. Oh, yes, did I then not suffer that fleeting bolt of cruelty, even though it might have been so justly deserved? But I loved her no less for it, knowing those many unjust burdens she herself had borne – oh, plumed little bird of paradise in your silk-spun cage!

Yet, during those many full seasons that I served her, were they not always so rich in intrigue and forbidden pleasures? Whenever she permitted that my ugly servant lips should suckle her delightful flowerbud, would I not already be in heaven? Her jasmine-scented dew was to me like the hot nectar of her restless soul, even if she made my cruel constriction fly my spume to her bosom like a dart of my own hot passion. Oh, magic frog, how must you trail your silver thread as you leap from your wicked confinement, but never to be permitted the soft velvety cushion of her warm portals!

Yet, I hope she will not scorn my unworthiness now that I set down on parchment those sad accounts. And if in a hundred years to come there should be sympathetic eyes that read my words, then I ask no more than that those same eyes should turn up to that celestial place of spirits and then to wonder if this humble writer's soul shall perhaps be floating there, and smiling fondly at his gracious Mistress.

One

My bare feet were cold on the marble floor as the Eunuch-guards hurried me into the huge chamber. The humbling nakedness of my body would have affronted me as much as it would have my poor ancestors, but the sheer terror that engulfed me was altogether a more powerful emotion. It obliterated all other thoughts or feelings.

'Move faster, boy!' snarled one of my escort Eunuch-guards, tightening his grip on my arm.

I had been brought into the Pavilion of the Divine Orchid Ladies of His Imperial Majesty. The only men who ever entered upon those hallowed precincts were those who were not whole men, or those who would shortly be deprived of that wholesomeness that made them so. And although I had at least eighteen full seasons behind me, I was enough of a man of youthful wisdom to know my purpose here. And it would have taken an unwise man or an idiot boy not to shake in fear at what rumour said happened in this awesome place.

There were perhaps as many as four dozen women who resided here. They were dressed in gowns of such rich finery that the many lanterns made them shimmer. The jewels adorning their hair, necks, arms and ankles glittered like a million stars in the heavens.

And the women's faces were both curious and critical as they looked upon the new male entrants. And there were a dozen of us, each naked, each chained at the feet, each of us stumbling along between two yellow-robed guards. Our fearful eyes blinked and darted stupidly around at these strange faces that explored our wretched nakedness with such cold intensity.

The Eunuch-guards halted before a raised dais. Upon this had been set three large thronelike wooden chairs, side by side. Each one was ornately carved and lacquered, with inlaid twirls of gold-leaf and jade. Three elderly women sat on the plush satin cushions with almost regal indifference. Their sagging jowls and faces were so heavily painted and thickly coated with *maquillage* that they were almost grotesque. Perhaps once endowed with youthful beauty these seemed now devoid of graceful features. They might have been sinister masks, from which only coldly twinkling eyes shone out at us, their slaves.

The woman in the middle, despite her hunched-up posture, had the most imperious bearing of the three women. Clearly she was the senior. Even the younger women in the chamber – some of them perhaps of no more seasons than myself – were diffident in her presence. She might have been the matriarch or grandmother, only her demeanour was one of haughty disdain to them and lacked the slightest display of affection.

We were paraded before her, lined up there still in our nakedness and our shackles. A heavy silence descended upon the huge chamber. Everyone – slaves, guards and women alike – stood respectfully there, waiting for her to speak. Even the clinking and slithering of our chains was hushed now. And I shivered in my fear and my so vulnerable nakedness.

I tried to cover myself with my hands, but my escort tapped my arm with his baton. 'Put your hands at your sides ... and do not hide yourself from the Grand Lady's eyes,' he whispered, adding, 'Or she will punish you ... and me.'

I was second from the left in the line, and I was slightly taller and of a more muscular frame than any of my sorrowful companions, so that it seemed to me that the stature of my birthright made me stand out from the other young men. It was as if a thousand glittering eyes were examining me, alone. And my shame made my cheeks burn like hot suns.

'Only one dozen?' she asked gruffly, peering at us.

'Yes, Your Grand Ladyship ... only that many. The net was cast wide, Your Ladyship, but alas, the catch was poor.' A tall man, a Eunuch, dressed in yellow but wearing a brilliant crimson sash across his shoulder, was bowing before her. 'But, Your Ladyship, I think you will find that the lack of quantity is rewarded in their quality. They are fine specimens.'

'Huh! If they are fine, then *I* shall judge it so ... and not *you*, Karif!'

'Indeed, Your Ladyship. I apologise for my hasty tongue, Your Grand Ladyship.' He was chastened now but his bearing still retained the dignity of authority.

'Make them approach, Karif!' She beckoned, and immediately we were prodded to go forwards.

By now these younger silk-clad women were gathering around, careful not to get between us and Her Grand Ladyship, or in front of the two women on the thrones at her side. There was muted giggling, and one or two astonished gasps, but Her Ladyship silenced the culprits with a stern look. And then her eyes returned to us, roaming over our bodies, although neither she nor the two other women beside her so much as moved a muscle. There was no chink in their painted masks. Had it not been for their cold eyes, we might have been under inspection by giant dolls.

I was aware that now Her Grand Ladyship was looking at me – or more precisely at the place between my legs. Of course, I at once knew why. It was the same as when that cold-fish official and his guards had come to our village and demanded to look at the young men and boys. And we had been made to strip and stand there naked in front of our Headman's hut while the official examined each of us in turn, peering into our mouths and our ears, feeling our lean muscles with his grasping fingers, even making us touch our toes so that he could look between the scarps of our rumps.

I recall how His Imperial Inspector of Servants – for that was his title – placed his hands roughly on my two flanks and then prized them wider so that he could look right into the very sump of that private place. And then he turned me, peering down at my young manhood, smiling with such evident satisfaction. 'The Heavenly Gods have favoured you, boy . . . not that this will be important to you,' he sneered, motioning his guards with a curt sweep of his hand.

At the time I had been puzzled by the strangeness of that remark, but the humiliation of this irreverent examination had made my cheeks smart with mortifying embarrassment, stifling all other thought. And then I had been taken from my village, and a small pouch containing a hundred silver taels had been left for my people – they who had been as my family since birth. Only my dear mother had wept, whereas the others had rejoiced. And, before taking his leave of the villagers, His Imperial Inspector of Servants had announced so patronisingly how much I was blessed with good fortune at being selected for His Imperial Majesty's household. But, if it were good fortune for the village of my birth, was it perhaps misfortune for me?

Her Grand Ladyship was holding a jewelled long-handled fan in her hand, and she pointed it at me. 'You! Come nearer.'

But I was paralysed with fear and embarrassment, such that my two escorts had to prod me forwards with their batons, making me stumble from the chains at my ankles. I stood there before the three women, wanting to die and shrivel up like a dead moth.

With snake-eyes she peered into my crotch. And it seemed to me that my flesh there had now become that same shrivelled moth. But I had known since a young child how my birth-endowment had grown beyond those of my village play-companions. Had not my poor dead father's eyes twinkled with amused pride?

'Son, you will be the prince of bulls! And your seeds will spume like an everlasting fountain of fertility. How your admiring princesses will shudder in their ecstasy!' This he had said, but how ironic his words seemed now.

Chief Eunuch Karif was hovering at my side, evidently pleased with Her Grand Ladyship's discerning scrutiny, no doubt thinking that his own improper observations about quality had been worthy, after all. But he said nothing, only watching Her Grand Ladyship with a sly expression that prudently concealed his own amusement.

'He is . . . an unusual specimen, I agree, Karif,' she conceded imperiously.

Karif bowed. 'Indeed, Your Grand Ladyship. You speak as always with such wisdom and grace, Madam.'

7

Her Grand Ladyship ignored the remark, still peering closely at me. 'His spheres hang low . . . like weighted marbles in their rose-pale pouch of velvet. It seems a pity . . .' she began but did not finish, a certain air of regret in her tone.

'Yes, my Lady. But he would still have his manly rod, at least. And, even though it will be bereft of its stiffening power, it shall still be a magnificent member . . . even in its quietened repose, Madam,' he pointed out solemnly, as if discussing an important matter of state.

'What measure has it got, Karif?'

The question came with such abruptness that he was flustered, as though caught out in some lacking of his duties. 'I did not think to –'

'Did not *think*, Karif? Did you wish to deprive my Royal Sisters of such interesting facts about a slave that comes to serve them?' She mocked him now, and there were amused titters of appreciation from the younger Sisters.

Karif bowed low, troubled by his oversight. 'If you permit me, my Lady, I shall measure it.'

But there was anxiety now in his face, since he had nothing to carry out that measuring with, should Her Grand Ladyship have demanded it. And now she did.

'I permit you, Karif. And measure also the hang of his pouch.'

'Yes, my Lady . . .' But Karif looked around him in desperation, gesticulating at one of his yellow-robed assistants to hasten away to fetch an instrument.

At this, Her Grand Ladyship became irritable. 'Use this, you idiot. And next time be equipped, Karif!'

She waved her long-handled fan at him, and bowing repeatedly Karif hurried to take it from her, before backing away obsequiously. 'Yes, my Lady.

Thank you, my Lady. I humbly apologise for my shortcomings.'

And then he came up to me, his face etched with his own displeasure, as if I were somehow responsible for his Mistress's rebuke. He knelt quickly in front of me, holding up the long handle of the fan. Then, with the palm of his other hand, he lifted up my soft shank that seemed ever more inclined to be a withered moth. And he laid the handle alongside it, marking where the tip of the mushroom-head came against it with his finger. He dropped me and returned immediately to his Mistress, careful to keep his finger precisely on the marked spot.

'It is this much length, my Lady.' He held the fan out for her.

Her Ladyship took it from him and, keeping her finger on the mark, held it up high so that the assembled women could view it. 'Behold, my Sisters! This Novice is a veritable bull-man. His rod comes to this ruby-stone here ... even though he's as limp as a kitten's tail.'

The women were not sure whether to gasp or giggle. And there was a mix of both sentiments.

'And what girth does it have, Karif?'

But this time Karif was prepared, as though his cunning mind had worked swifter now, knowing his Mistress's own cunning. And he came quickly back to kneel before me, and he circled my shank with his finger and thumb, adjusting the reach of them until he could gauge the circumference of my flesh. Then he rushed back to his Mistress, holding up the 'O' of his finger and thumb for all to see. 'It is like so, my Lady.'

Her Grand Ladyship nodded, and there were more gasps and sniggers. 'Ah-ha ... and what of the hang of his pouch?'

'I beg Your Ladyship's indulgence, but, if you will permit the use of Your Ladyship's fan again, I shall determine the answer, Madam.'

And again the Grand Lady handed him her jewelled fan and he came to kneel down, lower this time, between my legs. And I stood there trembling still, my head erect, but my eyes absent of direction or purpose.

'Don't move, slave,' he muttered under his breath.

But I was like a bronze statue. I felt him fumbling at my sac. The tips of his finger and thumb came together around it, just above the repose of my spheres. He pulled down slightly on me, as though to adjust the full vertical stretch of my sac. The top of the handle of Her Ladyship's fan nudged into the hard ridge between my legs, and the shaft measured me again.

He hurried back to his Mistress, marking the precise point on the handle for her.

'Good . . . but it came only to this humble sapphire, this time,' she announced with such mocking haughtiness.

And there was laughter. But it was the laughter of approval – whether as a result of Her Grand Ladyship's wit, or because of the hang of my sac, I was uncertain.

'This young bull would shame our Imperial Majesty and his Royal Princes! Is there any one of them that could measure up to this poor humble slave?'

There was a rumbling of consternation now. Perhaps our Grand Lady had ventured upon dangerous territory. But she was undaunted.

'And would Their Majesties not sacrifice their jewels and their lands to be able to boast the generous flesh of this slave? And, if so, would they not then be richer in their royal seed . . . and plant it more eagerly in our fertile beds, my poor lonely Sisters? Perhaps the bull-rod of this slave can dock in as many of us in one night as His Majesty can manage in ten!'

For several moments her unwise words seemed to hang in the air, but there was a certain bitterness to her tone. Then she laughed sardonically, looking around her. But the laughter that came from her Sisters was muted and uneasy. Many months later I wondered if she might have laid a trap for them, to see which of her Royal Sisters might have voiced agreement to so preposterous an insult.

Her Grand Ladyship looked at me again, perhaps a touch of pity in her eyes suddenly. She shook her head thoughtfully, but I had no way of knowing what things she was contemplating. Yet, it was perhaps that very moment that sealed my fate.

She waved me back to the line-up. Clearly the entertainment I had provided was at an end. She began to scrutinise the other Novices, who seemed to wilt yet more under her frightening gaze. But she did not select any of my companions for close appraisal. Perhaps her game had tired her.

Finally she finished her scrutiny. Her demeanour became stern, and she waved her hand at us. 'In future you will always prostrate yourselves before me. And you will take care to bow humbly at all my Sisters here. I am the Grand Lady of Royal Concubines to His Imperial Majesty, the Glorious Emperor. And my Royal Sisters here, depending upon their age and rank at this court, are also His Majesty's Royal Concubines. And just as we are the devoted and royal slaves to His Majesty, so are you now to be the devoted slaves of my Royal Sisters. And you should know that I hold the power of life and death over you. And if you displease me I shall not hesitate to demonstrate how well my wrath shall fall upon your lowly shoulders.'

11

She looked at each of us in turn again, and our eyes were downcast in temerity, our minds not wanting to contemplate such things, each of us not doubting for a second her dreadful power.

'You heard our Lady Mistress,' Karif addressed us calmly, his voice scarcely raised. 'Prostrate yourselves now!'

There was a moment's delay, each of us slow in our obedience, uncertain as to how we should comply. Were our minds not still numbed by all that had come so thick and fast upon our eyes and ears and our poor senses? Then I got down on my knees, as did my companions. We glanced at one another for reassurance, our chains rattling again. We knelt there stupidly, not knowing if that was enough. And clearly it was not.

One of the Eunuch-guards seized the boy on my left by the hair and flung him forwards, forcing his head to the ground. And quickly I threw myself down, copying that humbling posture, feeling the shock of cold marble on my chest and on my belly. But this was not the way. The Eunuch had kicked my neighbour's legs until he scrambled to kneel again, but in such a way that his chest and head were pushed down against the ground, his hands and arms spread forwards in front of him, and his backside thrust out tautly behind him. It was the most demeaning of postures, but it was one that we quickly learnt to adopt over those many seasons later.

We became accustomed to how our muscles strained to keep our balance, our spines arching so unnaturally and our feet splayed out behind us. Our rumps were so tensely spread that the covering of hide upon them seemed to stretch like the skins of unripe pomegranates, and the sheer tension of our bodies made every sinew and muscle tremble in our excruciation.

On that first morning as I prostrated myself in that debasing way, I had so much time to reflect upon my fate. We waited there for what felt like an eternity in that terrible posture, our straining muscles screaming out for relief. All the while we could hear those Honourable Ladies discussing us as if we were mere chattels. Sometimes there was mocking laughter; at other times we could hear Her Grand Ladyship's shrill voice chiding one of her Honourable Sisters; and meanwhile Karif was walking around us, occasionally prodding at some Novice and commanding him irritably to improve the manner of his posture.

At the very moment that I felt that my poor spine and limbs could take not a second more of that torture, I heard Her Grand Ladyship rise from her throne. There was a silence from the gathering of her Honourable Sisters as she made her way out of the vast hall. She shuffled away, her Eunuchs following discreetly behind. And finally the Honourable Sisters went from the hall, leaving us there in the echoing silence, still in the debasement of our prostration.

Eventually Karif spoke to us. 'You may rise, Novices. Now you will be taken to your quarters.'

And we rose shakily, glancing at one another, our eyes so uncomprehending of these strange events. It was perhaps at that moment that we could first begin to imagine what hardships were in store for us in the Pavilion of the Divine Orchid Ladies.

Thereafter, each and every morning we would have to assemble before Her Grand Ladyship. Sometimes she made us stay that way for a full hourglass if she had reason for displeasure, or even if she had no reason. And it was not just a matter of prostration alone, as we soon found out. It was about 'keeping a grace in the manner of your prostration'. I had been assigned to my Lady Jiang-Li – whose rank was Third Divinity – and it was she who taught me this and so much more about my duties and life at the Palace. And when she punished me, she did it not with anger usually, neither with any undue measure of severity, except when it was undeniably warranted. In fact, she tended to leave my punishments to Her Grand Ladyship's morning assemblies, and therefore at the hand of whichever of her Royal Sisters had been assigned the task that day.

And this task was undertaken with relish by many of the good Sisters. Indeed, it was an honour for them to be chosen by the Grand Lady to perform this ritual – for that was what it was, and one of many such rituals and ceremonies that seemed to serve no other purpose than to torment us poor Novices and to entertain the bored Sisters.

Whichever Sister had been chosen, she would walk behind us, while we waited there, prostrated in the exact manner prescribed. It was not permitted that our eyes should look either to the left or to the right, and our noses must always touch the cold marble. Our rumps must always be thrust high and tightly back, our knees and feet widely placed. We would hear only the vague whisper of the Royal Sister's silk slippers as she walked slowly behind our sprawled feet. Sometimes we might just catch the faint sound of the split-bamboo cane brushing against her robes.

Then Her Grand Ladyship's voice would call out. 'One of you Novices, for his impertinence to Senior Eunuch Ingor-Shon, will receive six stripes with the Bamboo Rod of Reformed Memory,' would be such example of a just sentence.

And perhaps only at that very moment would the poor culprit be aware of the beating he was about to receive. And, in our humiliating postures, our minds would be frantically working, hurrying to remember if we had been impertinent to that particular Senior Eunuch. But the chosen Sister would already have known the culprit and his whereabouts in the line, and she would quietly go up behind him. Immediately, and without warning, she would begin her task.

Such beatings for Novices were a matter of routine – a habitual phase in their tutoring. And the fact that the punishee would have no definite knowledge of his scheduled fate was an inherent part of his punishment.

My Mistress later told me that this was practised to enhance the punishee's wretchedness. 'A Novice who comes there to Assembly like a frightened lamb, knowing that he is guilty of some misdemeanour or imperfection in his work, but not knowing for certain how much he might have incurred his Mistress's wrath, will surely be all the more fearful at the unknown. All night he may toss and turn on his mattress. But only at Assembly will he know for sure whether or not Her Grand Ladyship will have been informed of his shortcomings. Then his pain shall be twofold.'

While recounting this, my Mistress would smile benevolently at me as though her words were said for my own benefit. 'First he will feel the cruel affliction of his mind and thoughts during that past night, and later the cruel affliction of his prostrated rump.' This was my Mistress's reasoning. And she imparted her many other philosophies of punishment during my first weeks at the Palace. Her wisdom and her patience with me were indisputable.

Here, in the Pavilion of the Divine Orchid Ladies of His Imperial Majesty alone, there were at any time no less than two hundred Eunuch-servants, and as many again of Maidservants. The Novices numbered three dozen and they were ranked according to the date of their indenture to the Palace. Depending upon the Novice's precise intended function, he would remain a Novice for at least two full seasons and perhaps three. Only then could he gain the honour of wearing the saffron-yellow robe. Before graduation to that honour he would be dressed simply in a short yellow skirt with a thin blue sash around his waist. To denote his year of seniority, a single tassel of white beading would be hung from his sash in his second year, and a second tassel in his third year.

But for the morning ritual of prostration, we Novices were always required to be completely naked – even those Novices in their second or third year. Apart from the purpose of ritual punishment with the Bamboo Rod of Reformed Memory, there were other reasons for Novices to be in that humbling state of nakedness at Assembly. Firstly, it enabled the Honourable Ladies to inspect their slaves closely for any signs of ill-health or damage. Secondly, it was as much for the Honourable Sisters themselves to know how their fellow Sisters treated their own assigned Novices. If, for example, a Novice appeared frequently at Assembly bearing numerous welts of his Mistress's whip, the Mistress herself might be judged by her fellow Sisters either as being too harsh or too lenient. If the welts were deep, then the Novice's Mistress might be accused of ill-treatment; or of being a poor tutor; or of simply being in a mood of the Black Moon. Minor domestic matters or even frustrations at not having been summoned to the Emperor's bed, or to the bed of one of his royal sons, were reasons frequently given – or she might just have been in the midst of her womanly cycle.

Discussion, sometimes heated, might take place even as the Novices remained in their acute prostrations while one Sister made critical comment of another Sister. During all that time they might be standing behind the poor wretch whose rump it was that had been the original source of the debate. The Grand Lady herself might be consulted. There might be tears, particularly if the Grand Lady were overly critical of the Sister whose Novice it was sporting such deep welts. And then perhaps other Sisters would gather round the raised-up rump of the errant slave, examining it with much prodding and jabbing of fingers into the cores of the welts. It was as if such clinical appraisal could somehow determine the psychological wellbeing of the slave's Honourable Mistress, rather than if it had anything to do with any matter of physical damage to the slave himself.

Such things were a part of everyday life in the Pavilion, considering that the Honourable Ladies lived in such close proximity, one with another. Many of them suffered from acute boredom, and there was much bickering, petty jealousies and side-swiping comments and all manner of unpleasantnesses. And there was always an atmosphere of competition between the concubines, many of whom might not have been visited by His Divine Majesty for several years. And the older those forgotten Ladies became, the smaller the chance of them ever finding favour with His Majesty again. They were the Faded Orchids.

The third reason for the Novices having to prostrate themselves naked at Assembly was so that Chief Eunuch Karif could himself inspect them. I did not find out the true purpose for some time, but it shocked me when I did. It seemed that for several decades some of the concubines, and even some of the senior Eunuchs, resorted to practices that did not meet with the Emperor's approval. It was well known that there were many concubines who, starved of sexual attention from either the Emperor or his nine sons, needed alternative consolations. While Novices were usually gelded in the first days of their arrival at the Palace in that terrible ceremony known as the Reverent Departure of Temptation, in the months thereafter, those castrated survivors were often seen as still retaining some sexual value. Whether symbolic or in a more practical way, some Novices might on occasion fall victim to their Mistress's frustrated desires, or even become surrogate sex-partners in some perverse manner of copulation, whereby – although lacking any means of actual penetrative arousal – the young man's body could be used in some alternative manner.

The forced abstinence from normal sexual activity – for which concubines had been well trained in those seductive arts – had perhaps inevitably led them to indulge in what they saw as being acts of almost defiance. Or perhaps they considered that such obscene practices were a richly deserved revenge upon the Royal Dynasty itself. And of course, whatever led the Honourable Ladies down this dangerous path, it would always be the hapless Novices who would most likely suffer the consequences, if ever discovered. Their dilemma was an appalling one. On the one hand they must obey their Mistresses' every order and desire, whereas on the other they knew the terrible penalties for such obscene and forbidden acts.

One of these, and that most frequently indulged in, was the practice known as Bracing the Pod. In this, the Mistress made the Novice stiffen himself artificially by means of a sheath. Made of light strands of leather and shaped in a tubular arrangement bound with threads of silk and goosebone, it fitted over the Novice's shank, being itself otherwise unable to attain any significant measure of stiffening – at least not with natural ability. Yet strangely, despite the obvious absence of his seed-sac and its potent spheres, the wearer of the sheath might nonetheless on occasion manage some small hardness of his own accord.

In fact, this phenomenon was not as rare as once supposed. It seems that the process of gelding does not always deprive the victim of every last vestige of his potency, such that it was not entirely uncommon for some of the older Eunuchs – as well as the young Novices – to retain some vague residue of potency. When that unforeseen event occurs it enables not only some degree of natural stiffening, but also a feeling of accompanying arousal. Yet, I cannot myself vouch for it.

There was, however, one forbidden and utterly perverse act that I can vouch for. It involved the Mistress herself using a bull's pizzle. This was stiffened with a mixture of coarse goat hair and sawdust. One end of the hardened black pizzle was then attached to a series of leather straps which were fastened around the Mistress's waist and thighs. Thus, she assumed the dominant role of surrogate male and wore the contraption with the shank reaching proud from her own loins. Yet it was not for use on her fellow Sisters. Such were the jealousies and rivalries, concubines could never be certain that their secrets would not be betrayed. One concubine might seem to acquiesce to such a sexual liaison, but in the end denounce her willing partner. The young Novices made far safer partners. They were but humble slaves, having nobody to listen to their complaints or believe them. A slave could so easily be condemned. Who would take the word of a slave over a Divine Orchid Lady of His Imperial Majesty?

And what then was this perverse act of coupling between Mistress and her slave? I myself learnt the nature of this quite early on in my days at the Pavilion of the Divine Orchid Ladies. A slave, ever anxious to do his Mistress's bidding, would himself be made to take the passive role that the redundant Mistress herself had once desired to fulfil.

This clandestine practice was known as Bowing Before the Unjust Bull, although such references to it were made only in hushed tones, and only in those concubinic circles where such forbidden acts might dare to be talked of. The Novice, having usually been tutored in the art of his debasement, would be called upon to kneel and bend over one of his Mistress's huge day-cushions. Then she would grease the inner precincts of his passage with a mixture of goose-fat and jasmine oil, and once having done this to her satisfaction she would mount behind him with the black bull's pizzle already strapped to her loins and with it so artificially proud in its thrusting poise.

I cannot say that this was a practice admired by my own dear Mistress, and I was grateful for that, even if she had her own particular proclivities. Fortunately those were ones I could satisfy, whereas my fellow Novices lacked the wherewithal with their own Mistresses.

However, my Mistress once lent me to her beloved Sister, Lin-Yao, who at that time had been particularly sorrowful and depressed. It seemed that His Imperial Majesty's youngest son, His Highness Fidram-Ong, had rejected her in a most callous manner. And Royal Sister Lin-Yao had been greatly offended, her pride damaged beyond repair. Thereafter she had sought to avenge her rejection in the only way she knew.

I can recall it vividly all these many years later. I know that my own dear Mistress had not intended for me to Bow Before the Unjust Bull, having supposed instead that her dear Sister Lin-Yao would have been content to have me serve in the same manner as I served my own true Mistress. After all, was I not more naturally equipped for her pleasures?

But Sister Lin-Yao had harboured other notions. And on that one occasion it had been I who provided that painful function, and I can remember how she rutted in me so frenziedly. Sister Lin-Yao had thighs like a buffalo's and they thudded against the flanks of my rump like claps of thunder. Moreover, that bull's pizzle had almost seemed to reach beyond the very core of my being. As she rode me she cried out insulting words all the while, not directed at me, but at His Imperial Highness. Yet even so I can recall how frightened I was at those dangerous insults, no less than I had been frightened by Sister Lin-Yao's frantic motions in my rear passage. Yet, it was strange that I had been so used, considering I had been spared that same disfigurement suffered by my peers.

How sore I was for several days after, even though my Mistress Jiang-Li had graciously tended to me herself with soothing tea-tree lotion and ky-ky berry-juice. Bowing Before the Unjust Bull was fortunately something I would never experience again, but I shudder still at the very notion of it. However, it was not always like that for other Novices. It seems that many of them found some strange affinity for this practice, being happy to please their Mistresses in this way. I can only think that those Honourable Mistresses possessed thighs that were less awesome than those of Sister Lin-Yao. Perhaps also the bull's pizzle was of smaller girth and of shorter length than the one I had accommodated.

But these many things of life at the Pavilion of the Divine Orchid Ladies came to me only gradually over

21

those first full seasons that I served there as a Novice Eunuch. Although my young mind was ever ready for enlightenment, how often was I to know the black mist of shock and terror. And, if on occasion I were to be permitted some brief pleasure in my slavery, how seldom it would come, and then so perversely, often catching me unawares like a leaping tiger in the grass; and always darkened by such dangerous shadows.

But it was to be those first few unwelcome sunrises at the Palace that brought so many miseries upon us. How much did we all look forward to sunset when we could go to the comfort of our mattresses and our linen covers. The Novice dormitories were at the very end of the Pavilion. Our teacher there was Senior Eunuch Kanchu, a thin man with birdlike features, whose robe hung from his skeletal frame so that he resembled a desert crow with saffron-yellow wings. He was strict with us, but not always unjustly so, having retained some small measure of humanity. Yet he had the cunning for survival, and this was his first instinct. We called him Brother-Master Kanchu to his face and Brother-Yellow-Crow behind his back.

We rose before sunrise and we lit the oil-lamps. Our first duty was to wash ourselves in the cold water of our communal bathing-pool. The manner of our bathing was closely monitored by a second-year Novice. We were given scented wild-coriander soap to cleanse every crevice of our bodies, before which we powdered ourselves with calc-dust. We ate a frugal meal of rice-cake and stewed fruit that was served to us by the young Maidservants. One of them was Li-Mei, her name meaning 'Beautiful Plum Blossom', on account of her pale colouring and small dainty shape. At once I was attracted to her, and she to me. Even so, a full cycle of the moon would pass before I ever managed to speak to her.

Apart from matters of household routine, Novices were, of course, not permitted to speak, except during recreation hour just after sunset. Moreover, any communication, no matter how fleeting, between Novices and Maidservants was also strictly forbidden. This we very quickly learnt, and any breach of either of those rules would result in swift punishment for all parties. Besides, there were often practical difficulties in communication, because not all slaves spoke a common language. After all, had we not been gathered up from so many far-flung outposts of His Majesty's Mighty Empire? Some of us were olive-skinned and with hair as dark as a horse's mane; some with skins that had the burnished hue of bronze; others the pure pale whiteness of coconut pulp; and of myself the golden tan that had come from unclothed childhood under a kindly sun.

On that first morning we were lined up in the main hall. It was deserted now. Apart from the Honourable Sister whose roster duty it was to be dressed and in attendance in the Reception Hall of Orchid Bloom, all the other concubines were in their individual quarters in the east wing of the Pavilion and seldom ventured out until the sun had risen to its highest point. Their Eunuchs and Novices would be tending to their needs, and there was much coming and going as these servants scurried about their duties, carrying platters from the kitchens, or freshly cleaned robes, or boxes of some delicacy or other, or messages and parchments to read, or flowers or jars of scent; and attending to so many other of their Mistresses' constant demands.

There were many rigid requirements of State that formed the daily regimentation and rituals of Palace life. Only Her Grand Ladyship could grant any change to the set routine, and only then provided His

Majesty's Chief Minister approved. For that to occur it was likely that considerable bribes would have to be paid before any proclamation would eventually be issued, and, even then, several moons might pass to allow due process of his deliberation.

Our transport-chains had already been removed from our ankles the night before, not that there was the remotest question of fleeing from the Palace. Its gates and outer walls were as heavily guarded as any fortress. And to go from one Pavilion to another required permission, which was never given lightly – and certainly never to lowly Novices.

Brother-Yellow-Crow was supervising us, standing there in front of us and watching us critically with those vulturelike eyes of his. Hovering in the background was one of the Senior Novices. He was the same one who had monitored us in the bathing-pool earlier, and now he carried a small silk cushion in his hand.

Brother-Yellow-Crow clapped his hands. 'Soon Her Ladyship Jiang-Li will come to inspect you,' he announced.

It was my very own Mistress who was on duty that morning, although I did not know I had been assigned to her then.

'She will pass you fit to proceed with today's studies,' Brother-Yellow-Crow continued, adding in ominous tones, 'If any one of you fails, there will be punishment.'

It was not clear what would constitute failure. Brother-Master Kanchu had not enlightened us at that time. But there was something else that had puzzled me. Every Eunuch and every Novice was shaven bald, whereas we new arrivals still had our full heads of hair, some dark, some less so, a few of us with hair of straw, like my own.

Now there came a soft rustling sound behind us and Brother-Yellow-Crow made a little bow in that direction. Of course, we did not turn around. We had by then already learnt that much about correctness of posture and what humbling manner of self-discipline was required for proper servant etiquette. We stood rigidly in our line, all one dozen of us, bare-footed and dressed only in our new yellow skirts, these being called Aprons of Good Modesty.

The Honourable Sister Jiang-Li was young, perhaps only a few more full seasons than I. She had about her a quality of beauty that radiated from her like a springtime sunbeam – one that came lazily, but glowing with gold-tinged luminescence, neither too vivid in its brightness nor too vague, but more with a tone of passive splendour. She was small and pretty, her face like a thin summer moon, lean but with high cheekbones and with slanted kitten-eyes that seemed to stretch across their entire width. Her hands and slippered feet were as dainty as a child's, and a sweet fragrance of honeysuckle drifted in her wake.

Yet, she was proud of face and bore herself with an air of regal haughtiness, although that particular morning she seemed to possess a certain uneasiness of demeanour, as though perhaps she had no desire to be here at all. She was almost nervous in our presence, despite her so elevated status. Later I was told how once she had been a favourite of His Majesty's third son, His Highness Fid-ram-Lo, but that his treatment of her had become rough and unkindly, and that the nature of those things she had to do for him was more than her youthful vulnerability could easily bear.

'May Your Ladyship's morning be blessed with a thousand pleasures, Madam,' Brother-Yellow-Crow said, bowing again in formal greeting.

Then he addressed us, his tone suddenly sharp again. 'Novices, unfasten your Aprons of Good Modesty and let them fall to the floor!'

It was not a command that we had been expecting, and we were mortified in our fresh shame that now we must bear our nakedness once more in front of so regal a lady. Perhaps we had already forgotten how much greater had been our shame only yesterday, when we assembled naked and in chains before so many watching and sniggering Sisters. But we obeyed quickly, some faster than others. I myself struggled to untie the knot of my own linen belt, and my thin garment fell awkwardly to the marble last of all. Brother-Yellow-Crow frowned at me but said nothing, although I could see that my ineptitude had been well noted. And from beneath my shamed eyelashes I saw that Her Ladyship was looking at me, although more perhaps with pity than displeasure.

Then Brother-Master Kanchu commanded us, 'Lift your arms and make them stretch to the ceiling . . . and spread your legs.'

In ragged unison we obeyed, holding our hands high, and shuffling our feet into this new debasing posture.

After a moment or two he turned again to the Honourable Mistress. 'Your humble new servants are ready for Your Ladyship's inspection,' he announced, bowing again slightly. His eyes were all the while warily upon us, as though in warning of our conduct.

She nodded, her lips unsmiling, but her eyes darted nervously from one to the other of us. But we were careful to keep our gaze from her, only looking straight ahead. Brother-Yellow-Crow gestured politely for her to approach the line-up. And she began to walk slowly to one end, then halted in front of the first of us, a young man called Lep-Spru. He was three slaves away from me, and he was flushed with both apprehension and fallen modesty. What things must be troubling his mind, but no less than they troubled mine! I had seen how all night long he had tossed on his mattress, muttering in his restless sleep. I wondered if he would survive in this dreadful Palace, which was yet to reveal so many cruelties.

Brother-Master Kanchu waved for the Senior Novice to come, and gestured for him to set the cushion down between Lep-Spru's bare feet. He bowed and, keeping himself with eyes cast down, the Senior Novice knelt and neatly arranged the cushion, before getting to his feet again and quickly going to stand behind our solemn tutor.

Out of the corner of my eye I saw how Her Ladyship seemed reluctant to proceed, even though this was clearly a duty she was accustomed to.

Brother-Yellow-Crow was waiting patiently for her to begin. Eventually, realising her hesitation, he said, 'Perhaps Your Ladyship would care to make a start on the slave's armpits?'

'Very well, Kanchu,' she replied in a small soft voice, but one that seemed to travel as clearly as the gentle song of a nightingale across a lily pond.

Whatever her apparent reluctance, she bent her head towards the Novice until her tiny nostrils came under one of his arms. She smelt him there, first under that arm, and then the other. She seemed to go into a prescribed sequence of the ritual, and slowly her nose travelled down the length of his body, taking in his scent. Her blue satin gown shone in the slender rays of the morning sun filtering through the tall window and the rich abundance of gold and jewelled bracelets on her wrists tinkled in the silence. Without looking down at the cushion beneath her, she gracefully sank to her knees and began to sniff at the young man's crotch, first one side of his small

27

member, and then the other. She lowered herself ever so slightly until her head was under him, and then she sniffed him there.

She got to her feet, lifting herself nimbly as if she were much practised at such a movement, her balance finely kept. She said nothing, as she moved to the next slave in line, and immediately the Senior Novice hurried to slide the cushion along until it was neatly positioned under that slave.

She began again with the ritual, more confidently than before, even though she had an air of perfunctory resignation in the performance of this strange duty. She sniffed at one armpit and then the other, just as before, before letting herself gently down on the cushion to smell him there. For a second I thought I could see her draw back. Her long eyelashes seemed to flutter, as if something perhaps might have given a momentary displeasure to her nostrils.

Brother-Yellow-Crow had noticed this and his face became even sterner than before, looking askance at the Novice. His build was heavier than most of ours, his legs sturdy and there was much hair to his body.

Brother-Yellow-Crow's eyes narrowed. Her Ladyship had risen, but she said nothing, about to move on to the next in line, which was I.

'Is Your Ladyship displeased with this slave?'

She hesitated for a second, not knowing what to say, confusion passing like a cloud before her eyes. 'It is . . . it is acceptable, Kanchu. Thank you.'

But Brother-Yellow-Crow sensed that her answer lacked sincerity. He glared at the poor Novice beside me, searching his frightened eyes. And without warning our Brother-Master got down quickly on to the floor. Holding on to the young man's legs he pulled himself up so that he could sniff under him, inhaling deeply and evidently finding reason for dissatisfaction. Then our Brother-Master leapt to his feet, his lips twisted in distaste and his face like thunder. 'Madam,' he addressed Her Ladyship, but not as obsequiously as before, 'This slave is lacking in reverence to His Imperial Majesty's property.'

At first I wondered if I had misunderstood his words, but then I realised. We slaves were His Imperial Majesty's own property. Our bodies were no longer ours to do with as we pleased. They must be made to the requirements of our purpose and duty here. And any neglect to our own persons was as if we had neglected His Majesty's.

Her Ladyship looked anxious now. She had been caught out in neglect of her own duty. Clearly she had been bound by the Palace rules to make complaint if His Majesty's property was found lacking. And clearly it had been so, and she – an Honourable Sister who owed as much duty to His Majesty as any slave here – had remained deceitfully silent. And if she had done so for reasons of pity or benevolence towards humble slaves, perhaps not wishing to bring punishment down upon them, she was misguided in harbouring those undutiful sentiments. And now it was a servant – a humble Senior Eunuch – who was taking her to task. And in the culture of the Palace she would be shamed, no less than we were shamed as we stood there in our nakedness, presenting our naked parts for such belittling attention.

'Perhaps. Kanchu . . . I was wrong. I am tired this morning. My Eunuch brought me a potion of ginger and crushed kankari-seed because of my indisposition,' she replied without so much as glancing at Brother-Yellow-Crow and in a way that could not be challenged by him.

For a moment he looked slyly at her. Then he bowed, smiling graciously. 'Your Ladyship, please accept my most earnest wishes that some warm sunlight in the Garden of Tranquillity – perhaps by the side of the lily pond – will banish your indisposition and make you glow with good health again.' He paused before continuing again, his tone with a yet more cunning edge to it. 'Would Your Ladyship desire to end the inspection . . . and for me to send word of your indisposition to Her Grand Ladyship?' His eyebrow rose quizzically.

'No . . . er . . . that will not be required . . . thank you, Kanchu,' the Honourable Sister Jiang-Li replied hurriedly.

Even though I tried not to look at her, I could see fleeting anxiety in her eyes. And she was a Royal Mistress! What hope did humble slaves have not to live in fear?

But she had recovered her superior demeanour again.

'I shall continue with my inspection. And this slave who offended my nostrils shall be reported for just punishment.'

Her Ladyship had become forceful now in her manner, the harshness in her voice returned, almost as if she were aware of how she must be seen to lack the smallest grain of compassion. She glared at the poor slave on my right who had given cause for Her Ladyship's offence, beholding him as if he were no better than a worm. The hapless Novice was as much fearful as bemused, wisdom not having come to him even now. And I could see from Brother-Master Kanchu's withering look that his displeasure would soon be vented.

Almost before I was aware of it she had come in front of me. Her sweet scent of honeysuckle seemed to overwhelm my very being, and the rustling of silk against her skin was magical. I was more than a head taller than she, so that I looked down on her, and her glossy jet-black hair was set high in a neat circular twist above her tiny ears and pinned by three sapphire and emerald butterfly-clips. Although she had not deigned to raise her chin so much as a fly-wing's length, her eyelashes made a dangerous flutter up at my face. For one terrifying moment my eyes met hers, and in that fleeting second I saw her sadness and her suppressed passion as if they were two opposing fountains waiting to spurt as one.

Her beauty was as radiant as a burst of early sunlight. And, by some manner that I could not conceive, I knew her desire for me in that second. I, too, standing there in my debasing nakedness in front of this richly clothed and so beautiful young woman, felt a surge of my own desire. Her lips were so ripe and soft and so delightfully formed. And her skin was unblemished, the colouring of a pale rose. I could see the delightful contours of her figure through the silk of her garment. Her small pert nose, its tiny nostrils as yet with unfinished work to do, was twitching so near to my bare chest that I knew she was smelling me, her sweet breath on my skin. I knew, too, that she had observed that almost imperceptible rise in my loins, no matter that I so desperately tried to contain it. My fear and humiliation were as before. Nonetheless those emotions were not enough to stop my dangerous surge of desire.

'Oh, be still and do not lift yourself and so disgrace me!' I told myself silently.

My upstretched hands seemed to waver as her nose came into my wispy-furred armpits. She smelt me there on each side, the tip of her nose almost touching me. Then, satisfied there, she moved down my body. I could see the cushion down there between my legs, and she sank gracefully on her knees. At once her face almost met the partial rise of my flesh.

For a second I thought I heard a little uttered gasp from her lips. Her eyes were taking in my length and girth, but I held myself in my rigid posture, hoping that I might quench my unwilled ardour. All this had clearly not escaped the attention of Brother-Yellow-Crow, and his eyes were like those of a cruel eagle waiting to swoop upon its prey.

Her face moved around to one side of my protrusion, and she sniffed me there. The hairs of my sac tingled, and again I felt a tiny seepage of my seed flowing into it. 'Oh Heavens, be merciful,' I silently cried.

Perhaps she heard my unuttered words, but still her nostrils drew in my scent. And almost ducking her head beneath my impudent rise, she smelt me on the other side. A sweat broke out on me, glistening in the muscled plain of my belly. But at last she disengaged, very slowly getting to her feet. For a moment she stood there before me, her face flushed even beneath her mask of soft *maquillage*. There might have been a slight tremor to her body, but her voice came as clearly as tinkling crystal in the night.

'This slave has passed,' she said simply, moving on to the next Novice without a further glance at me.

And then the hot tightness in my loins receded like the ebbing tide at the mouth of the Great River of Abundance.

For the whole of that day Brother-Yellow-Crow's fury was etched in his features, his vulturelike appearance all the more pronounced. The boy who had so displeased his Mistress had been taken away. None of us knew where. As for me, whatever displeasure I had caused, it was clear that I was living under a Summer Cloud of Bad Omen. My newfound companions kept their distance from me, as if somehow they suspected that I was cursed by one of Heaven's Dangerous

Spirits. Furtively my peers had glanced at my manly endowment, at first with curiosity, even admiration, but now it was as though my flesh were afflicted by the plague.

In a corner of the outer hall we were sitting cross-legged in an enclosure of ornate silk-covered screens that depicted colourful birds in lush foliage. How free were those birds; how caged were we in our Palace of Splendour.

Brother-Yellow-Crow had been lecturing us for many hours. The midday sun had long passed, and we had only been given water to drink, served by those same timid Maidservants. Once I dared to catch a fleeting glance as Li-Mei – she of the Beautiful Plum Blossom – quickly set down a pitcher of water and scuttled away. Our legs were stiff and our backs ached. Our Brother-Master had spoken of so many things; of how our bodies must never offend; of how to bow and to sit; the manner in which we should walk and stand; how our eyes must always be downcast, never to look directly at our Mistresses; and how we must be unobtrusive, as though we were but fleeting shadows that whispered silently along the corridors of the Pavilion. He instructed us in so many strange things, such that by nightfall we had forgotten more than we had learnt.

But I could see that he was apprehensive in his tutoring, as though expecting that at any moment Her Grand Ladyship might suddenly appear. But she did not. Only occasionally did we catch glimpses of the Honourable Sisters as they went about their Palace pursuits. Sometimes there were muted sounds of giggling and occasionally chiding female voices from beyond the screens. And always there were the silent hurrying forms of the yellow-clad Eunuchs as they attended to their Mistresses' wants.

The sun was low in the sky when Brother-Yellow-Crow clapped his hands for us to rise. 'These are your lessons for today, Novices. Remember them well so that you do not incur my displeasure. I must report everything to Her Grand Ladyship and when tomorrow you prostrate yourselves at Assembly you must hope that she has not chosen any of you for punishment.' Here, he seemed to glance at me, but he did not address me. 'You should sleep soundly this night, because tomorrow will be a special day for you. Remember, you have been selected for honourable service in this, His Majesty's Divine Palace. And there will be a ceremony called the Reverent Departure of Temptation and it shall take place in the Room of Glorious Transformation. And when it is over, you will be taken to a special place, which is called the Room of Joyous Reflection. Here you will be permitted to rest and, now as your hearts and minds shall become pure, you shall think upon your lives to come ... and of the devotions expected of you.'

One or two of the Novices – those possessed of curious, fertile minds – glanced at one another anxiously. What ceremony was this Reverent Departure of Temptation? What purpose had this Room of Glorious Transformation? But clearly our Brother-Master and Tutor had no intention of enlightening us further.

Of course, we knew something of the rumours. But in reality we could not grasp the perversity of them. While we knew of the word 'Eunuch', it meant little to us other than that these yellow-clad Eunuchs were Palace servants, and that it was each of our destinies to become one of them. Some of us perhaps knew enough from the rumours to suspect that these Eunuchs were, in some way, no longer whole men.

Perhaps they'd been born so, or in their infancy they'd been divested of their manhood, or alternatively perhaps some affliction had accounted for their loss. Yet, despite our uncertainty and our fear, we somehow could still not believe that we – as young men in our prime – would now be forcefully deprived of our manhood. What purpose could there be? If our bodies were as complete as nature had intended, could we not serve our Mistresses equally as well as if our bodies were not? All this was perplexing to us. Moreover, the peaceful décor of the Pavilion, with its fine tapestries and richly ornate furnishings, seemed to lull us into false feelings of security. Certainly there were strange perversities and beastly cruelties, but otherwise the very culture of the Divine Palace seemed somehow to defy the notion of cruelty for cruelty's sake. And was not the Palace the very centre of civilisation? And were we not honoured to be a humble part of it?

It was with these thoughts and this turmoil in our minds that we went to our straw mattresses that night.

Two

Our whispering bare feet scuttled across the marble floor as we came to Assembly. The Honourable Sisters were already seated there on their plush cushions around the dais. Her Grand Ladyship and her two Senior Ladies beside her were on their ornate thrones, looking down at us as we came before them.

We stood in three lines, one behind the other. I was in the first line. We were naked again, our Aprons of Good Modesty taken from us. Even those of the more senior second- and third-year Novices were once again discarded. As before, they formed up in rows behind us and now prostrated themselves as naked as the newly arrived Novices. However, it was only at these morning Assembly rituals that our Senior Novice brethren were ever as humbled as we were in such mutual nakedness, reduced then to our same lowly status. Otherwise they maintained a gulf of superiority between us, as if they were the masters and we the humbled slaves. We had yet to earn our seniority.

The Royal Ladies watched us in silence. I was careful not to let my eyes wander. Nonetheless I felt the curious gaze of several Ladies upon my own vulnerability, and my heart was thumping.

Chief Eunuch Karif was, as usual, in attendance. He too watched our arrival with a stern expression on his face. Today he carried a long thin black-lacquered rod in his hand as if it were his symbol of authority.

Brother-Master Kanchu had brought us here. Since dawn he had been preparing us. We had bathed, which this morning he himself had supervised, instructing us again in the manner of using such precious soap and powder. Once our frugal meal was out of the way he had again lectured us on posture and decorum, using one of us as a model. Paying particular attention to the proper manner of prostration, Brother-Yellow-Crow made each of us rehearse this, and also how we should form up in our lines for Assembly.

Bowing now to Her Grand Ladyship and then to the Honourable Sisters, and finally to Chief Eunuch Karif, Brother-Yellow-Crow moved away to one side to stand with a group of other Senior Eunuchs.

Karif clapped his hands. 'Prostrate yourselves, Novices.'

And, now knowing the precise manner of this, we quickly knelt on the marble and stretched ourselves in the required debasing manner. After allowing us a few moments to settle ourselves, he then walked stiffly behind the first line.

Every now and then, using his rod, he prodded at some Novice's feet, making him spread them wider. Or he would press the tip of his rod on the small of someone's back, making the poor Novice arch his spine further and tense his thrusting hindquarters more acutely. Palms down, hands must be stretched neatly on the marble, placed there in symmetrical precision; forearms and elbows set squarely; noses touching the ground; and toes curled under our feet so that bare soles faced backwards. No Novice must move a muscle. We were to be like bronze statues in that perversity of posture. Our silent breathing alone would show our human frailty.

Once his inspection of our three lines was completed, he walked quickly back and bowed before Her Grand Ladyship. 'The Novices are in good order, Your Ladyship.'

She nodded curtly at him, her gaze then sweeping with regal indifference over our ranks. The silence was oppressive. The morning heat had already risen. Despite the coldness of the marble beneath me, I felt the first prickle of sweat breaking out on my skin.

'Newly arrived Novices!' Her voice was shrill. 'Your Tutor has given me mixed reports of your progress. Here in the Pavilion of the Divine Orchid Ladies there is no room for mediocrity. Slaves must always give of their best. Their learning must be swift. Eyes and ears must be vigilant for the requirements of your Honourable Mistresses. There shall be no lazy spirits amongst our servants. No tolerance can be permitted.'

She paused then so that her words could sink into our humble brains.

'Soon comes your time for induction. The ceremony of Reverent Departure of Temptation shall be performed this very day on those of you to be so honoured. You should feel proud, my slaves . . . those of you who are deemed worthy! And you will be rewarded! Of course, the Room of Glorious Transformation is not a place devoid of suffering and pain. But that suffering and pain will be honourable . . . and, I hope, honourably borne by you. Whatever blood you may shed, you must think of it only as being worthy blood that has been shed for His Imperial Majesty and for his proud Orchid Ladies. You will be like brave warriors and when your wounds are healed you will feel the worthy freedom that your sacrifices have brought. As the evils of temptation are lifted from you, how pure will your hearts and minds become! Only then can you serve your Royal Mistresses with the devotion they require.'

These chilling words tumbled shockingly into our minds as we tried to make sense of it all. Were now our worst fears finally to be confirmed? Yet, even now we struggled to accept it. Perhaps her words were meant in some symbolic way that we could not fathom. And we clung to this slender straw of belief. But Her Grand Ladyship had not finished yet.

'Before we see whom amongst you is worthy of attending the ceremony of Reverent Departure of Temptation, let us first know of those slaves who have offended us already ... when not even three dawns have yet risen since your arrival.'

Of course, we could not look up, although our eyes perhaps strained to see what was happening around us. Without daring to move my nose even a fly-wing length from its point on the marble, all I could see were the nearby feet of some of the Honourable Sisters as they sat primly on their cushions. We Novices meanwhile remained tense in our prostrations, our minds filled with cold terror.

There was movement somewhere to the side of our ranks, and then Her Grand Ladyship spoke quietly to someone. I did not know it at the time, but Her Grand Ladyship had given the Bamboo Rod of Reformed Memory to one of her Junior Sisters. This was the usual procedure on those many mornings of Assembly. The Honourable Sister – chosen by Her Grand Ladyship each morning – would be given the name, or names, of the offending Novices. And then the chosen Sister, armed with her instrument of punishment, would quietly approach the back row of the prostrated slaves.

I heard her padding footsteps, the silk slippers coming nearer. Out of the corner of my eye I could see the swirling folds of her rich apricot-coloured robe, the embroidered clusters of garnets glittering suddenly as they caught the late rays of morning sun. Her tiny feet shuffled daintily towards us, and I could make out the cruel shaft of the bamboo cane that hung down at her side. It was a strange implement, and I beheld it with a certain fatalistic fascination. The main shaft, lacquered until it shone a deep-brownish hue, had the thickness of a man's big toe, but the bottom half of it had been split down the middle into several thin separate strips that sprouted from its core. They opened out in such a way that it resembled the shredded stem of some strange dead plant, its cluster of small tails waving menacingly at the end. But that was not all. Each of these waving strips had been bound with thin scarlet-dyed cotton thread all the way along and up to where the split section joined on to the main shaft. It was clear that the strips had been almost lovingly and intricately bound, and the bamboo itself had been freshly oiled, as though to keep each strip as flexed and supple as any whip.

The nimble little feet of the Honourable Sister disappeared from my view now. She had gone somewhere behind the line-up. So intense was the silence again. I could vaguely see Her Grand Ladyship looking haughtily down upon the scene, her eyes glittering like beads of black polished stone.

Then I heard it, the hairs on the nape of my neck bristling. The sound came like a dull thud, followed by a yelp of pain and shock. Then the bamboo tails lashed down again, more forcefully this time, as though the chosen Sister had gauged the correct angle and sweep of her delivery. And the young man's yelp was louder now.

Chief Eunuch Karif, who had been hovering near-by, called out sharply, 'Do not move, slave! Keep your posture or Her Ladyship will award you with extra strikes.'

The bamboo lashed down again, and thrice more in quick succession. Their wake caused little echoes in the hall, and the punishee gasped and moaned in his excruciation. There was a pause, and for a moment I thought that that was the last of it. Then I caught the faint swishing sound, as if the bamboo had flown back from a wider reach than before. This greater momentum made for a more solid impact, and now he yelped again breathlessly. And finally, as the last echo died away, he made a piteous whimpering sound.

'Seven cocks have crowed . . . and whimpered like puppy-dogs!' Her Grand Ladyship announced gleefully. 'That was your sentence, slave. You were reported for having a slothful attitude to your learning. Now the Bamboo Rod of Reformed Memory will serve to remind you in your future conduct. My dear Sister has done well in her kind service to you.'

Once his whimpering had quietened, there was silence again. And then I heard that soft approach of silk slippers behind me. They stopped. My heart was in my mouth. I remembered how I might have offended Brother-Yellow-Crow. But should I be punished for something unintended? Could that small but shameful rising of my flesh be cause for me to be beaten?

And the answer came swiftly. The first stinging impact made me rock on my knees. A scream started to rise in my throat, but I stifled it, only gasping in my shock. Then the second strike came, harder than the first. I jerked forwards involuntarily so that I lost my balance for a moment. And she waited until I recovered my posture before the bamboo lashed down again. This time I managed not to buck forwards and three more deliveries came quickly, one after the other. I gasped each time, the sweat breaking from my lower torso. Another pause, and then three more quick strikes, each hitting me on both cheeks of my rump simultaneously. I could feel how each of the bamboo strips seemed to spread across the taut skin of my peaks like separate wispy tails of pain. Although it was agony, somehow the growing numbness in my lean muscled flesh had an anaesthetising effect on my screaming nerve-ends, the stinging sensation at least partially diminished.

I had been too stunned to properly count the strikes, but Her Grand Ladyship had, after all, announced those strange words 'Seven cocks have crowed' and I had roughly counted those same number of strokes my companion had received. I felt sure that I had already received more than this number. Perhaps now my shortcomings had been adequately addressed.

I was on the point of believing that the Honourable Sister had indeed finished with me. I could hear her silk gown rustling behind me, as if she were preparing to move on. Yet, looking back under my legs, I could see that her slippers had not moved, still planted there behind me and pointing beneath my throbbing rump. And, without warning, another blow came. And it was a harsh one, more than before. I cried out now, as much in shock as in agony.

'Aaagh! Please, Mistress,' I heard myself gasp, and I fell forwards on to my chest, my knees crumbling under me.

Chief Eunuch Karif was there in a flash, standing in front of me, his feet almost in my face. 'Get up, dog! And reform yourself.'

I hurried, trembling, to get back on my knees. But my rump was not thrust back or taut enough for his liking, as though it feared to adopt the same acuteness as before.

'Nose to the ground, you disobedient dog! And make your miserable body into the required posture of debasement.'

I made myself settle back again, arching my spine and sticking my bottom out again until I felt the welts upon it stretch painfully as my flesh tautened.

Silence again. Her Ladyship was sizing me up, gauging the path of her downwards sweep.

Agony again, the impact like a dozen whip-tails striking me at once. So hard was her delivery that I heard her gasp at her expended effort.

And I moaned, every muscle and sinew in my body and limbs in a tremor of excruciation. But I managed not to move. But how many more could I take? How many more were to come?

I saw the bamboo being drawn back. I closed my eyes, and it struck again. The agony was intense. A million swamp-hornets had stung me. I think I cried out again, but I can no longer recall. My mind was in a swirling haze of pain and misery.

'One dozen strokes, my Honourable Grand Sister,' a small soft voice announced, but the words were of such clarity that they might have travelled as clearly as the gentle song of a nightingale across a lily-pond.

Even in my haze of pain I recognised that voice. It was that of my sweet Mistress Jiang-Li, that same sweet Mistress who only yesterday had smelt at me, and for whom my improper rising had shamed my loins and almost nudged against her beautiful face.

But I had no time to deliberate on this so cruel and shocking knowledge. Her Grand Ladyship was speaking again, and my sweet Mistress Jiang-Li was padding softly back towards her, carrying that dreadful implement of my punishment so gracefully in her tiny hand.

'You have done well, this morning, my dear Sister,' Her Grand Ladyship remarked pleasantly, taking the proffered cane from her and placing it across her lap. 'You must be tired from your skilful labours now, my poor exhausted Sister. You shall rest now. Tonight I shall offer you my bath-chamber and my peach-blossom scent that His Majesty gave me as a gift only yesterday. My Eunuchs shall prepare for your well-earned bathing. When the sun dips behind the West Wall you shall soak away the sweat of your labours from that pretty body of yours!'

Her Grand Ladyship turned towards me. 'Raise your head! Yes, you who crowed and whined like a puppy-dog. Surely a mere dozen strikes with the Bamboo Rod of Reformed Memory was not so hard to bear? After all, are you not the golden bull who can rise like a staff of iron?'

And there was laughter all around me. The Honourable Sisters were enjoying Her Grand Ladyship's mocking taunts at me.

Was I supposed to reply to Her Grand Ladyship? I did not know. And, as if to answer me, Karif sneered, 'Her Grand Ladyship asked you a question, slave! Is your mouth struck as dumb as the flesh of your rump has been struck?'

'Yes, Your Ladyship ... I mean, no, Your Ladyship ... I-I am h-happy to bear my p-punishment, Your Grand Ladyship,' I stammered humbly, hoping that my words were the right ones for her royal ears. My thighs were throbbing and I trembled visibly.

She laughed. So did the Honourable Sisters again, their eyes gloating upon my shamed and ravaged nakedness.

'Good. You answer well, my poor slave. You have redeemed yourself! There is hope for you yet. Remember well today's lesson. In future you will curtail your impertinent shamefulness.'

She turned to Chief Eunuch Karif. 'The Senior Novices may go to their duties,' she said, looking imperiously out towards the back of the Assembly.

At once he snarled the order and the Senior Novices hastened to their feet before scuffling away relieved. One of the Eunuch-tutors quickly followed behind them, turning to bow to Their Ladyships as he finally departed from the vast hall.

Only my newly arrived fellow Novices and I remained there in our wretched prostrations. The Honourable Sisters were still seated on their plush silk cushions watching us curiously. My Mistress Jiang-Li – she who had so cruelly wielded the bamboo rod – was amongst those silent watchers. I could feel her eyes upon me, even though my nose was against the marble floor. My heart was beating madly and my stinging buttocks throbbed. I was trembling, every joint and muscle of my body aching in my misery.

Her Grand Ladyship was looking down at us again. Her fan was open now and she waved it leisurely against the side of her face.

After a while she nodded curtly towards Karif and immediately he addressed us.

'Now you will be taken to where you shall undergo the first of your transformations. Your heads and bodies will be shaved. This is the state in which from now on you shall remain, as all of us Eunuchs are. The Maidservants will carry out this task at every fourth sunrise. Now you will dismiss and follow your Brother-Master. When the shaving is done, only then shall you proceed to the Room of Glorious Transformation.'

Brother-Yellow-Crow appeared in front of us. He clapped his hands for us to rise but, as I did so, Chief

46

Eunuch Karif yelled at me. 'Not you, slave! Remain in your debasement, nose to the floor. You have not been selected for the honour. Her Grand Ladyship has other plans for you!'

Despite the depleting wake of my agony, I felt another bolt of fear. Why should I be singled out, denied this privilege? Had I not been brought here to fulfil my servant role?

My companions scurried away, following Brother-Yellow-Crow, who strode ahead at a fast pace.

I was left there, prostrated alone in the vast expanse of marble floor. The three Grand Ladies had not stirred from their thrones. Neither had the Honourable Sisters moved from their plush cushions. All eyes were upon me. I shivered uncontrollably.

'I have decided,' Her Grand Ladyship began, 'that you shall not be accorded the virtue of full Eunuch status. Your name is Shani, I believe?'

'Yes, Your Ladyship,' I mumbled faintly, daring to look up at her face.

'Well, Shani, you will complete your Novitiate with the other Novices. And you shall be afforded the same rank as they. But you will not attend the Room of Glorious Transformation. Neither shall you be worthy of the ceremony of the Reverent Departure of Temptation. However, you will be assigned to one of my Honourable Sisters. And you will serve her as faithfully as any other Novice or Eunuch here. And any failing will be punished no less severely. Do you understand, Shani?'

I did not truly understand, but I knew that I could not ask, and I only mumbled a word of reply.

'Good. Perhaps your understanding is limited, Shani, but for the present it is enough for you to understand only what I have told you. Full knowledge will come later to you, just as the dawns come in the East.' She paused, watching me closely, her eyes narrowing. 'Stand up!'

I got hastily to my feet, and stood there, not knowing where to put my hands, but wanting to clasp them to my throbbing buttocks.

'Do not be bashful. What you are blessed with . . . what is your natural born flesh . . . is not to be ashamed of. It is the Bad Luck of a Grey Dragon that you are nothing more than a humble slave, otherwise you might have sown the seeds for a thousand princes . . . and become a golden bull with a horn of plenty.'

There was a ripple of laughter again and a rustling of silk gowns.

Her Ladyship's eyes were scrutinising my loins, a look of amusement crossing her heavily made-up features. For a moment she turned towards her Sisters. 'Come, my dear Sisters. Raise yourselves and gather round! It is not often that you can feast your eyes upon such magnificence.'

There was hurried movement and more busy rustling of royal gowns. The Honourable Sisters came quickly, gathering round me in a semi-circle, jostling one another for better positions, but being careful not to obscure the vision of the three Grand Ladies on their thrones. There were stifled giggles and amused glances beneath long eyelashes, some coyly lowered, others more blatantly open. And, finding myself in such close proximity to these Ladies dressed so magnificently in their fineries, I felt a new dimension to my humiliation. I knew where the Honourable Sisters' eyes were focussed. Again I felt that withering limpness, knowing how my member and my sac were drawn up like the puckered flesh of dried prunes.

'Oh, celestial Heaven, what mortification have you brought upon me,' I cried silently to myself.

Yet my perceived state of contraction seemed not to diminish the amused admiration of the Ladies. Some of them pointed and whispered to each other, giggling every now and then at those exchanges of impure comments. But, even though I tried to keep my eyes averted from the Sisters' irreverent gaze, I saw again Mistress Jiang-Li, she whose beauty had made me rise with such imprudent lack of respect; she who had wielded that cruel bamboo.

She was standing slightly apart from the others, as if perhaps having no wish to participate in their mocking scrutiny. Although she was watching me intently, her beautiful face was without expression – except perhaps for a certain sadness about her pale lips, as though she might even have regretted her dutiful punishment of me.

All the while I stood there, my hands against my sides. And, if my mortified embarrassment at my so scrutinised manhood was not already bad enough, the cheeks of my rump throbbed relentlessly. The smarting sensation heated them, making them as if to shine like two small red suns.

At last Her Grand Ladyship clapped her fan shut and tapped it against the arm of her throne. At once the Sisters fell silent.

'Very well, my dear Sisters. Enough of this frivolity! Now you have had your entertainment for the day. Let us attend to the travails of State.'

Slowly the gathering broke up, Their Ladyships going to their private quarters. Yet there was one amongst the Honourable Sisters who had not moved. Mistress Jiang-Li remained standing there patiently, still watching me. There was knowledge in her eyes, and whatever knowledge it was I could tell that at least one part of it concerned me.

Apart from her, only the three Grand Ladies remained, with Chief Eunuch Karif in attendance.

And he looked at me with a mixture of curiosity and disdain. I could tell how he, too, already knew my fate.

Her Grand Ladyship waved her fan at me. 'You will be shaven now and, like all Novices, your hair will be gathered and used by the cushion-makers.' She spoke in a matter-of-fact tone. 'And afterwards you shall be ringed and clamped.'

My mind swirled with apprehension, wondering what she meant. I had seen no rings on any other servants here, and the word 'clamped' was one that I had no understanding of.

For a moment Her Grand Ladyship paused, an amused twinkle coming to her eye. 'You have already made acquaintance, have you not, Shani, with my devoted Sister here?' She turned her head towards Sister Jiang-Li, at the same time sweeping her hand imperiously in her direction. She continued, looking down at me again. 'And your acquaintance with her was an inauspicious beginning to your service with her! For it is she who will henceforth be your own Honourable Mistress. This I have decreed. And you will be indentured to her personally and serve her faithfully. And as your very own Mistress she will supervise your tutoring in those many duties required of you. Do you understand, slave?'

'Yes, Your Grand Ladyship,' I muttered quickly, bowing low.

I at least half-understood, although I didn't know whether to be gladdened by these tidings or not. My mind slowly digested these many notions. Was Brother-Yellow-Crow not my Tutor? Or was my tutoring in need of yet closer attentiveness? And was there not some perverse measure of unkind irony that my newly designated Mistress should be she who smelt at me and made for my shameful rising, and who later beat me for it with such cruel delivery?

The Grand Lady was speaking again, her tone no less severe. 'You shall never be found wanting in your duties ... not ever again!' she said gravely, before adding with an air of finality, 'Your devotion to her shall be no less than a faithful dog who defends to the death his Mistress from the jaws of baying wolves.'

She rose from her throne, as did the other Grand Ladies. Chief Eunuch Karif bowed low. And, thinking that I should also do so, I bowed in my nakedness. The three Grand Ladies shuffled away, their Eunuchs silently walking behind them like yellow shadows.

Only Chief Eunuch Karif and my Mistress Jiang-Li remained in the hall. Karif bowed to her and motioned me to follow. He took me along the west corridor and our feet padded in the echoing silence. He neither looked round at me, nor spoke, knowing only that I followed meekly. I could hear my Mistress Jiang-Li coming behind me, her silky robe whispering as she walked. I could almost feel her eyes upon my striped and burning rump. Yet I could not determine whether those same eyes looked at my ravaged state with compassion or with smug satisfaction. All I knew was that my backside smarted as much as the cheeks of my face, such was the utter humiliation of my naked debasement. With my legs moving stiffly from the throbbing pain to my buttocks I felt like a whipped dog, its tail between its legs, divested of all manly dignity.

We passed between some lacquered doors and at once the splendour of the Pavilion was left behind. Clearly we had entered some kind of working area, and there were all manner of strange aromas from either side of the corridor. Karif stopped at an archway that led into a small chamber. He stood aside, signalling for me to go in, then he waited respectfully for my Mistress to follow.

Here there were so many strange things that my eyes at first could not take them all in. I could see a number of pails filled with steaming water and several wooden cabinets against the wall. Their doors were open and inside were peculiar tools and alien instruments and assorted unknown paraphernalia. There was a small square table, on which were set other instruments, a number of jars, brushes and linen cloths and various other unidentifiable objects. A large cast-iron pot mounted on a grille-like stand, like that of a cooking stove, had been set down on the ground. And in the middle of the chamber, standing on squat pillars, was a narrow raised slab. It could have been a stone bench or even a bed, the platform of which was at the height of my belly-button.

Chief Eunuch Karif bade me curtly get up on to the slab, motioning me to lie back on it. The stone was cold against my back and my buttocks as I lay down, my eyes darting anxiously about me. What menacing place was this, with its strange aromas and paraphernalia? There was a mixture of lilac scent and ripe hay, but more sinister was the odd fire-burning smell of sintering charcoal. And I could feel the heat of it coming from beneath the iron pot.

We were not alone in the chamber. Hovering around were three yellow-clad Eunuchs and a small bare-chested man wearing a leather apron. And three Maidservants stood timidly by the wall.

One of them was Li-Mei, she of the title Beautiful Plum Blossom. With downcast frightened eyes she glanced upon my nakedness. What thoughts were in that tiny head of hers I could not conceive.

I saw the Eunuchs and Maidservants bow as my Mistress entered. She neither spoke nor acknowledged them, only stood there silently in her regal poise, her hands tucked neatly in the wide sleeves of her robe.

'Begin!' Karif commanded.

And at once the Eunuchs came to stand beside me, one on either side of the slab, the other at my feet. Now the Maidservants busied themselves, coming behind my head. They had small bowls in their hands and there were instruments contained inside.

'Your head will be shaven first,' Karif announced, standing over me.

And immediately I felt small hands taking the straw-gold locks of my hair and metal beginning to cut them away, and not with any gentleness. Nobody spoke. There was only the sound of the cutting work. And, when I felt the strangeness of such unknown exposure of my skull, the work stopped for a moment. Then the Maidservants began again with other instruments that closely scraped the tufty residues of my golden birthright from every part of my scalp.

I dared not look at my Mistress, but I instinctively knew that she was looking at me all the while. It seemed to my poor humbled mind that the reposing flesh of my manhood stood out with such mortifying prominence between my legs. Her eyes and those of all her servants must be upon my once proud flesh. Yet the Maidservants showed no apparent interest, being so wholly engaged in their shaving work, their eyes etched with concentration. It must have been a task they were well accustomed to, because their fingers moved deftly and skilfully, and they needed no instruction or rebuking.

My head was bald and I could feel it wet with the soapy lather and water that trickled down to the floor. Without prompting, the Maidservants moved to either side of the slab.

'Lift your arms back, slave,' Karif ordered me, and then the Eunuchs grabbed my wrists and extended my arms outwards.

At once the Maidservants shaved my armpits. And, when this had been done, the attendants moved down to my groin. I could see their small bowls and brushes and the shaving blades and how every so often these were sharpened on strips of leather.

Two of the Maidservants came to stand on either side of me, the other girl hovering nearby and holding out the bowls. I could not help but look up at the sweet faces of my unwilled attendants, but it was only Li-Mei who had shyness in her eyes. And I could see how she wanted to look away, but all the same her gaze remained fixed upon my reposing manhood as if it were an object of fascination to her.

I was aware, too, that my Mistress had come forward now. I could smell her fragrance and hear the rustling of her silk. She bent slightly, peering down at me. And for a second the Maidservants stood back, not knowing whether to continue with their work upon me there.

For a moment my eyes imprudently met hers when she glanced down at my face. Her expression was inscrutable. But the moment passed and she stepped silently back, motioning for the attendants to continue.

I felt the blades coming against my lower belly, beginning to scrape at my hair on either side, then moving down on each side of my reposing flesh.

Karif grunted and motioned the Eunuchs to take my legs, and I felt them being spread outwards so that my groin was more exposed. At first there was no disturbance to my mound, the blades nimbly scraping around each side of it. But, when the work became more intricate, I felt my sac and my shank being gathered up in a soft warm hand.

'Oh, Mother, what new humiliation is this heaped upon me?' I cried out silently as I thought so fondly of my home, now so far away.

Although the hand that held my manhood held me gently enough, those slender fingers circled my seed-stones tightly, and stretched my sac away from its root-base. Every so often the hand moved my pulpy mass to one side or the other while the blade swept close in against the drawn-up sac, scraping delicately and into every nook and fold. And this time there was not even the merest stiffening of my shank, not even a rush of blood to its veins or any flooding of my sac. I was as good as gelded, my manliness departed me no less than the moisture of a sun-dried prune.

I opened my eyes. With a little shock I could see that it was Li-Mei, my Beautiful Plum Blossom attendant, who held me so. But at least the shaving in my crotch was completed. I felt her lay my flesh down again gently, neatly arranging it so that the mushroom-head of my pendulous shank touched the cold stone of the slab below, and she let me rest finely across the twin humps of my sac. How naked did I feel.

But my ordeal was far from over. Karif signalled the Eunuchs, and the Maidservants stood back, but they did not withdraw. Then I felt the Eunuchs seize me by my legs, and slide me down to the very end of the slab. They lifted me, pushing my knees back on to my stomach, so that immediately my thighs were forced wide apart, spreading the tautened scarps of my buttocks. This brought a further wave of agony as the cores of my welts seemed to split in the sudden stretching of my skin.

The Eunuchs held me in that freshly debasing posture, my feet in the air and on either side of me. I felt so helpless, not knowing what would come now.

Karif snapped, 'Keep still, slave. We have more work to do.' He had something in his hand, a smooth wooden implement like a small rod with a smooth conical end to it. He looked warningly at me from the end of the slab. 'Do not move. I shall not hurt you . . . unless you squirm.'

He stooped low over my ravaged and thrusting hindquarters, his bald head disappearing somewhere between my feet. My Mistress watched impassively. And I felt something nudge into the very sump of my forbidden passage, pressure coming at once to it.

Oh, celestial Heavens take me now and make me a spirit free from earthly misery!

The impure end of the wooden rod drove a small expansion in me, beginning immediately to manoeuvre itself against my so forceful and involuntary resistance. Every muscle there in my lower body seemed to seize up like unyielding rock, closing themselves against this vile intrusion. And, not knowing what manner of debasing perversity this was, I could only gasp in despair and fresh humiliation. What torment was this? In my innocence I could make no speculation, knowing only that my so wickedly ruptured passage had hitherto only one evacuating purpose. And now some other unnatural thing of impurity had entered me and travelled inwards, defying the habitual tidal direction allowed by that so private domain.

Then, as quickly as the rod had entered, it was withdrawn. I gasped again, perhaps with relief. Had I not felt as if that rotten wood had been intent upon forging a path to the other side of my very being? Karif stood up, apparently satisfied with whatever exploration he had desired to achieve. I saw him turn towards my Mistress, who had observed these irreverent proceedings without expression or movement.

'My Lady, I can humbly report that the examination ordered by Her Grand Ladyship and the Royal Physicians is complete,' Karif announced, bowing.

'And I am pleased that I can humbly verify that there is no need for concern in that matter. The slave is pure there. His flesh is unsoiled by the entry of man. I find no unnatural expansion there, Your Ladyship. His innocence is as that of a lamb, and his passage is no less intact than the flowerbud of a young virgin girl.'

These words were so strange to me. But my Mistress only nodded. Her expression was as inscrutable as ever, even though for a second her gaze alighted on my shamed face. But still the two Eunuchs held me in that evil posture, as though I were to suffer some fresh indignity.

Karif motioned to the Maidservants, and they came quickly between my thighs, taking their shaving brushes and blades again to me. And it was Li-Mei with her sweet plum-blossom cheeks that wielded the blade, scraping first the outer scarps and then deeper with delicate little sweeps. In my unenquiring innocence I had not even known that I was possessed with any growth there at all. This Pavilion was such a place of mystery, and a place where unknown secrets were revealed like the rotting pulp of a slowly peeled pear.

When I was done, the Eunuchs lowered me, at the same time sliding me back along the slab again. I could hear the other Eunuch removing things noisily from the big cabinet by the wall, but I could not see what these things were.

As if in answer to the questions in my mind, Chief Eunuch Karif said, 'You will be bound now. It is better that this should be so. You body is strong and it must be held by straps and chains while we ring and clamp you.'

Again these words 'ring and clamp' floated unwillingly into my ears. But I had no time to deliberate.

My arms were seized and pulled down on either side of the stone slab. I felt straps cuffing my wrists, and then being secured somewhere beneath. The Eunuchs came to my legs, and split them roughly to the sides, pulling them right under the slab so that my knees were bent right back and jammed taut against the stonework. My ankles were fastened and drawn even further back so that the muscles of my legs and arms were as tense as bowstrings. My back and my still throbbing buttocks were hard against the cold slab, my sweating body astride it, trussed like some sacrificial beast awaiting its demise.

But my binding was not quite finished. If it were not already enough, my poor wrists and ankles aching with the tightness of the straps, a length of chain was placed across my lower belly, tightened and finally hooked beneath the slab. Now there was no possibility for me to move, except for my head and neck, and these in futile desperation I raised up in order to look down at my own tethered nakedness.

But the smell of burning charcoal came again to my nostrils. The huge iron pot was being heated, and the small bare-chested man was bent over it, holding some kind of implements in the fire. Terrified but helpless, all I could do was to try to see out of the corner of my eye what fresh torment was being prepared for me.

Again it seemed that Karif had read my mind. 'It will hurt you, Shani . . . but you are strong and brave. And it is surely better than the ceremony of Reverent Departure of Temptation. Her Grand Ladyship has mercifully spared you that at least.'

It was the first time that the Chief Eunuch had addressed me by name, and perhaps a fleeting wave of compassion had washed over his stern countenance. He spoke again, softly now. 'They will ring you first. A circle of gold will be inserted at the end of your pizzle and you shall wear it proudly for the remainder of your days here.'

At that moment my Mistress came closer. Still with her hands calmly folded in her sleeves she stood there beside me, her eyes for the first time looking down with pity at me. Her beautiful face was as serene as the reflection of a summer moon in a lake.

Karif stood back patiently, waiting for her to speak. And clearly she would do so. On this occasion she seemed so full of confidence and majesty. And for the first time in my lifespan at the Pavilion I heard her wisdom, her words floating down to me so gently. 'Shani, you are to be my servant . . . and I, in turn, will be your Mistress and Tutor. For this I need you to know that what your tortured mind now thinks must be no less than the wicked cruelty of demon-gods is in fact a gift to you.' She paused for a second, letting her wisdom come slowly to me. 'It is Her Grand Ladyship's gift . . . and one that I begged from her. I prostrated myself before her before I could find pleading words enough to secure her favour.'

She looked at me, seeing the puzzlement that had for a moment displaced my terror. 'Oh, yes, Shani. This is so. But I was not alone amongst my Honourable Sisters here. Many of them would have wished to save you from the cruel disfigurement that, even now as I speak, is the fate of your companions in the Room of Glorious Transformation. But I alone, as your Mistress, dared to ask Her Grand Ladyship. And for that I made many concessions, including the gifting of my favourite opal and emerald necklace . . . that same one given me in person by His Imperial Majesty. And not only that, Shani, but I lost face in asking our Mother Sister for her mercy.' She turned suddenly to the Chief Eunuch. 'Is this not so, Karif?'

Karif bowed low, smiling obsequiously. 'That is so, Your Ladyship. But, if I may be bold in my humble reverence to both of my Honourable Mistresses, you were both so generous in your compassion for this unworthy slave. How favoured he is to have two such benevolent Mistresses! And, my Lady, although you were gracious in your gift of your necklace, it went justly to a merciful Lady . . . with only well-meaning loss of face by you, my Lady.'

My Mistress nodded, before turning to me again. 'Whatever my own loss, you have been saved the loss of your natural-born manliness, Shani. Perhaps even Karif here shall be envious of your good fortune . . .'

Karif smiled again, but his lips were frosty, as though caught for a moment in deceptive thoughts. 'My Lady, it is not good for your humble servant to be envious of his good fortune to be in this Divine Palace and for the honour to serve –'

But my Mistress waved him to silence, and he bowed again. She continued speaking to me, perhaps seeing how my body shook with fear and from the aching discomfort of my bonds. 'Your companions will by now no longer be true men, Shani. Their seed-sacs will have been cut from them in their transformation into Novice Eunuch-servants and their blood will have flowed like the blood of slaughtered pigs.' Her voice was as soft and crystal clear again as if it had floated across a moon-bright lily-pond. And, if I did not comprehend all her words, I knew at least the sincerity of them.

It was only much later, in my many quiet discussions with my Brother Novices – they who indeed had been worthy of the ceremony of Reverent Departure of Temptation, and who thereafter were only my half-Brothers and in name only – that I heard the full accounts of what happened in that feared Room of Glorious Transformation.

In that same season of my arrival only six of my ten remaining comrades survived their ordeal. Those who did not had gushed their life's blood from their torn wounds, their white staunching-pads not sufficient to stem the deadly flow. Although the Royal Physicians were skilled at their work, and their healing herbs were as potent as any known to man, the ritualistic cuts of such delicate flesh were frequently more than the victim could endure, either to his flesh or to his sanity. And in that first crucial hour, if the flow of blood could itself be stemmed, there was always the risk of putrification. This was despite the surgeon's skill and how cleanly his knife cut, and despite those healing poultices that he afterwards applied. And then would come the agony that was said on occasion to drive the now gelded victim to a state of madness. And sometimes the madness would come even before the knife itself had begun its task. Moreover, that same madness gave him such inhuman strength that the skin of his arms and legs would be burnt from the straps that bound him.

One night, many seasons after my arrival, I went secretly to the Room of Glorious Transformation, even though it was a forbidden place for me. To reach it one had to cross the Garden of Tranquillity on the west side of the Pavilion. This in itself was such a deceiving irony because the Novices would first have to walk to their fate through the peaceful and fragrant lushness of those beautiful gardens before arriving at the stone building at the end. And it was this quietly unobtrusive place that housed the Room of Glorious Transformation. To look at those huge external doors as those many young men came upon them would have surely given so little notion of what awaited beyond. Yet, as the naked Novices meekly followed their yellow-robed Eunuch-masters across the gardens, they were perhaps suffused with peacefulness and reassurance by all those sweet scents of magnolia and hibiscus, so that by the time they had reached the thick wooden doors every Novice was filled with awe, lulled into his compliant fate.

There was a bright half-moon when I ventured furtively across the gardens, the forbidden doors looming before me so suddenly. They creaked loudly as I opened them, first one set and then a second, as if two had been required to contain the secrets beyond. Inside, it was as silent as the grave and the shadows of night fell upon it as eerily as if the restless spirits of countless dead Novices lurked all around in the archways overhead and behind the great pillars. The marble floor was like ice to my bare feet. And the three ceremonial trestles seemed to stand there so ominously, as though eagerly awaiting new candidates for transformation. Each wooden trestle was fashioned in the shape of a giant cross, and I shuddered as I imagined the Novices stretched out upon them and strapped in their terrible prostration, like young spread-eagled fawns, all so utterly helpless in their terror. And, as I stood there, closing my eyes, I would make an oath this day that I could hear the echoing screams of a thousand demented souls.

I remember fleeing from that haunted place, and never more did I return there.

But my gracious Mistress had not finished with her wisdom. And, as I lay there on the cold slab that was wet beneath me from my sweat and the soapy water, it was more difficult to concentrate on her words, each one coming so thick and fast upon me that I could scarcely understand each dreadful meaning.

'Shani, I may weep tonight from the pain you must bear, but you must bear it well . . . and when you cry out it will offend my ears. But in this Palace there are so many fearful cries and yours will be of no greater significance than many others.' For a moment she paused, smiling sadly down at me, before she continued. 'The ring you must bear is for a purpose, and the size of it shall have no less purpose. It will be to stop those things that temptation will bring about . . . not just your temptation, but as much that of my dear Sisters.'

I heard these words so clearly, but my thoughts were dulled by fear. Whatever temptations she referred to were far from my mind. It was only later that Brother-Yellow-Crow would reveal to me the fullness of all these puzzling things. But for now all I could think of was the ordeal awaiting me. My nostrils were invaded by burning smells and my eyes swivelled about fearfully as they tried to make sense of all that was happening around me.

For a moment my Mistress let her gaze travel from my face down to where my legs were splayed open so irreverently. She looked at me in that place with what perhaps might have been a mixture of critical appraisal and fascination. And my shank reposed there motionless, its gnarled veins empty of stiffening blood and humbled by her gaze. It might have been for just a brief moment, but it seemed as if she were on the point of reaching out and taking my flesh in her hand, but she did not. Instead she stepped back a pace and nodded her head curtly at Karif. And he took my flesh in his hand, pulling me upwards, stretching me, and his fingers held me in a vicelike grip so that the mushroom-head – that which had been exposed from the cut of my infancy – was raised up so prominently. 'Pierce him now,' he ordered.

The small bare-chested man with the leather apron came at once to the end of the slab and bent down over me. I strained to look down, not wanting to, but needing to. The point of the long bulbous needle was red with heat and it moved nearer to me.

Karif nodded at Li-Mei, who came quickly to his side, her timid eyes glancing down at me. 'Take this fold of skin here,' he ordered, moving his fingers to pull at the tight skin of my sheath just below the grooved slit of my mushroom. 'Pinch him here, girl, with your finger and thumb – and hurry yourself.'

The Maidservant reached out with her small dainty hand. Ever so hesitantly she took the skin of my flesh.

'Draw it out, girl!' Karif was impatient now. The needle was cooling, its point no longer red with heat. 'More!' he snapped.

I felt a sore tightening of that so intimate and vulnerable part of me.

Li-Mei obeyed, stretching the elongation of my skin. Her lips were pursed with concentration, her eyes so bright in their intensity. She could no longer glance back at my face in sympathy. And all the while our Honourable Mistress was watching us.

'Keep it like so!' Karif's voice was harsh, and he glared warningly at the Maidservant. 'Do not release it until I order you!'

The needle came swiftly and I felt the sudden agony as it pierced my delicate fold. I wanted to make my legs kick out at this defilement, but they were tethered so securely under me. All that I could do in that moment of excruciation was to heave my chest out, my lungs breathless, my spine arching involuntarily, and I uttered a long gasping moan.

But the metal was still in me, as if its work were not yet done. The bare-chested man kept it there for a few seconds before pushing it further along, expanding the incision until eventually the much wider and blunt end of the needle passed out of me. But Karif still held my shaft and Li-Mei had not dared to release the freshly pierced fold.

I closed my eyes, but I was aware of the bare-chested man standing over his charcoal stove again. I could smell hot metal, and there was the sound of tongs and pincers fashioning it.

'Keep still, Shani,' Karif said quietly to me, his tone not unkindly. 'Now he will put the ring of gold in you and seal it. The pain will be more, but it will pass quickly enough ... unless you struggle. Then it will be greater.'

I did not watch. My trembling was like the ague of mosquito-sickness. But soon I felt another stretching of my flesh and a surge of new agony. This time it was a burning rather than a tearing agony, but a certain throbbing numbness began to diminish it. There was a weightiness, and I felt another brief searing of hot pain as the metal was sealed by pincers.

Karif grunted something that I did not hear, but I felt my shank being gently laid down. There was an alien heaviness at the end of it, and I caught a tiny metallic sound that the ring made as it came to rest against the stone slab below.

'That part is done,' Karif announced abruptly. 'Now we shall do the clamping of his sac.'

If, at least, I could vaguely understand the alien ring, I had no understanding of what meaning there was to these other words. What manner could there be to this clamping of my sac?

As if my Mistress had read my thoughts, she came again to my side, looking down at my pain-racked face. 'Shani, your manhood sac will now be circled by a band of gold. Our learned Physicians advise us that in time this will impede the rising of your sap.' She was speaking slowly so that every word that came so unwillingly to my ears might enlighten my feeble brain. 'The Physicians say that, each time you shall begin to be overwhelmed by temptation, the band will constrict the rising and quell the brewing of your seed.'

She glanced down at my ringed manhood suddenly, studying its new adornment, but continuing to speak to me all the while. 'And even if the seed should still rise from your sac it will pain you there, and so lessen the temptation. And, if that is not sufficient, whatever sap shall still spume from your eye-spout would be no greater than an infant boy's.'

How many times thereafter did I recall her words? Yet, had I not detected a certain insincerity in her tone – as if she herself doubted those words? And much later I was indeed to learn that those wise Physicians were not altogether correct in their predictions. Certainly I would have pain, but the pain was never enough to quench the lust of youth. And, as for temptation, my Honourable Mistress in all her beauty – and indeed in the beauty of other Honourable Ladies in the confines of the Pavilion, and even that of my sweet little Li-Mei – was always there constantly around me to offer such imprudent temptations. And those temptations were never mine alone, which indeed had been my Mistress's own wise prediction. But there was always that other impediment to stop my unwisely brewed seed from entering forbidden places. But all this would soon be explained to me by my Brother-Master Kanchu, and later by my dear Mistress herself.

Once more she stood back, making way for the bare-chested man to come again between my open legs. I could just see the small gold band that he held in his tongs, and I could see that it was hot. It was

66

more in horror that I cried out, for he had not even touched me. But suddenly Karif pushed my ringed shank to one side and seized my low-slung sac in his fingers. He made a circle around me with his finger and thumb and slid it down my limp pouch until it came up against the small spheres contained within. And, tightening his grip, he pulled at me, stretching me outwards to the full extent of my natural elasticity. The pressure on my twin spheres was as if he intended to crush them, but he pulled no further, only holding me out for the band to be curled around the lower sac and just above the base of its attachment to my groin.

I screamed because the heat was unbearable, even though the man worked speedily and nimbly, twisting and bending the malleable gold until it neatly circled me. My bellowing and my helpless writhing made me as a wild animal, and the sweat ran from my heaving torso. But the chain across me and the straps around my wrists and ankles were unyielding, biting into my struggling flesh.

'Oh, Mother . . . oh, Mother! No!' I yelled, careless of the echoing din.

But it was over, and the searing heat began to evaporate, even though the soreness would remain for several days after.

'There now!' My Mistress was once more standing over me, her poise ever so graceful and dignified. Without lowering her chin she looked down at me, smiling wistfully. Her hands were always clasped together in her silk sleeves. Every now and then she glanced down at my new adornments with a lazy but nonetheless furtive sweep of her eyes.

'It is done now, Shani. Your pain is over. Although Her Grand Ladyship mercifully denied you the honour of Glorious Transformation, you are nonetheless indentured now, and with scarcely less honour than your fellow Novices. And remember, my poor slave, that their agonies are threefold more than yours. With each cut of the surgeon's Knife of Transformation it will not be just their flesh that is parted from them, but also the lustful thoughts of manhood. Whereas your mind is left with those natural thoughts, theirs are left only with memories.'

If it had not been for the words themselves my Mistress's voice would have sounded like the music of harps.

She turned to Karif. 'See that he is well bathed down, and that the lotion is soothingly administered to where the gold has burnt him . . . and also where the bamboo has flayed him. Then he should be oiled and rested.' She glanced down at me again, her face severe now. 'Tomorrow, bring him to my chamber . . . and then we shall judge his manner. If his temperament is pleasing enough, he shall stay in my service. But if his demeanour is as if cursed like one of Heaven's Dangerous Spirits, then . . .' But she did not finish, only turning away and gliding out of that dreadful place like a gracious cloud of shimmering silk.

Three

I would always so vividly remember the day of my ringing and clamping, and also afterwards how, when my Mistress had departed, Karif had ordered the Eunuchs and Maidservants to attend to my sore throbbing body.

Once my chain and straps had been removed, I lay there panting, my back and buttocks still against the stone slab. First the Maidservants had washed me down with cool rose-water, their soft towels so soothing on my skin as they gently sponged away the sweat of my terror and agony. More than the other servants, it was Li-Mei who was like a heavenly angel as she stood there over me, her towel working so tenderly over my chest and belly and under my arms. Her face was the very picture of concern, and perhaps much more, but she worked under Karif's wary darting eyes and he was ever vigilant.

The Eunuchs sponged my arms, legs and feet, carefully attending to the inflamed marks made by my wild tugging against the straps. When it came for Li-Mei to sponge between my legs, I could see how shy her face became, a small pinkish glow appearing in her cheeks like an instant blemish of plum-blossom. Her eyes focused on my newly ringed shank as if they desired to take in every small detail, but at the same time fearing to linger there for longer than her duty required. She held her wet towel so daintily with her shy fingers as she sponged down on each side of my bonded manhood, scarcely daring to touch it until Karif snarled impatiently at her. 'It will not bite you, girl. It is just the flesh of a slave . . . as is your own. Lift him there and make your towel sponge all around it. Do your duty with all earnestness, Li-Mei . . . or I shall do mine on you with my leather Learning Tails!'

And immediately she was chastened, her pretty face crestfallen, her wistful smile gone in a second. She became brisk in her work, taking my flesh in her fingers almost irreverently and wiping underneath and in all the damaged and undamaged folds. Even though the cool wetness came pleasingly on to my throbbing soreness, I still gasped aloud at the numbing shock of it. But my eyes were on her face, seeing the beauty of it and the slender shapeliness of her small arm. Moreover, the thought of her busy fingers working on my masculine flesh was altogether enough to cause an impudent stirring in me. And the brewing seed that my Mistress had spoken of was not at all quenched, neither by my prostrated humiliation, nor by all those stern faces hovering over me. It occurred to me at that very moment that the pain and wickedness that I had endured had failed to achieve that unwilled state of departed temptation. Had not those learned Physicians so assured my Mistress and her Honourable Sisters that it would be so? Those words were still so fresh in my troubled mind. 'Each time you shall begin to be overwhelmed by temptation, the band will constrict the rising, and quell the brewing of your seed . . . and lessen the temptation.'

Yet scarcely had more than a few grains of sand flowed to the bottom of the hourglass since my ringing and clamping than already I felt some rising of my sap. And was this not despite all those contrary influences that had been heaped upon me? And in this, my first impudent stirring since those quenching measures had been fixed upon me, was I not still with those same manly feelings as before? As for the withering prediction that 'if your seed should still rise from your sac it will pain you there', I could not at that time confirm it to be true or otherwise, because the throbbing and stinging pain was all about me there, and not confined to the brewing place of my now banded sac.

But fortunately my stirring amounted to little more than a brief swell to the veins of my shank, not enough to cause an impetuous stiffening, but more a languid expansion. But I am sure that Li-Mei must have felt this in her fingers, the sudden intensity in her eyes telling me as much. Fearfully, perhaps for both of us, she laid me down. And, whatever measure of my expansion had occurred, it was insufficient to keep the ring from touching the stone slab beneath me, and I reposed there once more, the moment having passed.

It was not Li-Mei who poured the soothing ointment over my tender manhood, or who massaged me there, working the greasy balm into my moist pulp and making me groan. This task had been assigned to one of the other young Maidservants, and she performed it without the slightest show of emotion. My flesh might have been no more than dead meat on a chopping slab. Her face was without expression, a pale mask of indifference and unconcern as she stood there moving her fingers about me in so perfunctory a manner. I wondered what thoughts must have been inside her head.

Soon the Eunuchs and Maidservants had finished with the front of my body and Karif ordered me to turn. I did so stiffly, feeling the new heaviness of tight gold dragging down at my vulnerable flesh as I settled myself face-down on the stone slab. It was difficult to know where the stinging and throbbing soreness began and ended, my whole lower body seeming to be afflicted by so many different assaults on its nerve-ends.

Karif was giving orders and the same perfunctory Maidservant was beside me again, standing there with a small earthenware pot. At once I felt an oily coldness come upon the lashed cheeks of my rump.

'Her Honourable Ladyship, your Mistress, has streaked your flesh so harshly with the Bamboo Rod of Reformed Memory,' Karif sneered. 'She has left its gnarled imprints on your white skin like crimson furrows made by the plough of a she-devil.'

Out of the corner of one eye I could see that he was on the other side of me, bent over my ravaged cheeks and examining them critically. All the while the Maidservant was massaging them with the balm, not tenderly, the motion making me wince and gasp as she worked. Her fingers travelled over the bumps of my ridges with no apparent discern, as if they might have been defects of nature that required her dutiful attention.

'Your Mistress inflicts deserved punishment on you, but then afterwards orders me to have your punished flesh soothed with healing balm!' Karif scoffed, his tone rich with impudent sarcasm.

Clearly he did not approve of my Mistress's orders. But she was no longer there to rebuke him.

'Make your fingers rub the balm with more vigour!' he told the Maidservant impatiently.

At once she obeyed, her rotating actions becoming more painful on my rump and making their firm peaks contort and quiver beneath her busy hands.

Whatever balm it was, it stung like the bites of a thousand hornets. I groaned, my eye catching hers, but her face was still a mask of uncaring indifference and there was no respite in her task for even a second. Whatever compassion she possessed, clearly none of it was for me.

I could not know why. Might it have been that she performed this duty with such regularity that her heart was dead to kindly feelings? Or perhaps she despised the flesh she tended to, each time finding it becoming more repugnant to her touch. It was to be much later that Li-Mei gave me an explanation, but for now she hovered in the background watching me with such tenderness. Why could it not have been her to minister to my sore cheeks – or beforehand to my perversely ringed and banded flesh? Perhaps Karif had deliberately wanted to deny her that assignment, and also to deny me that assuredly more gentle attention.

Nearly a whole season in the Pavilion would go by before Li-Mei told me about this uncaring Maidservant. She was called Huan-Yue, a name that meant 'One of Joy'. I laughed at such irony of fate, but Li-Mei rebuked me for my rash condemnation. 'She is a lonely creature with a damaged heart, Shani. If she hates men it is for a reason. But, whatever that reason may be, it is hidden too deep in her. So do not be too harsh in your judgement of her.'

'Too harsh on *her*?' I snorted indignantly. 'Shall I not always remember how harsh she was on me?'

At that time Li-Mei and I were in the Garden of Tranquillity. It was a moonlit night and we stood together in the shadows, speaking quietly to each other. It was after the hour that we should have been in our separate dormitories. Our meeting was therefore a clandestine one, and so fraught with danger. We could not linger there too long. The more we did so, the greater was the risk of discovery. At the very least it would have meant a whipping for both of us. And in my case how displeased my Honourable Mistress would have been. To her there was no greater sin than disloyalty.

I can no longer recall why Li-Mei was speaking to me about Huan-Yue. Perhaps it was to keep our minds away from dangerous passion. And the Garden of Tranquillity was scarcely the place to unleash it, there being always so little time to indulge in any illicit outpouring of our mutual affection.

'Huan-Yue is . . . is attracted to me, Shani,' Li-Mei whispered hesitantly, her soft voice etched with guilt. She waited to see my reaction, but I said nothing, only looking into her eyes.

'On lonely nights she sometimes comes to me in the darkness. She lies on my mattress . . . and . . . and she massages me.' For a second her lips quivered, her eyes round as they looked into mine. 'Here . . . in this sensitive place between my legs,' she added in a whisper.

I saw Li-Mei touch her flimsy robe down in that place, and I felt a pang of sudden jealousy. The notion of her lying naked with another naked girl was at once both intriguing and hurtful. I myself had never seen that place she spoke of now, except on one fleeting occasion. Even then I had only glimpsed its covered outline.

She had been seated on the stone floor of the laundry-chamber, wringing out her Mistress's washing in a basin. Her own servant's robe had been wet from her work, and I caught sight of the delicate formation of those delightful twin humps, but only through the tightly transparent folds of her garment.

But now Li-Mei was looking at me, searching my eyes, knowing what I would ask.

'Do you . . . welcome her when she comes to your mattress?' I did indeed ask. 'And when she does those intimate things to you, Li-Mei, does it . . . er . . . please you?' I could not help myself. I had to know her feelings.

She replied coyly, but with a kind of sadness. 'Shani, it is difficult for you to understand those things.' She sighed, reaching out and gently taking my hand in hers. 'We Maidservants live so close together . . . like young nesting birds, our plumes brushing against each other in our caged confinement. We are deprived of so much. Our restless spirits crave so many things, but above all we crave companionship and comfort . . . and loving company.'

She wanted so eagerly to reassure me. 'And we have no men to give us those things, Shani. All we have is our own bodies. So do not judge us badly when we form our own relationships, one with another . . . for mutual comfort, as comrades who share the same hardships and deprivations, and as much to ease our loneliness.'

She ran her finger across my bare chest, tracing the muscled curve of my breast, and added softly, 'It is not for the sensual act of pleasure itself, Shani. Believe me. I ache for you . . . to have you close to me. But are we not slaves here? And, although we must be grateful to our Royal Mistresses, we still have feelings. And, although our good Mistresses put food in our mouths and a roof over our lowly heads, we are denied so much else. Even as we talk, it is forbidden . . .' Here she looked at me again with such bright wistful eyes before continuing. 'And although I always desire to feel your manly muscled body against mine, and to know how the warm presence of your huge flesh in mine would be, how can that happen? Your ring makes it impossible. And, even if it were not so, if we should be caught in such a dangerous act, would we not be flogged, or worse . . . or be sent away from this place which has become our home?'

I could not reply, knowing my own feelings for her and my loneliness, but at the same time feeling guilt. How disloyal that would have been to my Honourable Mistress – she who had saved me from the Reverent Departure of Temptation. Despite my desires and affection for Li-Mei, how should I ever cast aside the constant shadow of my Mistress, her serene, regal image always dancing into my vision?

Li-Mei continued with her reasoning, and I listened without a word. 'As a Novice Eunuch who can never be a true Eunuch, have you not been blessed with celestial good fortune, Shani? Apart from being like other Novices – I mean, in name and in all other ways apart from one – you are at least as whole as any other man, and not like your poor Novice Brothers. And they are without feelings towards us girl servants, so how then shall we know how to release our own natural feelings towards other men? We have no means . . . because there are no true men here. Therefore should we not seek comfort and pleasures amongst ourselves?'

What she said made sense to me, and I was at once ashamed of my insensitive questioning. But she had spoken of my celestial good fortune, which both angered and saddened me at that moment, because it was clear to me that she had little understanding of my own plight.

'How should that be my good fortune, Li-Mei?' I asked hotly. 'Do I not also crave to put myself in you, and to spume my seed in you with loving passion? And do you really believe that my ring and the band around me stifle the rising of my sap and all my desires? Do you not drive me wild as I stand beside you, knowing that I can never enter you? And when my Mistress teases me and makes my flesh stiffen like a mast, am I not reminded of my potency ... that same potency that is denied me to spume anywhere, in her, or in you? And, in my frustrated lust, is not my fledgling spume forced back to sink again like stale milk in my sac, making me ache as the unspent fluid of my passion seeps back so painfully into my pod?'

I was almost breathless with my angry words. But she smiled sadly at me, running her fingers fondly down my belly. She could see my anguish, and perhaps she regretted her words, but I would not be silenced yet.

'No, Li-Mei, I am *not* fortunate! And if it is good fortune, then I curse it with all my heart. Sometimes I think it would have been better to have suffered the ritual cut in that terrible Room of Glorious Transformation, rather than to have been made into something that is neither a Eunuch nor a whole man. I am even without honour amongst my Brother Eunuchs, for they see me as an outcast, not one of them, but an alien creature without place or purpose.' I sighed heavily, my anger vented.

She continued to brush her fingers over the warm contours of my belly, her eyes so full of sadness.

'The other Novices cannot help it, Li-Mei,' I went on. 'They both envy and despise me. Perhaps they are tormented by my sac, knowing that it makes me different from them, knowing that I was spared their terrible ordeal only because my natural-born flesh was more prized than theirs.'

Li-Mei knew the truth of that. Had she not seen my endowment with her own eyes and touched me with her dainty fingers? No less had she known the rumours of how those Honourable Sisters in the Pavilion of the Divine Orchid Ladies had been permitted to retain me as a kind of trophy – one that was for giving pleasure to the sight, but nothing more, and never to be touched, except by some cruel act of perversity or punishment.

After all, many of the Honourable Sisters were bereft of His Imperial Majesty's company, being summoned only infrequently, or sometimes never at all. He was no more the bull-emperor of his younger days. And his sons, although numerous, were less prolific than their father. Besides, they favoured only the more youthful of the Royal Concubines, and not particularly those who were favoured by their own father. Moreover, many of them were said to seek their pleasures elsewhere, some of them with manly flesh, or even with the younger Eunuchs, although this was forbidden on pain of death.

It was this scarcity of royal summonses to imperial or princely bedchambers that made for discontent in the Pavilion. In that first full season of my service there, how many times was I to witness the unleashing of so much spite and cruel perversities. And it seemed to me that my destiny was nothing more than to be a sort of royal plaything amongst the Honourable Sisters. And Her Grand Ladyship did nothing to discourage it. Indeed, she took a remote secret pleasure from it, watching her Sisters at their play, and watching me. Perhaps she wished to catch her own dear Sisters in some forbidden act. Certainly it had been out of no benevolent act of compassion on her part to deprive me of the ceremony in the Room of Glorious Transformation.

It was only much later that I learnt how much my Honourable Mistress Jiang-Li had risked to save me from that transforming ordeal. That generous gifting of her favourite opal and emerald necklace given to her in person by His Imperial Majesty had not been her only sacrifice on my account. Her Grand Ladyship had wished to exact much more than that. And regardless of my Mistress's often capricious moods, and her sudden outpouring of cruelty, how much I owed her my undying devotion, even if on occasion I should seem unworthy.

And so there should not have been bitterness in my words to Li-Mei, at least not in respect of my Mistress's good intentions. But good intentions are not always for the best in the final outcome of reality. And on that particular day of my meeting with Li-Mei – both of us mere servant slaves – reality had a bitter taste to it. I went on with my complaint about my very existence, caring not of my ungracious words or of my disloyalty to my Mistress.

'It is true what they say of me, Li-Mei. I am a false Eunuch – one that is like a freak to be gaped at. And they know that I am only kept this way because my presence gives some strange pleasure to Their Honourable Ladyships. They mock me and taunt me mercilessly, and at their fanciful whim order me to remove my Apron of Good Modesty, so that they can gaze curiously at me, or even prod me with their lace fans or tickle me thereabouts with ostrich-feathers, and humiliate me in whatever way they choose. And I must obey unquestioningly or face cruel punishment at morning Prostration Assembly. And when I complain to my dear Mistress – she who saved me from the sac-knife – she only tells me angrily to be compliant and obey implicitly and to stop my petulant complaining, or that she herself will beat me for my insolence.'

During all this outpouring of my despair Li-Mei listened in quiet sorrow, unable to comfort me. Nor could she release the hardening frustrations of my flesh in my desire for her. Or so I thought.

'My poor Shani, he who wants me . . . as I want him. How cruel is the wall our Mistresses have put between us,' she whispered huskily.

We stood there together under the bright stars of the heavens. The Garden of Tranquillity was bathed in such ghostly silver shades of night. Our thoughts were both at once so full of melancholy and desire. We were silent for a while, only looking at each other in the solitude. No living thing stirred.

And then, ever so swiftly, Li-Mei undid the ties at the sides of her servant-robe and slipped the garment over her head, before letting it drop silently to the ground. She was naked and her soft bare skin glistened in a pale sheen of reflected moonlight. The shapely moulding of her breasts made them as two perfect shining orbs, each of their darkly circled buds like a tiny orbiting planet.

How frozen to the spot I was. My eyes were helpless in their thirsty gaze of her beauty. She stepped closer and, despite the terrible danger, I felt her hand reach out suddenly to my Apron of Good Modesty and unfasten the tie, so that the wretched cloth fell to my feet. For a moment she only looked down at me, seeing the first bloom of my rising. But then she reached out and, the very second that her illicit touch came upon me, I was jacked instantly in my swollen rigidity.

Certainly I felt that same spasm of aching pain whenever the surge of my sap breached the constricting band around me, but my veins filled and swelled my trunk just as ever they had done before. And in the potent silence of those forbidden gardens my taut protrusion hung there like some majestic span bridging our two naked bodies, its slight upward curve only enhancing the magnificence of its length and girth.

I heard a little gasp come from her lips. She had never seen me in that swollen way before, and her expression was as though she had been struck by a sudden awesome vision. 'Oh, Shani –' she breathed in sharply – I did not think . . .' Her words trailed off into the silence.

Her fingers were clasping my flesh, fondling it as if in astonished wonderment. And all the while I stood there brazenly, thrusting out the full rod of my glory to her.

But it was the ugly ring at its extremity that might perhaps have marred her perception of my magnificence. Yet, strangely she seemed undaunted by it, or even fascinated by its grotesque clasp of my bulging head.

'My sweet bull-man,' she murmured. 'But the iron of your flesh is stronger than even that cruel metal of your ring.'

She held me there, looking down on it, the gold glinting in the moonlight. And, smiling with a sort of sweet tender sadness, she began to pump me lightly, knowing my desperation. And, before a handful of strokes of her delicious motion, already my latent sap began to ferment irreversibly in the sump of my loins. Soon the rush of seed rose up in me like volcanic lava. I knew that I could not contain its hot urgency.

'Oh, Li-Mei . . . I want . . .'

But she did not stop, and I could not.

Whatever suppression had been intended by my cruel ringing and clamping, how strange it was that, ever since then, the surge of my seed was made more potent. And, as it burst forth, all that pent-up power made the shooting spume fly like a bolt of white lightning across the cool air of the night. The slender tracer hung there in the wake of its leaping mass, caught for a second in the moonlight. The sweet-scented honeysuckle bush behind Li-Mei gave a tiny fleeting sigh of protest as the blooming gold-red petals took the vented splatter of my seed.

But the agony of my constricted climax was excruciating, and I cried out in the silence that had been the cloak of safety for our dangerous liaison. The peace of the Garden of Tranquillity was shattered in that instant. And the eyes of those millions of stars above were suddenly hostile, making ears hark to the trespassers in that forbidden place.

Oh, my poor Li-Mei!

We had stirred the demons that night.

After I was separated from my companions, those first many sunrises and sunsets came and went in a swirling haze of strangeness. For the moment there was no sign of my Brother Novices. My Tutor Brother-Yellow-Crow told me that my Brother Novices were resting in the Room of Joyous Reflection. Yet he told me nothing of the four who had not survived the ceremony of the Reverent Departure of Temptation, saying only that my companions would join me soon in the resumption of our lessons. So I was alone in the dormitory and it was I who attended to the daily duties of sweeping and tidying there, and of whatever other small chores he bade me do. For much of my time I, too, had been permitted to rest. Often I would lie on my straw mattress, looking about me in my silent solitude; wondering at my new home; thinking of my comrades and their empty mattresses around me; but above all thinking of my new Honourable Mistress.

Then, one morning when the sun was still lazy, there was a hushed scuffling sound and my Brother

Novices returned to the dormitory – but only six of them. They came not joyously or with boisterous demeanour, but meekly and with despondent downcast eyes. And they walked stiffly, as if their gait had been impeded by things that were concealed beneath their Aprons of Good Modesty. They greeted me, but sullenly, almost as if they resented my presence, and they went to their mattresses and lay on them, gazing vacantly up at the domed ceiling above.

At that time I was squatting on the cool marble floor, filing the nails of my toes, just as my Brother-Master Kanchu had instructed me to do. It seemed that for a Eunuch or a Novice to have nails – either on fingers or toes – that grew too long was an abhorrence to Their Ladyships. This was just another small matter of strangeness in the Pavilion, because Her Grand Ladyship had nails on her fingers that were as long as my big toe.

I turned to the silent occupant of the mattress beside mine. I knew his name was Mimtu. I had been shackled to him when they brought us here, and at that time he had been of a more optimistic disposition than mine. He had often told me during that long journey how it would be an honour to serve at the Imperial Palace, and how I should cast aside my despair and my fearfulness.

Perhaps now was not the moment to ask him, but my curiosity was insatiable.

'Have they – have you been ... made as Brother Kanchu is?' I began hesitantly.

But Mimtu did not even turn his head, and his legs were kept apart, as if one limb did not wish to touch against the other.

'I mean, have you received that honour that he, Brother-Yellow-Crow, told us would be granted in the Room of Glorious Transformation?'

Still there was no response, and I morosely returned to my nail-filing devotions. After a while he spoke. 'You have been fortunate, Shani. You must have a guardian up there in the Heavens to have spared you this fate of mine. The pain was unbearable, and the blood flowed from my wound so much that I fell into a stupor of black nightmares. I felt as if the cloak of death had come to smother me, and I even yearned for it to take me. Such was the agony it made my body shake and my mouth cry out like banshee-demons.'

That much I could already believe. Not that I was without compassion for him, but I wanted to know much more, and he was slow in enlightening me.

'Do you feel . . . a different man?' I ventured.

Then he turned his head angrily towards me. 'Different man? I am not a man, Shani. Not now. I am a half-man, a slave, and one to be done with as the Mistresses desire.' He spat the words at me before calming himself again.

And what should I reply to that? But I still needed to know. 'But is not the Glorious Transformation an honour – an honour that they've seen fit not to bestow on me, Mimtu?' I asked. But my words seemed clumsy and I regretted them immediately, fearing another outburst of his bitterness.

At length he replied calmly enough. 'What honour is there in having my sac cut from me, or for squealing like a stuck pig? And was it not foolish of me to submit myself so compliantly?'

'But did they not tether you?' My question came indelicately and in a rush from my desire to know of the ceremony.

He stared at me as if I were a fool. 'Of course they tethered us! How else should we have endured such agony? Do you think that we stood there like silent lambs while they cut us?' he demanded hotly.

Reflecting on his words, he continued more sombrely. 'At first I walked to that place compliantly, and then I drank the potion they gave me, saying to us how the pain would be numbed, and that whatever pain was left should be endured happily in the knowledge of the honour being bestowed upon us. And when my turn came I submitted without protest to being bound to the wooden trestle-beam. It is called the ceremonial table, and I lay on it meekly, like all the other mindless slaves.'

He turned again to me, his eyes blazing. 'You see, Shani, the potion was strong and it dulled my mind more than it dulled my agony. And all the while they spoke such rich words of encouragement and reassurance to us so that we obeyed willingly. We were like flies in the spider's web! And, before we knew it, the straps held us to the beams. Then it was too late to become unwilling.'

I waited for him to go on, seeing the dreadful turmoil churning in his mind.

There was a tremor in his voice as he continued. 'That is what I meant by submission, Shani. But when they bound us to those ceremonial tables, how then did we wish to flee from that place and save our poor skins! Honour and loyalty to His Imperial Majesty were no more in our minds. Now there was only terror. And it was worse for those of us Novices who had to wait our turn. There were but three ceremonial tables, and ten of us! And we stood there shaking, having to watch the ritual cutting of our Brother Novices who had gone before us, prostrated there on the three tables. And, while we waited, the Eunuchs held us tightly, placing sash-cords around our necks to tighten around us should we show resistance. But the potion was so strong that I felt as weak as a stumbling newborn puppy. And even when

85

the screams came so loud in my ears, still did I stand there so obediently. When it was my turn I walked to the table with my head held high, but my bare feet on the marble were wet with the blood shed from the Novice who had gone before me.'

I was too stunned to speak, scarcely wanting more detail. But Mimtu was not finished yet.

'One of the surgeons took hold of my sac in one hand, pulling me out, making me yell at this alone, and another surgeon took his cutting tool and quickly sliced my sac from me, as cleanly as if he'd cut silk. And then I bellowed like a bull ... only I was no longer one. And mercifully I fell into the stupor, and when I awoke from it I was bound between my legs with linen cloths. I lay there in the Room of Joyous Reflection for several sunsets without having desire to move.'

How sorry I felt for him, but I also felt relief for myself. I was watching him, and he sensed it, knowing the limitless boundaries of my curiosity.

'See for yourself, Shani.'

He pulled up the skirt of his Apron of Good Modesty, opening his legs wider to me, and at the same time lifting his shank to reveal where once his sac had been. That vacant space was so evident, the scar at once visible.

So this was the mark of the true Eunuch, and I was gladdened not to be one!

He told me much more of those events, and how four Novice candidates had died a short while later from their wounds. He told me also about the days after in the Room of Joyous Reflection, and how slowly he and his companions had recovered, and how every day they had been lectured about the honour of their new status at the Imperial Palace. He told me how their dressings were changed daily by the

Physicians; how hot poultices were pressed against the raw wounds; and how his mind had swum in a turmoil of despair and indignation. He told me so much that my ears no longer wished to hear more.

I think it was on the fifth day of my arrival that I was summoned by her. And it was not Brother-Yellow-Crow who came with the summons, but Chief Eunuch Karif himself. He only ever deigned to speak directly to Novices if he himself had been despatched by one of Their Ladyships with a particular purpose for coming to us.

At that moment I had been on my knees beside my mattress, arranging it ever so neatly in the manner already taught me. It was a while after dawn but the summer heat was already rising. I was lonely, and my state of dejection hung upon my bare shoulders like a hot rag. My Novice brethren at that time had not yet returned from the Room of Joyous Reflection.

I had bathed alone in the Novices' wash-pool. By then the second-year Novices had already left the chamber, which smelt always of so many rich moist scents and herbs. It seemed that Their Ladyships desired that their servants' skins should always smell that way – neither like the skins of men, nor yet like those of women. A third-year Novice by the name of Accassoo had been assigned to inspect me, and he carried out his duty with sneering disdain, looking into my intimate places and smelling at me with such critical appraisal.

'The nails of your toes are not evenly rounded,' he said at last.

But it had not been my nails that his eyes had dwelt on for so long. It was now that I could understand the resentment. I was different from the other Novices, and I was condemned for it.

'Attend to your imperfections, and tomorrow let me not find any!' Accassoo admonished me, before letting me depart.

Chief Eunuch Karif came into the dormitory so silently that I did not hear him, and therefore I did not rise respectfully from my knees to greet him.

'Get up!' he barked impatiently. 'Her Ladyship, your Mistress, desires your presence. Hurry. Let me look at you.'

I scrambled to my feet. 'Yes, Brother-Master Karif,' I said meekly, standing there while he examined me.

He was carrying his black-lacquered rod and he lifted my Apron of Good Modesty with it, before bending down and sniffing at me there. He grunted, in evident approval. 'Follow me ... and walk with your head downcast. And do not forget to bow to Her Ladyship. Do not raise your chin again until she bids you so.'

I padded behind him as we went through the labyrinth of vaulted chambers and down those long corridors of the Pavilion of the Divine Orchid Ladies. We entered the east wing and passed by many pairs of ornately lacquered doors, beyond which were the private chambers of Their Concubinic Ladyships. We stopped eventually outside one door that was no different to the others, except that the design carved into the wood was unique to the Honourable Royal Sister who resided in those particular quarters. The motif of my Mistress comprised the Imperial Dragon and a symbolic boat sailing on a river.

Karif knocked with his black rod and then went in, beckoning me to follow.

When I came that first time into my Mistress's chambers, it seemed to me a place that was as much pleasingly cosy as it was rich in its adornments and furnishings. It was a blissful contrast to the more subdued and sometimes gloomy splendour of the rest of the Pavilion. Here, there was so much light and so many colours, and such symmetry of graceful shapes. All around were many exotic plumes of birds, threads of glittering beads, embroidered tapestries depicting scenes of rivers and lush foliage and birds of paradise; and there were beautifully lacquered screens and hanging drapes of silks.

I had come to a place of bright dreams. My bare feet came so pleasantly upon the plush rugs and there were no echoing sounds here. The tranquil splendour of the interior was as though shut away from the outside hostility of the Pavilion beyond. It might have been a haven of peace, its stillness as if brought there by a gentle summer breeze – one scented with the perfumed blooms of a million flowers.

Although so meekly downcast, my furtive eyes were at once overwhelmed by so many exotic images. In the middle of the chamber was something I had never seen before. It was certainly a bed, but the finery of its cushions and its laced covers made it much more than just a place to sleep in. It might have been a throne, except that it was immense and rounded in such a way that it could have been a brilliant cloud of cumulous silk, and its magnificence was only enhanced by the serene figure waiting there upon it.

Her Ladyship Jiang-Li was seated there in regal poise with her back propped up against a mound of ornate and gold-braided cushions. She was wearing a long silk gown that seemed to shimmer in the morning light. The small dainty feet that protruded from the folds of the garment were bare and they rested on a small blue satin cushion.

She did not look up as we entered, a placid and almost insouciant expression on her beautiful face.

The only sound came from beyond the huge meshed windows. There, the playful morning chattering of birds could be heard.

'Your Ladyship, I have brought the Novice,' Karif announced, bowing low.

I did likewise, the bow that I had practised a thousand times in those few days coming as naturally as if I had been born for it.

'You may leave us, Karif.' My Mistress's voice was as clear as ever, her tone authoritative but lacking any discerning indication of her temperament. Still she did not look up at him, nor at me. She was looking at the painted nails of her long delicate fingers.

Karif bowed again, casting me a final warning look, before departing silently from the chamber. I stood there near that vast bed, although it was as much a throne as a bed. My chin was lowered respectfully, my eyes only able to glimpse her bare feet. She said nothing for a while. The silence – except for the birds beyond the window – made me wilt with anticipation. Had I displeased her already? Was I to be punished for some unknown misdemeanour for her to keep me thus in cruel suspense?

'Have you been well cared for, Shani?'

I was at once flustered by this question. Should I suppose that a Royal Lady would be interested in the welfare of a mere servant slave? I looked up at her beautiful face, as if for inspiration for my reply. But she admonished me immediately.

'I did not permit you to raise your head, nor to gaze upon my face, Shani.'

Yet her admonishment was not unkindly spoken. I dropped my chin quickly though, making it push into my neck. I mumbled something, but she admonished me again.

'You will not make a good servant to me if you only mutter like a Kangitaboo bird and do not answer me clearly when I ask a question of you.'

This only flustered me all the more and I struggled stupidly for suitable words to reply. 'Your Ladyship,' I began timidly, still keeping my chin down, 'I have been well cared for, I thank you. I have been fed and . . . and rested.'

I could tell by the amusement in her voice that she was playing with me. 'Should I be interested in your feeding and your resting, or of the bodily pamperings of my servant? Have you been taught nothing yet? Should you not be concerned only with the requirements of your Royal Mistress, Shani?' Her tone was patient and not even unfriendly, yet nonetheless there was severity in her meaning.

'Of course, Your Ladyship, I am here . . . I know it . . . to s-serve you, and . . . er . . . n-nothing more,' I stammered hastily, having chosen my words as carefully as I could.

She laughed, but became serious again. 'So you have been taught your duties already?'

'Yes, Your Ladyship. I have learnt what I must do . . . to serve you.' I was hurrying to say what I thought she desired to hear. 'And I have learnt how to serve in a respectful manner . . . and a humble one.'

I was confident that I had answered well, but in my haste and gushing enthusiasm to please my Mistress I had committed another impetuous breach of compliance.

'Why then, Shani, is your chin uplifted again and why do your impudent eyes look into my face?' she demanded, glaring at me now, her eyebrows lifted in sly triumph.

I dropped my head quickly again, cursing myself and muttering a pathetic apology.

'For lesser misdemeanours than that, Shani, your rump might feel the sting of my brush-whip or, worse, the Bamboo Rod of Reformed Memory at this morning's ritual of Prostration!'

'Yes, Your Ladyship,' was all I could mumble hoarsely.

But she took pity on my wretchedness. 'You may raise your head and look upon me,' she condescended. And when I looked at her – a trifle hesitantly – I saw the regal smile on her pale lips.

'There is much for you to learn, Shani. And there is also much time for you to become proficient in those many things you must learn. It will take the passing of three full seasons before you may presume to be worthy of the honour of being a Eunuch-servant.' She paused for a moment, studying my face. 'Until then, Shani, you must strive harder. And in your daily striving, from time to time, you will undoubtedly incur my impatient wrath ... and so you will often be punished for it.'

She smiled again wistfully, and her voice was as soft as wild bush-cotton, no malice to its tone, when she continued. 'But when you are, Shani, you should feel no resentment for it, because each time I should punish you it will be because of my caring for you, and because I desire you to remain as my servant ... and for you to be safe from those many other dangers that lurk in this Palace. And, if I did not myself punish you, there would be criticism of my leniency. And my dear Honourable Sisters might punish you all the more severely for faults that I have not myself had beaten out of you.'

For a moment she lowered her head, not wanting me to see the sudden cloud of sadness pass across her beauty.

'You see, Shani, even we Royal Sisters ourselves are not above punishment ... or even banishment.

And Her Grand Ladyship has the eyes of a hawk and the ears of an elephant, and her heart is made of iron.'

Then, as though realising the irreverence of her words, she quickly went on in a more businesslike tone. 'It is loyalty that I most desire in you, Shani, as much as devotion to your duties towards me. Those, I shall try to teach you. Your loyalty you must yourself acquire. All that happens in my chambers shall be between you and me. If I should hear that you gossip about these private things, then I shall not even punish you for your loose tongue. No, Shani, I shall have you banished! And if they take you to another place – and make you as a true Eunuch should be – then you will become a pitiful broken creature, lacking not only his freedom but the natural functions of his youth. And you will wither and die early and toil like the lowest of slaves. Do you understand me?'

I nodded. But there was so much I did not understand, so much that I wanted to ask my Mistress but did not dare to.

'Come closer. More so! Do not fear me, Shani. I am not a snake.'

Yet, despite her beauty and her regal face, her eyes might have been those of a beguiling serpent.

'Have your stripes from my rendering of the Bamboo Rod of Reformed Memory yet healed on your rump, Shani?'

I was again struck dumb by the slowness of my mind to think of my response, and I could only mumble incoherently in my shame. But this made her impatient, her placid expression at once wiped from her face.

'Drop your Apron of Good Modesty!' she commanded. 'And make your reply so that I shall hear it clearly and truthfully! You have yet to attend the morning Assembly of Novices . . . and I can still earn favour with Her Grand Ladyship and beat you again, just as before, while you prostrate yourself with the other Novices . . . there with your rumps held out so invitingly.'

'Yes, Your Ladyship,' I answered in a clear voice now and quickly fumbled with the cord, then dropped the apron to my feet.

'Turn yourself!'

I did so hastily, feeling her eyes at once on the streaked bareness of my rump.

She grunted. 'My hand is stronger than I thought!' she remarked thoughtfully and with a lightness to her voice. 'Your welts are raised up and black-yellowed from where the rod struck you. But, if they are sore, the soreness will serve to remind you of the need to obey implicitly. You may wear them proudly, Shani, like the scars of a warrior. And, if I should take the rod to you again, be content that I deem you worthy of my efforts. And then you can be proud to bear the new welts as much as the old.'

I stood there rigidly, feeling my shame and feeling her curious eyes upon me. How strange those words seemed. How should I be proud to have my flesh ravaged by a rod of such humiliating cruelty?

'Turn around and face me,' she ordered, then added haughtily, 'The sight of your hindquarters tires my eyes.'

I turned, trying to retain my composure, even though I was long since stripped of my dignity. Her eyes dropped immediately to where my manhood still reposed between my legs. She scrutinised me there silently for some moments, as though perhaps in a secretive deliberation of my endowment.

The shame of having to display myself in such abandoned grace might have been less humbling than before. After all, by this time was I not accustomed to exposing my naked debasement to so many curious eyes? But it was not so much the endowment of my natural flesh that gave rise to such scrutiny. It was rather more the presence of that so prominent ring at the head of my shank. The obtrusive circle of gold hung there so heavily, the encumbrance so perversely round and large. Had it been flipped back like a hoop over my mushroom-head – even when at its boldest – there would have been girth enough for the head and four more of them to fit easily into its embrace. There was also the band around my hanging sac. My sorry flesh felt to me as though an unseen hand grasped me tightly there, condensing my twin orbs beneath.

'Step nearer, Shani,' my Mistress said quietly. 'You must not be bashful with me. Besides, are you not a man who should have no shame of his natural-born flesh? You are clearly a man amongst men! A golden bull-man! That should make you proud.'

My Honourable Mistress was so intense in her study of me there, her mind as if momentarily absent of all other things. But, despite her flattering words, I could not discern whether the objects of her scrutiny pleased her entirely. Whatever had been the reason for her intervention on my behalf, was she perhaps regretting saving me from disfigurement?

I recalled how she had told me of the concessions she made to Her Grand Ladyship to spare me from the fate of my companions in the Room of Glorious Transformation. And had not my Mistress been daring in her presumptuous pleadings for a humble slave, and had she not lost her opal and emerald necklace, as well as having lost face in asking Her Grand Ladyship's mercy?

As I stood there, not knowing where to look, I wondered if I were worthy of my Mistress's sacrifices.

But her face was inscrutable and the grains of sand trickled slowly in the hourglass, the silence so profound.

She reached out and gently touched the ring. She took it between finger and thumb and lifted me, peering beneath. At that moment I felt that familiar stirring, and the veins of my unwilling shank swelled. And I could not stop it.

A tiny laugh that might almost have been one of delight came from her lips. 'Oh, Shani, I can see how our wise Physicians have not succeeded in stemming the flow of your manly fluids! Your trunk rises and swells before my very eyes! Clearly the band of gold was not enough to stunt the natural potency of your poor sac.'

Her smile was radiant and her eyes twinkled mischievously as she suddenly glanced up at my flushed face. At least she did not admonish me. I could not speak, and all the while my shank grew and she was still holding the ring, fascinated by the way it lifted so brazenly towards her. Despite the strangely thrilling mixture of anxiety and desire in me, I could do nothing to impede my impetuous thrust.

There was another expression on her face, her inscrutability lost for a moment and replaced by some distant emotion that I could not discern. But she continued to hold the ring lightly. I was by now almost in the full extremity of my span, its potency making it curve upwards, such that the eye of my mushroom-slit seemed to stare provocatively back at her. How I wanted her delicate fingers to touch my flesh, rather than just to hold the cruel ring of my slavery.

Suddenly a stern look of reproach slipped back across her features, as if perhaps reality had returned to her. The moment of such impudent indulgence had passed, her moment of unacceptable pleasure at once removed. She let go of my ring, but the fullness of my jutting span remained there, stretching out towards her.

'It seems you do not learn swiftly enough from your impetuousness, Shani. Have you not already felt the bamboo cut your flesh for such brazen impudence?' she rebuked, looking up at me severely.

Her hands were folded again in the sleeves of her gown, as if wanting to distance them from my blatant flesh. Yet, despite her apparent vexation, I could see the reluctance in her words and in her withdrawal. It was as if she had needed to make herself return to her regal superiority. Whatever dangerous emotions there had been between us in those few brief moments, they were suddenly vanquished. The aching of my constricted loins began to throb. Her eyes dropped again to my rapidly depleting thrust, and she watched its sagging progress as though with pretended disdain, until at last the ring again hung weightily between my legs.

I was unsure whether to speak; to beg my forgiveness and to plead my inability to control my so blatant feelings. I stood there helplessly in my nakedness, wanting to pick up my apron and cover myself with it again, and to hide myself from her gaze.

She could see my embarrassment and my wretchedness, but she seemed to take pity on me. The hardness of her face evaporated, making it brighten with a kind of sad beauty. 'Shani, these walls have many eyes and ears,' she said quietly, almost in a whisper. 'If Karif had happened to enter my chambers when you were . . . in that way, I would have had to order him to remove you from my presence. And at the morning Ritual of Prostration I would have taken the Bamboo Rod of Reformed Memory to your rump . . . and beaten you with it until you screamed. Only then would Her Grand Ladyship have been convinced that I had done my duty. Do you understand?'

'Yes, Your Ladyship,' I mumbled, my head bowed.

But she had much more to say to me. 'As I told you, I have taken risks for you, Shani. I alone saved you from the Room of Glorious Transformation. Even though my dear Sisters also wanted it so, having themselves looked upon your manly magnificence, it was not *they* who dared to lose face and appeal to Her Grand Ladyship, and it was not *they* who were willing to sacrifice their most favoured possession to save you from the Knife of Transformation. No, Shani, it was I, your Mistress. And I have earned your obedience and your loyalty.'

'I am indebted to you, Your Ladyship, and I pledge you my devoted loyalty and obedience,' I said quickly. 'And I shall try to be as you want me to be ... and, if I shall still have failings, I shall rectify them as swiftly as you rebuke me for them, Your Ladyship.'

I spoke my words clearly, raising my chin so that I could look directly at her. I went on, needing to tell her of my unwilled feelings. After all, what if they should come again and make my flesh rise insouciantly on some future occasion?

'I did not mean to defy you, Your Ladyship. It is only that ... that I could not help myself. I am still a whole man,' I blurted out helplessly. 'And I cannot contain those same manly feelings ... and you are not only my Mistress, but I see you also as a woman ... a woman blessed with beauty ... and when you reached out and touched my ring ...' My voice trailed off into silence, and once again I bowed my head, regretting my fumbling outburst.

She smiled at me kindly. 'So, you have words to speak at last!' she teased. 'You are not just a dumb bull of the fields without emotions or things to say. That is good, Shani. If I had saved but a dumb bull from the knife, what use would it have been to me? My sacrifices would surely have been so much for so little. But I can see that you have spirit! It is not only the impetuous flight of your flesh, but the impetuous flight of words from your lips that comes forth now! And you speak from the heart, and even a servant must have a heart.'

She regarded me silently for some moments. Then she waved her hand imperiously towards the end of the huge bed. 'You will sit there. And you will take my foot in your lap and massage it.'

I was confused. Should I first pick up my apron and restore my modesty? But she had not ordered it thus. Her eyes were piercing into me, mockingly so. I swallowed nervously and lifted myself awkwardly on to the silk coverings of the bed-throne, feeling the sudden soft coolness to my rump as I slid myself over to where her dainty feet awaited me.

'Move closer. They will not bite you! Turn your body to me. Yes, like so. Now, make your legs lie out towards me, so that I can rest my foot on them. Good. You may relax yourself. I do not wish you to be a bronze statue that has no feeling!'

'Yes, Your Ladyship,' I said feebly, beholding the small deliciously shaped foot that was thrust on to my leg. The touch of her hard coolness on my skin was instantly electrifying, making a pulsating bolt fly like a shooting star across the expanse of my naked body.

'Henceforth, you shall call me Mistress, for that is what I am to you.'

'Yes, Mistress.'

'This shall be your first duty every morning, Shani. You will come here just after first light, and sit as you are now and you will learn how to give pleasure to

99

my feet. Your fingers shall be smooth and they shall tenderly take each of my toes in turn and caress them as though you love each one of them with equal devotion. Then you shall take my whole foot and rub the shape of it in your hands so that I shall feel them on me firmly but sensually. Do you understand?'

I nodded meekly, daring to glance up at her face. It was as divine and magnificent as a radiant moon, but the serenity of it had been replaced by some other potency now; a look perhaps that promised a hidden mystery there, one that wished to remain concealed. I fought it desperately, but again I felt a stirring between my legs. I could see that she was looking there, and the ring was starting a lazy elevation from its repose.

'You may begin,' she commanded in a sultry voice, her eyes shining with intensity.

I took her foot in both hands as if it had been made of fragile crystal. Not knowing how to do it, but nonetheless instinctively beginning to massage her largest toe, I soon achieved a rhythm that was evidently pleasing to her. All the while she lectured me quietly, directing how my fingers should be, at times soft and slow, then more robust, and then to glide soothingly over her delicately boned contours, or to wipe beneath the soft arch of her sole.

'Repeat that movement until I tell you to stop.' Her voice was dreamy, and she lay back on her cushions, her eyes never leaving me. I could tell how busily her mind was working.

'It would have been a sin to have had you cut by the Knife of Transformation,' she announced distantly, but her voice travelled as clearly as the gentle song of a nightingale across a lily-pond.

'And it is the good fortune of a winter orchid bloom that the Imperial Physicians have failed to quell your natural manly desires, even though they are such impudent desires and make you stand like a branch of iron!' She laughed, and her laughter thrilled me to the very core of my being.

From then on I did not mind my Mistress's teasing. It was only when her mood was one of a Black Moon that her teasing was tinged with dangerous malice, and then I had to heed every minuscule sign of her potential displeasure. Those clouds could race across her features quicker than a summer storm.

For now, at least, I was absorbed in my task, and it made my senses tingle within me like hot icicles. My hands and fingers moved on her with such natural ease that it might have been a labour of love for them, and one that they had performed many times before. Although it was just a foot – and one that like any other made such lowly contact between the purity of her body and the dirt of the soil – it was a part of her that was no less erotic in my fingers than if it had been one of her soft breasts.

She spoke again, her words at once shocking me. 'You may lift my foot and kiss it.'

Had my ears deceived me? I looked up from my work, at once seeing how her eyes were staring at me with wicked amusement. Yet, I was hesitant, uncertain whether she meant it as some act of benevolence towards me, or whether it was intended as some further servile ministration to her foot. I looked at her stupidly, wanting her guidance.

Immediately she answered my unspoken question. 'If you should wish, you may kiss me there with your lips. I shall know then whether you are a doting servant who is truly happy to please his Mistress . . . or whether you are just an unthinking servant who carries out his duties only because he must obey.'

Cupping my hand under her heel, I quickly lifted her foot, bending my head to it, seeing its exquisite detail.

'Be warned, Shani! For I shall know by the manner of your kissing whether you do it with passion ... and if it is to please yourself or if it is only to please me.' Her smile was provocative, and as dazzling as a burst of sunlight.

Her toes – now so near to my eyes – were splayed slightly, tensed and curling back, making them stand out like dainty little pillars. My nostrils took in her scent as I bent lower and kissed her on the soft part of her sole, just beneath the taut line of her larger toes. Then I kissed her more, working my way across to her smallest toe, and then kissing each one in turn.

She wiggled them. 'Take them into your mouth – one at a time – and suckle them like a lamb at its mother's teats,' she commanded huskily. Her voice lacked the same passiveness as before. There was an intensity to it, just as much as there was intensity in her eyes.

I felt my stirring, the ring moving against my leg and upwards from its repose. I did as she commanded me, but I delighted in it. The taste came to my lips with such wondrous intrigue that the juices of my mouth flowed readily. Never before had I experienced such an act and, being so unaccustomed to it, I perhaps nibbled her at first with fumbling ineptitude. But gradually I became bolder and more sensual and I heard her sigh. And by now my shank had hardened and the ring hung there in such close proximity to the sole of her foot.

I do not know how many grains of sand must have trickled down in the hourglass before she spoke again, breaking such an intimate silent moment. 'Now take my other foot ... and do with it what you did with the other. Start from the beginning.'

'Yes, Your Ladyship, I mean, Mistress.'

I gently lowered the moist foot in my hand almost reluctantly, watching her face from beneath my eyebrows, needing her reassurance. I lifted her right foot on to my leg and clasped it reverently. At that moment I perceived a change in her countenance. Her kitten-eyes had narrowed and her lips formed an impish curl to her smile. 'Sometimes I desire that you shall massage my feet with scented balm, and not only with the dry touch of your fingers,' she said ever so quietly and with a mischievous inflection to her tone that I could not fathom.

I began to search around the room with my eyes to see whether perhaps there might have been a bowl of scented herbs or some jar of special balm that I should have been aware of. Had I so soon been neglectful in my duties? I wondered. But I saw no such scented lotions or balm or any other likely substance to aid my massaging task. I glanced back in puzzlement at her, fearful that I had perhaps broken the new intimate bond that had formed between servant and Mistress. I was a foolish servant, after all, who had massaged his Mistress's foot with his dry hands.

Her eyes were fixed admiringly upon my swollen shank, which seemed to stand like a white tower between my belly and my legs and with such dangerous prominence. The ring lay slightly at right angles. She lifted her foot out of my hand and reached up with it towards the ring. At first her foot only hovered there as she tried to locate the golden circle with her big toe. Although I saw her intention, I could not control the involuntary pulsing of my brazen mushroom-head, and I was powerless to facilitate her capture of its vulnerable ring. But eventually I was motionless long enough for her to slip her toe into the embrace. Instantly, as if she had hooked a fish with her rod, she tugged gently upwards, making my shank lean towards her. She held me there for some moments, her long leg stretched out so tautly and gracefully, the coupling locking us so utterly perversely. The skin of her toe had scarcely touched my head, but I felt that every nerve-end in my loins was on fire.

'A good servant should always be ready to improvise, Shani. If there is no lotion, he should provide it in other ways.'

Her eyes were like bright black beads of intensity. But I could not understand her words. And still she held me with her toe, waiting for my response.

'How shall I improvise, Mistress? Or – or provide balm to massage you with, if there is none?' I asked innocently, fearing rebuke again.

But she only laughed, teasing me cruelly. Her gaze was one of mischievous provocation, and she tugged at me with her toe, making me wince at such impure movement.

'Did I not say that a good servant shall improvise, Shani? And I see you there in your full rampant glory that no apparent means of ringing or banding can destroy!'

But still I understood nothing, even though her mocking eyes were everywhere upon me, as if challenging my inspiration. 'Please tell me, Mistress. I am a lowly fool-servant who is as slow as a feeble goat to comprehend.'

'But it is not a goat that I wish for, but a bull!' she exclaimed in exasperation. Her toe was moving me around in teasing little flourishes that jerked my head and made me wince all the more. 'Is it not yet clear to you? I cannot milk you as a nanny-goat but a bull can spurt his cream . . . and you are still a bull, are you not?'

And then it came to me, her riddle no less shocking for its deciphering. 'You mean . . .?' I began, incredulous and unable to finish.

'I mean only as much as a wise servant should desire for his Mistress,' she said evenly. 'And this Mistress desires only that you should massage her foot with soothing lotion. And, if you have none, then you should move heaven and earth to acquire it for her!'

'But, Mistress, w-what you ask . . . is forbidden! And what if Karif should enter here?' I stammered.

But her face had become stony, her eyes narrowing in that dangerous way I learnt to know over the years.

There was an awkward silence between us before she spoke again. 'You sit on my bed-throne with your back to the doors. And, if that sneaky servant should enter here into my quarters, would he not only see your back and your seated rump? And if his lowly eyes should cunningly look upon my bed what more would he observe other than how you engage in the duty that I have commanded you to perform?' Her eyebrows rose quizzically, challenging me.

'Yes, Mistress,' I answered uneasily. The tugging pressure from the ring made me uncomfortable, even causing a slight floundering of my shank.

'Then, have I saved a bull-man from the knife just for him to be a mouse?' she demanded sourly, giving another tug.

'No, Mistress.'

'Then, I command you to do what I desire! Provide the creamy sap for your hands to massage my foot soothingly.'

There was no doubt in my mind. Yet how should I do as she had commanded? I swallowed nervously, watching her. And then she smiled so radiantly that such irresistible beauty rushed across her face in a trice. She knew my thoughts and she enjoyed her wicked game, as would a cat with the mouse. Suddenly she released my ring from her toe, letting me bob back so ungraciously in my freedom.

'You may begin!' she said playfully. 'Massage yourself first and, when you yield the lotion, only then shall you massage my foot.'

I was mortified in my new shame. To do the thing she bade me do affronted the swirling fibres of my mind. How could I do that wretched thing to myself in front of another living soul? But my Mistress was looking at me with sly intensity, defying me to disobey, determined that I should not.

'Begin!' she prompted me, leaving me no alternative.

I held myself, just as I had done as a man-child. My breathing was harsh. Whatever pride and dignity that once I had was truly vanquished now. I was neither a bull nor a mouse, but a monkey performing the tricks for his demanding Mistress. Yet my lustful feelings had made any wilting of my flesh be halted, and I was standing brazenly again, my unwilling hand clasping its proud hardness, if not eagerly, then with a certain impure purpose.

Her smile spread wider, her eyes piercing into me. Her toes nudged at the golden clamp of my sac, then came gliding up my trunk, feeling along the network of its swollen veins. Without a word, she opened her silk garment, and I saw, for the first time, the small orbs of her perfectly moulded breasts. I drew a quick intake of my breath. Oh, what provocative beauty my Mistress possessed! I was iron in my hand, and I could not stop myself from those irreverent motions that brought up the hot sap from its deep sump in my loins.

She watched me with utter fascination and, when once I faltered under her scrutiny, she ordered me on breathlessly, 'Pump harder, you magnificent bull!'

Every vestige of my shame forgotten, I was on my knees, towering above the stretch of her long legs. I worked myself not with any frenzy, but in measured strokes. The frothing turmoil within me scarcely needed much to bring it to conclusion. Certainly there was pain from ring and clamp, but this pain was worthy of its suffering. All the while, my eyes could not take in enough of her and, as if sensing this, she opened her garment more. At once I saw the place that would forever be forbidden me. Only would my servant lips and impure tongue ever be permitted there, and then only whenever my Mistress graciously favoured me with such benevolence.

But, for now at least, just a glimpse of her delicious bud was sufficient to bring my surge onwards. I marvelled at the tiny peeping folds of crimson tissue that issued from between that divinely twinned hump. I marvelled, too, at the exquisitely contoured plain of her belly, and not least at those polished orbs above. Their tiny pink knurls were raised now in their hardness, as if having become the succulent stalks of some forbidden magical fruit. And they seemed to urge me on like wicked sirens.

'Oh, Mistress!' came the stumbling utterance from my lips, as I was lost in my lustful stupor.

Her eyes glittered, tempting me on. Her voice came as clear as a nightingale across a lily-pond. 'Release your passion now, my bull. Let me see you fly!'

But was I not to make lotion for my Mistress's dainty feet? How should I then gather it if it flew its vented force across her? And I knew how the straining force was contained within me by that wicked band of gold, and how my wretched loins felt as if on the point of bursting like a volcano.

'Let fly!' she commanded urgently, perhaps having seen my confusion.

'Ah, Mistress, I am! I – I . . . cannot . . .' But I could not finish my words, a little moan escaping me as I finally burst the leaping passion from my core.

When my eye-vent let forth its desperate eruption, I heard her gasp, and the membrane of my spume streaked like silver lightning to her orbs and across the plain of her waiting belly.

'Oh, Mistress, forgive me!'

She laughed. Perhaps there was delight in it, but there was a mocking edge to it, no less. Her eyes looked down at her breasts as if to appraise the glistening threads that soiled the unblemished perfection of her skin.

'Shani, not only do you have the magnificence of a bull, but the spring of a mountain-ram.' She giggled. 'And your lotion comes gushing like a hot fountain from the very bowels of the earth!'

She looked down at where I knelt in my still blatant poise. My thrusting span was not yet ready to wane and she observed it critically, a patronising smile on her lips. The golden adornments of my flesh seemed to intrigue her all the more.

In the trembling wake of my excruciation, my shame and degradation surged back into me like black writing-ink. So I was again the lowly servant with his ring and clamp, and deserving only to be cruelly mocked. If my passion were depleted, what passion had there been in her? I sat back on my haunches, nursing the throbbing agony that still coursed through my constricted veins, feeling her eyes upon me.

After a short silence she looked away, unsmiling. She reached beside her, took a small square of silk in her hand and held it out to me. 'You may clean me of your seed,' she commanded icily. 'Then with it you shall complete the task I gave you.'

She nudged me with her foot.

'Yes, Mistress,' I muttered, beginning to slide myself nearer to where her open garment still exposed her nakedness.

I took the square of silk in trembling hands and leant over her. What divine fragrance of her body came at once to my nostrils, the scent of her skin one of both jasmine and honeysuckle. Her breasts lay in their reposed pertness, the roundels at their peaks like tiny circles of pale-rouge satin. Her nipple-buds were still hard, as if inviting me, and I could not draw my gaze from them. She watched me all the while, but remotely so. That sparkling fire in her eyes was gone now. Perhaps I had become a Summer Cloud of Bad Omen.

Yet, for one moment I thought she was about to reach out and touch me, but she did not, and her voice was cold. 'Do your work. Wipe me with care and then attend to my feet. There is little time before your morning Assembly of Prostration, and your duties to me are behind.'

I had forgotten about that dreadful ritual. But surely I had pleased my Mistress enough to spare me risk of unworthy punishment. Yet with her I could never know for sure. Over those many seasons of my Novice-hood there would be times when I believed that I had served her with such diligence and loving devotion, giving pleasure to her as she commanded, yet, even so, punishment would sometimes follow. And often it was my Mistress herself who rendered it, not often harshly but nonetheless painfully. Later, in the quiet cosiness of her chamber, she would always tell me her reasons. And even when I saw no rational justice in them, I would thank her meekly and attend to her lovingly just as before. How often would she say that she must be strict in her discipline of me, because Her Grand Ladyship demanded it of her. It was to be the constant burden that I must bear. After all, had she, my Mistress, not spared me the Room of Glorious Transformation? And had she not risked so much on my behalf?

Her face was inscrutable again as she closed her garment, settling herself back on her cushions. I resumed my squatting posture at the end of the vast bed and I lifted her foot. I massaged her in silence, my mind so full of conflicting emotions.

Four

Those first unfamiliar days at the Pavilion of the Divine Orchid Ladies were the hardest of all to bear. Had I been a small bird I would surely have flown from there to my distant village. But that cosy childhood place with its sweetly scented fields was no longer my nest now, nor could it ever be again. Even my memories of it were fading into the grey horizon. Try as I might I could not even picture my poor mother's anxious face, even though the image of that jingling money-pouch of taels was etched so vividly on my mind.

Now my world was of whispering shadows in their silk-clad fineries, of the stifling quietness of those marble-floored halls, of sullen faces, of stern rebukes, and no less of fear and hardship. The Imperial Palace was a place of neither joy nor freedom, even that it possessed such beauty and richness of décor, and that it smelt blissfully of honeysuckle and jasmine.

The Black Crow's Wing of Gloom had cast its shadow over me. I had seen nothing of Li-Mei, she of the Beautiful Plum Blossom. I had missed seeing her sweet shy face. And with regards to my Mistress I had only glimpsed her from afar.

Since my recent summons to her quarters I had not, even once thereafter, been brought to her. That strangely enthralling encounter was so fresh in my mind, making me sleep restlessly. I was always wondering when I might be summoned by her again. Even the morning task she had given me of massaging her dainty feet had apparently been forgotten. Or perhaps she no longer desired such intimate attention. I did not know, but it made me anxious. If I had displeased her, why had she not punished me for her displeasure? All I knew was that one of the third-year Senior Novices attended her daily, and that he had been in regular attendance of her, long before my arrival.

His name was Ling and he despised me. That was so clearly evident by his haughty countenance whenever he looked upon me. Each time it seemed as if he were casting a spell of evil misfortune over me. His jealousy was like a cat deprived by another of its mouse. Moreover, his despising of me was more than that of my other Brother Novices. They tended only to keep a wary distance from me, as if I were cursed by one of Heaven's Dangerous Spirits.

It was only at morning Assemblies that I was able to catch a furtive glimpse of my Honourable Mistress. But as far as I could tell she gave no sign of acknowledging my humble presence. She, who was only of the Third Divinity, had remained unobtrusively in the background with her other Royal Sisters, all seated there on their silk cushions and dressed in their splendid fineries. Her Grand Ladyship would preside as usual, and she would survey us as contemptuously as if our stations in life were no more than those of scuttling ants. And, when we Novices prostrated ourselves in our naked debasement, it had not been my Honourable Mistress who carried the Bamboo Rod of Reformed Memory, nor she who had then walked silently behind the upturned soles of our trembling feet.

I knew this only because I could see from beneath my fearful eyelashes that Her Grand Ladyship had not chosen her to perform those soul-cleansing duties of punishment. During these first few Novitiate days of ours at the Pavilion, it seemed that this cruel duty was to be allotted to another of the Royal Sisters. However, this was not in itself any reason for my sullenness, because it was never once I who became the subject of Her Grand Ladyship's displeasure, or who required the learning for a Reformed Memory. At least not then.

During those first of many morning Assemblies, when we Novices were obviously in such constant need of instruction, the Bamboo Rod of Reformed Memory was never idle. Its relentless favours on unsuspecting rumps were an everyday occurrence. How often did the Great Hall echo to the cries of distress. This was particularly so whenever a certain Royal Sister by the name of Her Ladyship Bo-An was given the task of wielding the bamboo rod. The meaning of her name was 'Precious Peace'. What cruel irony! She possessed the malevolent character of a poisonous snake. Her arms were like those of one of the Warrior-guards who patrolled the Palace grounds, and she performed her task harshly and with relish.

On one such occasion my heart fluttered like a stricken sparrow when she came up behind me. Between my trembling feet I observed her standing there. I smelt her perfume, which was different to that of my dear Mistress. I could see the splayed tips of the Bamboo Rod against her long satin robe. For some moments she stood there. Perhaps she was only gazing down at my hanging sac, or at my listless shank, the ring pulling down its head towards the marble floor like a lead weight. But eventually she moved on along the row to some other hapless Brother Novice. I breathed then a guilty sigh of relief at hearing those first dreadful lashes pounding his thrusting rump.

But whatever the reasons for my Honourable Mistress to shun me, they were absent that particular day. I remember it as clearly now as I see my own reflection in the Silver Pond in the Garden of Tranquillity.

The morning heat was already up, even though it was little past dawn. It was after the ritual of morning bathing and I was standing in the habitual line of inspection with my Brother Novices.

Brother-Yellow-Crow looked at me reproachfully. 'Your face is darker than the Black Moon, boy.'

'Yes, Brother-Master Kanchu,' was all I could reply, keeping my eyes respectfully downcast.

He studied me curiously before bending stiffly to smell at me. He grunted, looking at my golden adornments with perhaps a measure of tolerant disdain. 'If your mood shall not quickly pass, it will be taken for insolence and ingratitude. You will be like an unwelcome Summer Cloud of Bad Omen for Their Ladyships at morning Assembly. You would do well to improve your demeanour.'

'Yes, Brother-Master.'

I felt his eyes piercing into me in that moment of silence.

'You shall go to your Honourable Mistress after Assembly,' he announced imperiously, as if he himself had deemed it so.

I cannot say that my heart leapt so much with joy as with an emotion that combined one of both relief and anticipation.

So, my dear Mistress desired my unworthy presence again! Was this not evidence of her capricious nature? She should shun me one day, and summon me the next! And one moment she might smile radiantly at me, but sneer in my face soon after!

Yet, after all, a speck of imperfection on a jade-stone need not obscure its brilliance.

My Brother Novices glanced at me with envy as they stood there naked in the line.

'You may now put on your Aprons of Good Modesty,' Brother-Master Kanchu ordered, his inspection obviously at an end.

We dressed ourselves hurriedly and went to our duties.

Morning Assembly came and went, but not before the habitual accompaniment of those wretched sounds of bamboo on flesh, and not least the howls from some unfortunate Novice.

I did not know it until afterwards, but the culprit in need of reform that day was none other than Senior Novice Ling, he who was in his third year and who had served my Mistress for so long. Nor did I realise it at that time, but it was rare that a Novice of his seniority would suffer the Bamboo Rod of Reformed Memory at Assembly. This was more usually reserved for new Novices or sometimes those in their second year.

When his howls had finally died away, Her Grand Ladyship addressed him coldly. 'One of my Honourable Sisters reported her displeasure to me. You were sullen and neglectful in your duties to her. You dropped her jar of jasmine-scent and your lowly servant face lacked sufficient remorse for one belonging to such a clumsy slave.'

She paused for a moment, looking slowly along the rows of her prostrated Novices. Her eyes were like those of a snake. But it was from her twisted lips that her venom came. 'Let that serve as a warning to all of you to strive in the performance of your duties to my Royal Sisters, lest I have the skins stripped from your ugly flesh and devoured by the scavenger rats beyond the Palace walls.'

Her voice rose shrilly and for a moment the Great Hall seemed to tremble in the wake of her wrath. The scavenger rats would surely have waited eagerly at the Palace gates.

Then, as if she had vented enough of her venom that morning, she rose from her throne-chair and walked stiffly away to her chambers, followed by the two other Grand Ladyships and her retinue of Senior Eunuchs.

The other Royal Sisters remained, beginning to talk quietly amongst themselves and seemingly in no haste to rise from their silk cushions. From time to time they regarded us with amusement. I noticed then my Mistress Jiang-Li sitting there amongst her Royal Sisters, not that she was looking at me, even if they were. They always did, and their eyes vied for the best position to behold my manly flesh – that same manly and adorned flesh which alone among us Novice Eunuchs had not suffered departure in the Room of Glorious Transformation.

Chief Eunuch Karif stood there in front of us. He still held the Bamboo Rod of Reformed Memory in his hand, and he watched us like a vulture. The only sounds in the Great Hall were of Their Ladyships' low babble of conversation, and from time to time the gasping moans of the unfortunate Ling.

'You are not keeping grace enough in the manner of your prostration,' Karif announced to us in a matter-of-fact tone, as the bamboo twitched threateningly in his hand.

At once there was a stirring of weary Novice bodies as they hurried to tense their limbs and torsos in yet

116

more acutely stressed postures. I, no less than my Brother Novices, arched my spine more and pushed my rump higher until every muscle in my body ached. But out of the corner of my eye I could see my dear Honourable Mistress, and, just for a second, our eyes met. Hers glittered like black gemstones; mine were humble and perhaps glazed with pleading desperation before I prudently made them downcast again.

The Royal Sisters got up from their cushions, not with any haste. It was, after all, not they who were in any discomfort. They ambled over to us, chatting all the while, oblivious to our debasing prostrations, ignoring us as if we might not have been there at all.

Karif bowed low to Their Ladyships, but they had no eyes for him, only walking around us. At least they were looking down upon us, our existences as though suddenly of at least casual interest to them. I heard slippered feet scuffling behind me, and I smelt so many wafting fragrances. I even once thought I smelt the familiar fragrance of my own dear Mistress, but I could not be sure. But my eyes and nose were kept so close to the marble tiles below, not daring to look between my feet to see whether I could identify hers.

I heard muted giggling. But I often did when Their Ladyships came behind me in Assembly. But today it seemed that their Pleasing Release of Mischievous Spirits was reserved that morning for Senior Novice Ling, although at that moment I still did not know that it was he. I only knew that it was one of the Senior Novices, by virtue of where he prostrated himself. Third-year Novices were always at the back row of Assembly.

From what I could tell, Their Ladyships stood behind him for some considerable while. Certainly his distress was more than that of his other Brother Novices, yet all the same my poor limbs and arching spine cried out for Their Ladyships' scrutiny of him to quickly end. I wished that he'd been more careful in the performance of his duties and in the manner of his demeanour. A disgruntled servant is surely no more desirable than a dog that bites its unsuspecting Mistress. And the whipping of that dog occupies time and energy, even though it might assuage the victim of its imprudent jaws. But during its whipping the other household dogs must cower silently and fearfully.

At last! Their Ladyships were departing, leaving their perfumed wake. And I needed no reminder of Brother-Yellow-Crow's emotive words. Was I not now to be taken to my dear Mistress's plush chambers, there to attend to her every whim and desire?

'Get up now and put on your Aprons of Good Modesty,' Chief Eunuch Karif commanded.

A ripple of relief surged amongst us as we got stiffly to our feet, hurrying then to cover our modesties again. The day's dutiful chores could now resume. The Novices were at least glad of that. And I was perhaps gladdened at the summons that awaited me.

If my heart made little fluttering pulses in my breast, I was also like a nervous mouse. Particularly when I learnt that the sorely punished victim of the bamboo that morning was none other than Senior Novice Ling – he who served my own dear Honourable Mistress; and he who had without doubt so offended her that she had cruelly reported his misdemeanours to Her Grand Ladyship.

I saw Senior Novice Ling standing there, trying to retain some vague semblance of his dignity. Even in our humbled status, we slaves must at least salvage our upright bearing and our servile pride. However, poor Ling looked no better than a whipped dog with its tail between its legs, shivering with the ague of excruciating agony. His face was ashen and his limbs trembled uncontrollably. Unable to keep his body completely erect, he tried to walk but his movement was stilted, the flayed skin of his buttocks as if not daring to stretch taut across them.

If, before that moment, my loins had dared to stir at the prospect of being in my Mistress's presence again, those stirrings were at once chilled as if by an icy breeze. It seemed that not only was my Mistress capricious in her moods, she was also harsh or even cruel in her ways. Moreover, if the dropping of her scent-jar were alone sufficient to precipitate her wrath, what chance was there for me to serve her without some hazardous mishap occurring at some time in the future? What if I were to fail in my task, if she again desired my silver-tailed frog to burst forth and leap to her bosom? Or if she desired some other intimate performance from me, what dreadful consequences might there be if that miserable performance proved not to her liking?

But I had no time to reflect further on these troubling thoughts. Brother-Yellow-Crow had appeared by my side and he was scowling at me, seeing how my anxious eyes were gazing upon Senior Novice Ling's humiliation and distress.

'Look inwards at your own unworthy imperfections and your humbleness, boy,' he admonished. 'Or you may find yourself soon enough laying bare not only your soul but also your hindquarters!'

I wanted neither, having already known only a few days ago the agony of bamboo upon my flesh. The trace-marks were still there for all to see. But at least it had been my Mistress's own fair hand that had wielded the bamboo, and hers had been considerably more merciful than that of her Royal Sister Bo-An in the punishment of poor Senior Novice Ling.

I looked away, mumbling my apology to Brother-Yellow-Crow, hurrying to fasten my Apron of Good Modesty.

'When Senior Novice Ling has sufficiently recovered himself he will escort you to your Mistress's chambers,' Brother-Yellow-Crow informed me. He was still studying me critically, as if perhaps he could still not entirely fathom out the purpose of my special status in the Pavilion.

All Eunuchs, I knew, were as much immersed in the tradition and protocol of the Palace, as were the various Imperial Ministers who directed those stately matters. The Senior Eunuchs adhered strictly to these rules, which not only governed their daily lives but, of course, also made them indispensable to Their Royal Ladyships – as much as to the whole Imperial system and the perverse culture surrounding it, and no doubt to His Imperial Majesty himself. And the fact that I was here like some unwanted interloper, defying the very essence of a Eunuch's credentials, did certainly make me an unworthy Novice, and one who had so unwittingly ruffled the saffron-yellow feathers of my elder Brother Eunuchs.

I had disturbed the shuffling silk shadows in the Pavilion of the Divine Orchid Ladies, even if the Orchid Ladies had desired it so themselves. My fettered flesh – but yet so intact – was of the quiet bull who treads a dangerous path between those china urns and silk-spun screens.

Brother-Master Kanchu addressed me sternly again. 'Her Ladyship will be awaiting you, and you had better serve her with utmost care and devotion in whatever service she may demand of you,' he warned. 'This day she is under the spell of a Black Moon, and unless you wish to feel the bamboo on your rump at next Assembly you would do well to heed my words.'

Indeed, Brother-Yellow-Crow's words sounded as ominous as his voice sounded grave. I wondered why my Mistress should be under the spell of a Black Moon. Perhaps I could be her instrument for casting away her dark curse. But I was being presumptuous now.

Brother-Yellow-Crow clapped his hands and at once the Novices were attentive. 'Everyone to his duties! Perform them diligently, or fear my wrath!' he said, waving his hand for my fellow Novices to disperse.

He turned then to look at Senior Novice Ling, who had to some extent managed to recover some grace in his posture and demeanour, even though he was still trembling and his face was no less ashen than before.

'You will take Novice Shani to Her Ladyship Jiang-Li,' Brother-Master Kanchu announced before adding in a more kindly tone, 'I hope you will not incur her displeasure again, Senior Novice Ling, because, from what I saw of your flesh, it could ill afford anything other than her absolute satisfaction.'

'Yes, Brother-Master,' Ling mumbled, bowing his head so that I could see its bald crown glistening with perspiration.

Brother-Yellow-Crow nodded. 'Take him there now then,' he ordered, turning to leave.

Senior Novice Ling looked at me with what I can only believe was pure hatred. But why I should deserve it was not fully apparent to me then.

'Follow me,' he snarled.

And I did, walking behind him so that I could see how stiffly his legs moved and how his body bent slightly backwards like a beanstalk in the wind, his buttocks as if wanting to distance themselves from his Apron of Good Modesty. Nonetheless he moved quickly, fearing perhaps that even now the cruel bamboo chased his shadow with its dragon-fire.

Our feet padded quietly in rhythm together across the marble tiles and into the east wing, where the corridor was empty and hushed with respectful awe. When we got to that familiar ornately carved door that I knew to be the entrance to my Honourable Mistress's private chambers, he stopped before it. He turned and hissed at me. 'I choose not to think what vile reasons my dear Mistress has for favouring you. Or why, after I have served her so faithfully, she treats me no better than if I were a mangy dog to be whipped away from her side. I only know that she purrs like a contented cat when she mentions your lowly name. Moreover, she does so to see the hurt in my eyes.'

He broke off, fearful that his snarled words might have been overheard, all the while listening out for any sign of it. Then he continued in a low growl. 'I shall not easily forget my humiliation this day, pretty slave-boy with his putrid flesh so pitifully ringed! I hope it withers away like a poisoned weed, and then Their Ladyships will quickly discard you like an old songbird that can no longer sing.'

I shook my head vigorously, my hand reaching out in a conciliatory gesture of denial. 'But, I beg you, Brother Ling, I have done nothing that I was not made to do,' I protested meekly.

He pushed my hand abruptly away. 'I am *not* your brother,' he hissed. 'You are not one of us. You've not suffered our same fate that makes me a Brother of my true Brothers. You are a false Brother . . . and a scorned plaything of the Royal Sisters.'

'I am not!' I retorted hotly, even though this guilty notion slopped like poisonous ink in my mind.

He sneered dismissively at me, his eyes blazing with contempt. 'She told me how you made your filthy bull-rod stand for her! And then how it flew your vile seed at her! *She* told me that and more!' he challenged, even forgetting his respect for our mutual Honourable Mistress. 'She' was scarcely a fitting word for reference to a Divine Orchid Lady of His Imperial Majesty.

I could say nothing in my defence. I felt no anger at him, only my shame and also a small pulse of shock, and even foreboding. How could my Mistress have betrayed such an intimate secret that might perhaps stir dangerous dragons from their lair? I began to wish that I had suffered that same fate as Senior Novice Ling had suffered in the Room of Glorious Transformation.

He could see that he had wounded me now, and his black eyes sparkled with triumph. 'Ah yes, my golden-ringed worm! You see how much I know! I have been nearly three full seasons in this cursed Palace, and soon I would have become a full Brother and have been granted the long Yellow Robe of Honour to wear – that which marks out the status of the true-fledged Eunuch here, and which would have ended my debasing hardships as a lowly Novice.'

I looked into his eyes, perhaps with pity. Pity for him, and pity for me. I could only suppose that his humiliating beating must in some way have deprived him of his seniority. Yet this could hardly be something he should blame on me.

I was about to protest again when he reached out with his hand and rapped his knuckles on the lacquered timber of the door. 'It is me, your servant Ling, Mistress,' he called out softly, his voice now so sickly sweet and humble, his angry venom gone.

He listened with his ear to the door, but before opening it he turned again to me and hissed in that ugly tone of his. 'Remember two things, my golden-ringed worm with your stuck-up rod,' he said smugly.

'Firstly, these Palace walls have whispering tongues that make bad-mouth secrets spread like spilt vinegar. Secondly, our Mistress's honeyed mouth conceals a daggered heart!'

And with that he pushed open the door and went quickly inside.

My Mistress was not alone. She was lounging on the cushions of her huge bed-throne. So were two of her Royal Sisters, whose names I did not know. Their Ladyships looked immediately at me, not as if I were quite a worm, but more an object of amused interest.

The other two Royal Sisters were propped up beside my Mistress on a mound of cushions and in such a way that all three Royal Ladies were stretched out beside each other, my Mistress in the middle. They were dressed in almost identical robes of pure silk, except that each of these bedchamber garments was of a different colour and pattern. They had those huge billowing sleeves, and the robes were loosely fastened across the belly by a braided cord of gold lace. Their Ladyships' feet were bare, protruding from under the hem almost provocatively so, and resting on small cushions, just as my Mistress's had been on that previous occasion of my visit there.

I confess to having been both shocked and disappointed to find that my Mistress was not alone. It seemed strange to me that she should be sharing her bed-throne with two of her Sisters. But then, I was not yet familiar with all those many contradictions that abounded in the Pavilion of the Divine Orchid Ladies.

One of the Senior Eunuchs stood respectfully beside the bed-throne, as if ready to retire from Their Ladyships' presence. There was a silver platter of tea-drinking chinaware and a small brewing-urn resting by the edge of the bed.

'You may go and fetch the Maidservant now, Shek,' my Mistress said curtly to the Senior Eunuch without deigning to look his way. But there was a smug smile on her lips, and her eyes alternated between me and Senior Novice Ling.

'Yes, Your Ladyship,' Senior Eunuch Shek replied, bowing with all correctness.

He glanced at us both before hurrying away from the chamber and quietly closing the door behind him.

My Mistress beckoned us both, and we came nearer, not forgetting to bow low and doing so in unison.

Brother-Yellow-Crow had taught us that creed, which we repeated aloud together before retiring to our night mattresses: 'Bow low or not at all; so that you shall see the horizon behind you from between your legs.'

For a moment or so my Mistress continued to regard us in that haughty amused air of hers. Then she spoke abruptly. 'Drop your Aprons of Good Modesty.'

That sudden habitual flood of shame came to us, but we complied quickly, our fingers fumbling to untie the cords, aware of Their Ladyships' eyes upon us.

'So, my poor Ling,' she addressed him pleasantly. 'Have you reformed your memory now? Did my beloved Sister Bo-An not do justice to your rump with her bamboo, and apply its stinging tails by such a gentle hand? And is your face as sullen as it was when its impudence offended me?'

'No, I mean, yes, Honourable Mistress. My memory is greatly reformed. And my face is now as respectful as it should have been, Mistress.'

'And are your hands less clumsy than they were before?'

Out of the corner of my eye, I saw him swallow nervously. 'Yes – No, Mistress. They are not any more clumsy.'

'In that case you shall remove the platter from my bed and put it on the floor rug.'

'Yes, Mistress.'

He went to where the platter was and reached out to take it.

It was only now that I saw how well reformed his memory must have been. Her Ladyship Bo-An had been far from gentle with her bamboo-wielding hand. The cheeks of his rump were covered with such an abundance of livid crimson stripes that his glistening flesh was more akin to that of a ripe pomegranate flayed to pulp, rather than the flesh of a human slave.

I continued to stand there rigidly, hands at my sides, which was the correct posture, even if my manhood was so blatant in its reposed exposure. I did not wish to move in any way that might be perceived as remotely offensive, nor to have my memory reformed in the same way as poor Senior Novice Ling's.

My Mistress was speaking to him again. 'Our ears – neither mine nor those of my dear Sisters – shall not wish to be offended by the clink and clatter of china cup against china cup when you lift the platter.'

'No, Mistress,' he said timidly, but I could see by the way his hands trembled and by the sweat that bathed his torso that he was far from confident in his objective. He took hold of the platter and lifted it as cautiously as if his life depended upon it.

However, before he could set the tray down upon the ground, my Mistress suddenly held her hand up. 'Wait!' she commanded, causing him to freeze with the platter midway between bed and floor. 'Perhaps my dear Sisters would care for some more refreshment before you dispose of the platter?'

The Honourable Lady on the far side of the bed-throne spoke now, scarcely trying to conceal the mischievous grin on her lips. 'Oh, I should. Indeed so.' She could not stifle a giggle, either. 'Thank you, my beloved and considerate Sister,' she added more sombrely now, as though remembering her regal station. All the while she pretended to cool her face with her peacock-feathered fan, watching Ling with benign interest.

She was about the same age as my Mistress. The other Honourable Royal Sister on the nearside of the bed had been perhaps a few full seasons older than either of them, and it was she who now spoke. 'I require no more refreshment at present. Perhaps later.' She was addressing Senior Novice Ling, her smile more of a sneer. All the while she looked critically at him. 'But, like my two beloved Sisters here, I shall not wish my ears to catch that irritating clatter of porcelain!' she went on. 'Slaves would be mindful to be silent in their work, even when they must perform it as nakedly as newborn puppies . . . and when so freshly whipped for their previous imperfections.'

My Mistress laughed. 'Our beloved Sister Yon speaks so wisely,' she said, tapping her beloved Sister's leg playfully with her fan. But she watched Ling through narrowed hawk's eyes.

I was being ignored. But I was glad of it, since it was not I who was providing their Ladyships' entertainment. I stood there as motionless as any statue, but my ears and eyes took everything in.

'Our beloved Sister Xia requires more lotus-tea, Senior Novice Ling,' my Mistress said, needlessly so. 'You may serve her now.'

In order to do this, poor Ling had to carry the platter over to the other side of the bed-throne. I could see how his face was such a miserable picture of fearful concentration, and the sweat seemed to come from every pore of his nakedness. The platter journeyed precariously in his hands, but nonetheless as level as the Silver Pond in the Garden of Tranquillity.

Just as he reached the other side, my Mistress stopped him in his tracks. 'Ah yes, I forgot to enquire, my poor Ling, how does your lowly rump feel now ... after its so justly deserved punishment from our Royal Sister Bo-An?'

He hesitated for a second, keeping the tray so carefully balanced. 'It is – I am ... richly sore, Mistress.' He chose his words as if having pondered each one carefully beforehand. 'But my mind is greatly improved in health, my Mistress. Thank you.' Then he added hastily, 'And – and my demeanour is as a devoted slave's should be.'

Our Honourable Mistress seemed pleased at this respectful reply, but she was not yet finished with him. 'Then your mind glows with happiness, Ling, even if your cheeks glow with their painful memory of the bamboo?'

'Indeed, Mistress. Your words are always so wise ... and I glow at their kindly wisdom.'

Their Ladyships were momentarily silenced by so reverent and skilful a response. Yet perhaps it had been too much so.

My Mistress now regarded him through narrowed eyes. Then with mock severity she glanced firstly at her Sister Xia, and then at Sister Yon, who both were so clearly enjoying their host's unkindly torment.

'Our dear Sister Bo-An clearly made such a worthwhile impression on Senior Novice Ling. Don't you think, my Sisters?'

'Mmmm. She has the hand of a true warrior!' Sister Xia admitted, nodding as if with admiration at such worthiness.

But Sister Yon shook her head in disagreement. 'Certainly she swings the bamboo like a sword, but she is more of a demon than a warrior. She cuts the flesh of her victims as though she desires to milk their blood afterwards. Perhaps she sometimes does ... and it gives her strength!'

My Mistress laughed, although not as loudly as did Sister Xia. Then there was a moment of silence, all three Ladyships continuing to study poor Senior Novice Ling with amused disdain – he all the while so wretched in his servile nakedness and still holding the platter with such utter determination.

My Mistress said quietly to him, her voice sweet as honey, 'Turn your poor rump to us, Ling, so we can better appreciate our dear Sister's skill ... and then we ourselves can judge if you have been well enough attended to by her.'

Up until that moment he had been exercising great care to keep his backside turned away from Their Ladyships' view, although I remembered that, in the Great Hall at Assembly, they had already walked behind him. While he had still been trying to keep a grace in the manner of his prostration, Their Royal Ladyships had already inspected the damage to his rump. Therefore, surely they had seen at first hand how skilfully Royal Sister Bo-An had administered to it?

Senior Novice Ling was crestfallen, his face like the Last Weeping Moon of Autumn. Saying nothing, he turned his back slowly, holding himself as erect as he could and trying to contain his trembling ague. By the Grace of Friendly Spirits, there was no rattling sound from the platter.

'Come nearer,' my Mistress said sharply.

And now he had to back himself towards Their Ladyships.

'Nearer, I said. If we shall become offended by the nearness of your lowly rump, you shall soon enough know of it.'

He backed closer. I saw the mortified expression on his face.

Their Ladyships studied him with morbid curiosity, seeing close up the evidence of their Royal Sister Bo-An's skilful work.

'I told a silk-edged lie,' Sister Yon considered, her eyes peering at his welts. 'Our beloved Sister Bo-An is not just a demon, she's a merciless warrior with a hand of iron. If she'd cut him with the sword and not the bamboo, his rump would be none the wiser for it.'

Royal Sister Xia grunted. 'It must surely sting him no less than if he'd sat upon a wild hornets' nest,' she ventured. 'He'll not sit down for seven suns! Or, if he did, surely his cheeks would scorch the seat he sat upon.'

Then suddenly – being near enough to him to do so – she lunged forwards and with her fan prodded him experimentally on one cheek.

It was at that very moment that a small tinkling rattle of porcelain came from the tray. Senior Novice Ling had flinched unwisely, his concentration momentarily flawed. The fan, after all, had not been employed for its habitual cooling of Their Ladyships' royal cheeks.

'This slave is impudent and careless!' Sister Xia declared gleefully. 'He learns not to work silently at his chores . . . and his clumsiness is surely not yet cured by the bamboo.'

My Mistress joined in her companions' laughter, although hers was a trifle forced. I stood as motionless as a dead tree, wishing I could melt into the wall behind me. I even felt sorry now for Senior Novice Ling. His face was stricken with terror and he was still frozen to the spot, desperate to keep the platter level. It was clearly evident that his hatred of me was momentarily suspended. Fear now was an altogether more potent emotion. I was no longer sure whether his trembling ague was from the painful aftermath of his beating, or from his fear of another, or perhaps a combination of both.

I could not believe that my Mistress could be possessed by such apparent cruelty. But now she was like a spider slyly contemplating the moths caught in her web. Yet, had I not been in her gracious company before, and known those intimate moments with her, I perhaps would not have noticed that measure of tenderness and pity in her soft eyes.

Imprudently now, I dared to raise my head a fraction from its downcast respectfulness, and I looked into those same eyes. But the softness was certainly gone from them. At least for now.

Suddenly she met my disrespectful gaze and I felt a tiny leap of fear in my heart. I bowed my head quickly, feeling her displeasure, regretting my impetuousness. But perhaps in that moment the capricious cloud of her mood was passing away, the black streak of cruelty finally spent. A burst of sunshine cast its radiance suddenly across the bed-throne, making those robes and covers of silk and satin shimmer in its welcome beam. And such richness of fragrances came thick and fast upon my nostrils. I could see her dainty little toes twitching, and there was silence now in that delightful chamber. But how could that cosy place, with its rich tapestries and hanging drapes of silk, and its beautifully lacquered screens depicting such tranquil scenes of nature's wonders, harbour so many dark shadows of woe?

Before my Mistress could speak, there was a rap on the door and someone I recognised as Senior Eunuch

Shek spoke shrilly from beyond. 'It is I, Madam, with the Maidservant.'

'You may enter,' my Mistress ordered curtly, barely raising her voice, but beginning to fan herself briskly again.

I should not have turned my head as he entered, nor looked upon the face of the timid Maidservant who followed behind him. At once I saw that it was Li-Mei, she of the Beautiful Plum Blossom and of those pretty pale features that could have graced a celestial angel. Her large brown eyes were wide with apprehension, but her head was not downcast enough in respectful humility.

For a dangerous second she glanced at me, and then at Senior Novice Ling, seeing us standing there in our debasing nakedness. Yet, to observe the nakedness of Novices was as commonplace as observing cockroaches scuttling across the stone floors of the kitchens. Besides, had she not herself handled my own naked flesh and seen it being adorned in its unwilled splendour of golden rings and clamps? Thus, the debasing exposure of naked man-slaves should have meant no more to her than if she were watching those same scuttling cockroaches.

'Do you forget yourself, slave-girl?' Senior Eunuch Shek demanded angrily, having turned on her, his eyes blazing at such blatant irreverence.

For a moment Li-Mei seemed as if overcome by so many grim faces and perverse images in that silent chamber. Then she quickly bowed as low as a bending willow branch, dropping her head so that her long dark hair hung almost to the floor. The tightness of her white servant-smock made the thin cotton fabric stretch tautly across her girlish thighs.

'You redeem yourself just in time,' Senior Eunuch Shek snarled.

But Li-Mei had instinctively sensed that need for her redemption, knowing that such an impertinent omission of reverence was justly worthy of punishment. Bowing still lower, she held herself in that acute posture, and it made the hem of her servant-smock lift above the tops of her legs. I could see then how divinely sculpted they were, every muscle and sinew tensed as taut as bowstrings.

'You may stand, Li-Mei,' my Mistress condescended, showing no sign of her displeasure. And for that, at least, I felt relieved for the plum-blossom girl who had once handled my flesh so tenderly.

Now as she raised herself, standing there meekly, hands clasped together in front of her, I could see how the small pert mounds of her breasts pushed against the linen. I remember thinking how they were like two impetuous buds waiting to burst forth impatiently into bloom.

All this while Senior Novice Ling was just standing there, still holding his platter, uncertain what to do with it. The Royal Ladies on either side of my Mistress were still reposing there, their faces impassive. But perhaps there was a glimmer of disappointment in them, now that it seemed that Their Ladyships' entertainment might have been so cruelly interrupted.

Certainly it appeared that the malicious cloud of black mischief had finally left my Mistress's face. She had ridden the devil's humps and fallen back to the warm bosom of merciful normality. Whatever it had been that caused the wickedness of her mood, I could not know. Not then. Besides, I scarcely knew my Mistress, other than to know her capriciousness and the soft exquisiteness of her feet.

She was speaking again to Li-Mei. 'You will go with Ling and bathe his sweat from him. Then you shall cleanse his punished flesh with onion-tears and tea-tree oil. And, when the stinging has eased, finally you shall massage him with ky-ky-berry lotion. Is that clear?' She spoke like someone with concern for a battle-wounded soldier.

Li-Mei nodded. 'Yes, Mistress,' she mumbled shyly.

So now my sweet little Plum Blossom was to minister to the intimate flesh of one of my brothers! Moreover she would do so with those same soft and dainty little hands that had ministered to my own flesh.

I could see by her expression that she could scarcely believe her ears, any more than Senior Novice Ling dared believe his. Relief had come hesitantly to him, like a sunburst defying a winter-clad sky and which might at any moment be snuffed out again. He was wondering whether this was yet to be some other torment to endure – one that was deceptively cloaked in his Mistress's sudden kindness. The bald confusion in his mind was all too evident. His Mistress had caused him first to be humiliatingly flogged, then to be tormented in her bedchamber with a tray of tea-brewing porcelain, and then – at the very moment that more punishment threatened – she ordered him to be soothingly healed by one of her own slave-girls!

But in the Pavilion of the Divine Orchid Ladies there were always so many unfathomable contradictions and conflicting emotions. Yet, surely Senior Novice Ling, having served there for nearly three full seasons, must already have known of these whimsical realities? In my case, I had not yet seen my first new moon through the window of my miserable dormitory, but had I not already acquired such profoundness of knowledge in my Mistress's ways?

'You may put on your Apron of Good Modesty, Ling. And then go with Maidservant Li-Mei for your healing treatment. But, now that you are with re-formed memory, let it not lapse again,' my Mistress warned. 'Or you shall know my wrath soon enough.'

'Yes, Mistress.'

Finally he could believe his good fortune and it showed in his face and in the way his words came so eagerly from his lips. But he still held the silver platter awkwardly, not quite knowing what to do with it. For a moment it seemed that Royal Sister Xia would be denied the refreshment that had been promised her before. In his eagerness, he clearly had forgotten that duty.

My Mistress, however, had not. 'Junior Novice Shani shall take your tray and serve my dear Sister's tea,' she declared, without looking in my direction.

I gulped, feeling a cold stab of alarm as if a dagger had struck my heart. This unwelcome mention of my name brought me back in a trice to the forefront of Their Ladyships' scrutiny. The source of entertainment was now passing from one miserable Novice to another, and I was immediately conscious of it.

I hesitated for only a second, knowing how orders could so easily be misconstrued. But the meaning in this case seemed clear enough. I was to put on my Apron of Good Modesty, take the tray from Senior Novice Ling and serve Her Ladyship Xia with her refreshment.

'Yes, Mistress,' I answered, quickly bending down to retrieve the apron at my feet, aware that not only were Their Ladyships and Senior Novice Ling watching me, but so were Maidservant Li-Mei and Senior Eunuch Shek.

And it was he who admonished me with the bark of a jackal. 'You insolent puppy! Did Her

Honourable Ladyship command you to dress yourself? Stand straight, slave, and drop the apron down where it was!'

My eyes must have told of my consternation. I could certainly not deny the truth of what he had said, nor did my Mistress's scowl suggest that she thought otherwise. Shamefaced and blushing, I quickly dropped the garment back to my toes and made myself as straight as an iron rod, arms by my sides and head bowed again. My words stumbled stupidly from my mouth. 'I thought – I mean, I did not think that – that I was not to dress myself . . . before I took the tray and went to serve Her Honourable Ladyship Xia.'

'Be silent!' Senior Eunuch Shek roared, red-faced with anger.

Much later I was to learn that Senior Eunuchs were held to account for any indiscipline of Novices in Their Ladyships' presence. No ripple of disorder must ever disturb the silk-spun tranquillity of the Pavilion of the Divine Orchid Ladies.

I stared at my toes, cursing my innocent folly.

It was my Mistress who spoke next, but her words were not unkind when they came. 'Senior Eunuch Shek spoke justly. You have much to learn still, Novice Shani. But there is time enough to teach you. And the Bamboo Rod of Reformed Memory is always there to assist your tutors. Is that not so, Shek?

'Indeed it is so, Your Ladyship,' he answered eagerly, adding as an afterthought, 'If you should desire it, Madam, I can report Your Ladyship's displeasure with this slave to Her Grand Ladyship in time for tomorrow's Assembly?'

A cold rush of fear chilled my blood. The dreadful image of Senior Novice Ling's welt-ravaged rump came at once to my mind, and I most fervently wished that it would not be Royal Sister Bo-An who would be assigned that performance of duty. How should I sleep at all, this night?

But my Mistress seemed not disposed to accept Senior Eunuch Shek's offer. Relief flooded over me as if an angel had brushed against my skin.

'Your wise offer is noted, Shek. I shall closely observe how well this Novice attends to us, until whenever we shall dismiss him. If he fails again in his devotions then I myself shall inform Her Grand Ladyship of his lacking.'

So, I was yet far from the Bright Edge of the Forest, and my ears burnt.

'You may go now, Shek.' My Mistress waved her hand at him. 'And take Maidservant Li-Mei and Senior Novice Ling with you ... and see that his healing is attended to as I have decreed.'

Senior Eunuch Shek bowed his acknowledgement.

My Mistress addressed me. 'You shall take the tray now and serve lotus-tea to my dear Sister ... and take care not to offend our ears with the rattling of porcelain, Shani.'

'Yes, Mistress.'

I had never before even held a silver platter, nor been instructed in the art of tea-serving, which I knew to be a custom amongst high-up people across the vastness of His Majesty's Empire. Nonetheless, I hurried to the other side of the bed-throne to where Ling was still standing with the platter. As I reached out with trembling hands to take it from him, I saw a smug look of malevolence spread across his face.

He was the gloating wolf; I the pitiful rabbit caught in his gaze.

But I held the tray squarely, no longer having any regard for him, nor for Li-Mei. Any fleeting moment of envy I might have had – in the knowledge of the intimate duty she was soon to perform on Brother Ling's flesh – was all but extinguished. Li-Mei was standing beside Senior Eunuch Shek, and they were both waiting for Senior Novice Ling. Only for a second did I wonder what thoughts were in her mind, and whether she was watching me with pity or disgust.

But my attention was taken up fully with keeping the porcelain vessels and the tea-urn from sliding in any direction on the glittering surface. Such was my concentration, I was not even aware that my fellow servants had already scurried from my Mistress's chamber.

All the while her two Sisters had reposed there in silence, watching the proceedings with amused interest. Their gaze was again focused upon me as they looked beneath my proffered tray, and I could feel their eyes upon my ringed and clamped manhood-flesh. Their Ladyships were not to be deprived of their entertainment. Only now, the source of it had changed.

Royal Sister Xia had the eyes of a cunning cat. And I was her nervous mouse. I could see her peacock-feathered fan, and the way she held it suggested mischievous intent. And I was not wrong.

As I came up to her, holding out the tray, she reached forwards with the fan and nudged my shank with it.

'Your Novice has certainly the pizzle of a bull Sister Jiang-Li,' she remarked casually to my Mistress, moving me to one side with her fan and peering under there. 'And his seed-sac hangs like a jute bag with two fat onions in it.'

I could tell that there was a measure of jealousy in her tone, as if perhaps she had been denied some chattel that my Mistress possessed.

Sister Yon giggled. 'But surely, dear Sisters, as much as he *looks* to have the potency of a rutting boar, has his sac not been clamped to make his pizzle safe?' she asked.

My Mistress was silent, pretending indifference. But it was Sister Xia who answered, and her voice was like wet silk. 'The Pavilion walls tell me otherwise. I hear whispers that he can still rise like a sprung branch unleashed and that, when it stands out, its reach and its length is enough to hang a dead cockerel from, without it once sagging to the ground.'

She turned her head slyly to my Mistress, enquiring innocently enough, 'Is that not so, Sister Jiang-Li?'

If my Mistress had been alarmed, she disguised it well, shrugging her shoulders and giving a dismissive little laugh. 'Certainly he can rise. I have witnessed it myself when I was at a morning's inspection duty. That was why I beat him at Assembly. And, my Sisters, if you look at his rump you will see that the marks and bruising of my displeasure are still there upon him.' She waved her hand at me. 'Turn yourself, Shani!'

I complied meekly, still holding the tray as level as I could.

'Come closer!'

I took a pace backwards, feeling the silk covers of the bed-throne touch against the backs of my legs. I stood there stupidly, my bare feet anchored to the rug beneath them. I was by now past the stage of embarrassed mortification. It was an affliction to bear, if not willingly, then without a murmur of protest. If my Mistresses should take pleasure from my nakedness, or from viewing the adornments of my manhood, or from peering at my marked backside, it was surely no more than a slave's humble duty.

Sister Xia leant forwards, peering curiously at my

rump. 'Hmmm, yes. He still has a few faint black stripes, Sister, I grant you.'

I felt her trace the end of her fan gently across one of the stripes that were undoubtedly there.

'But, from what I can observe of his lean flesh, his punishment was hardly of the severity you awarded Senior Novice Ling,' she declared, prodding me with the fan as if to make me move away.

Her remark had seemed innocent enough, I thought. But out of the corner of my eye I could see that her eyes glittered with mischief.

But my clever Mistress was quick with her reply. 'That is so, dear Sister!' she exclaimed airily. 'But in Senior Novice Ling's case it was Her Grand Ladyship who presented the bamboo to Warrior-Sister Bo-An . . . and not to me, if you remember? Alas, my dear Sisters, I have the hand and arm of a weak virgin, and I cannot make the bamboo fly like a demented buzzard, whereas she can!'

Then she added, as if it might have been a concession to Sister Xia's observations, 'But in future I shall endeavour to be more harsh whenever Her Grand Ladyship entrusts the rod to my feeble little hands.'

Her Honourable Sisters laughed now at such a worthy response. But, before their laughter had subsided, my Mistress signalled for me to turn myself again. Now that my hindquarters had provided such a joyous diversion, it was clear that I must once more revert to being the servant with the proffered tray. In any case, it was evident to me that my Mistress herself did not wish to dwell upon those comparisons that Sister Xia had made. If my Mistress had dealt more harshly with Senior Novice Ling than she had with me, surely that was a matter for her own conscience. Moreover, if my scars were fading, whereas Senior Novice Ling's were still but ripening, I myself could scarcely harbour any desire for this topic of Their Ladyships' discussion to continue.

Thinking that I should complete my task, I held out the tray again to Royal Sister Xia, but she waved me away impatiently. Evidently the lotus-tea was no longer of fancy to her, even if my golden adornments still were. Her eyes were again upon them. I could see, too, that she had more questions to ask, as if perhaps my Mistress's previously dismissive assurances had not been entirely satisfactory.

'So, the slave was punished for the impertinent rising of his pizzle? But I am curious, dear Sister,' she enquired of my Mistress without looking at her, 'as to what manner of things should have made him stiffen?'

Her eyes were more those of a crafty cat than a hooded vulture, and her voice had lowered itself to the husky croak of a bullfrog. 'Does his flesh rise to your command, Sister? And, if so, does it rise as much as was whispered to me? Or was this just a bland rumour made hot with pepper-spice? And, when he rose, was he truly as much as the sturdy branch of a maple tree . . . or was he more of a skinny twig, or even a limp weed that is soon bowed by a gentle breeze? Tell me, I beg you, beloved Sister Jiang-Li, for I am cursed with curiosity and I shall die from my affliction!'

My Mistress glanced sideways at her with an expression that might have been patient tolerance or guarded amusement. 'He is not a street-monkey that performs tricks for the crowds, dear Sister! And nor is it I who tugs at his leash to make him dance,' my Mistress said with mock indignation.

Nonetheless Royal Sister Xia was undaunted in her stubborn persistence. Perhaps she detected that first faint smell of blood. It was either her wicked curiosity, or her green jealousy of my Mistress having something that she herself had been denied, that was undoubtedly behind her sly inquisitiveness. As for my own humble slave thoughts at being the object of such friendly rivalry, I was not commanded to share them with Their Royal Ladyships. Besides, how should a slave's opinion count, even though I could perhaps have ventured one? Yet I was certainly glad not to have been commanded to do so. Such intimate and personal details would surely have issued from my pitiful lips with stuttering shamefulness. And how should I have expected such regal Ladies to understand the perverse intricacies of male flesh, particularly when it had been so cruelly festooned?

Sister Xia smiled provocatively, her eyebrows lifting. 'I have no desire to see your monkey *dance*, my dearly beloved Sister. I only desire to see him *rise* . . . and to see if his ring is a big enough hoop for him to jump through!'

She was looking mockingly at that vile adornment at the head of my shank, as if pretending to consider that such a perverse act might have been possible.

But my Mistress was scornful. 'Ah! So now he must be a juggling monkey, too?' she demanded sarcastically, smirking with pretended disdain.

But she carefully ignored Sister Xia's so boldly stated request. Clearly my Mistress had no wish for me to perform any rising in the presence of her Royal Sisters. And for that I was grateful, if for no other reason than that I would have found it hard to comply with such an order.

But Sister Xia was not about to let the matter drop. 'No, I would not say a juggler, Sister. Surely he would be more one of those street contortionists who contrive to twist their limbs and bodies inside out? A juggler is a less agile street-player who throws balls

142

and clubs and rings from one hand to another,' she argued, yawning now. 'But *your* slave's ringed club and balls are surely not for acrobatic displays? The Imperial Physicians would be truly astonished that their wisdom had been found so lacking!'

Her tone was no less sarcastic than my Mistress's, but Sister Xia had not finished yet. She looked cunningly at her now, her challenge all too evident. 'We – that is, we three beloved Sisters here – can keep the secret that the whispering walls will never hear, dearest Sister Jiang-Li.'

She paused, grinning wickedly. 'Let us see him rise, Sister,' she continued, no less stubbornly than an overladen mule. 'Would it not be a welcome diversion from our boredom?'

It was Sister Yon who broke the sudden uneasy silence that followed. She gurgled with laughter. The banter between her beloved Sisters was entertaining enough, but it was where her eyes were focused that appeared to provide more entertainment for her. That I could see, even though the silver platter obscured my own view. And, now that the monkey was surely about to be ordered to perform, her entertainment would be all the greater.

My Mistress was thinking of her reply, and now she was certainly trapped into giving one. I saw in her eyes that she was weakening. Now that the secret was so clearly exposed, would it not be better to indulge her dear Sisters boldly, in the hope that the secret would be contained within the walls of her bedchamber?

But it seemed to me that the logic in such a notion must surely be flawed, at least in one respect. I thought this because, only a few minutes earlier, had not Senior Novice Ling's words been so stinging to my ears? He knew – since my Mistress had told him so – that my 'filthy bull-rod had stood for her and

143

how then it had flown its vile seed at her'. Now, surely, my Mistress must regret having taunted a mere slave with such a dangerous secret – a slave whose harsh punishment she had so recently occasioned! Even if his respectful fear of his Mistress were enough to seal his lips, a brief moment of sudden vengeance might make them slippery loose.

It was little wonder, I reflected ruefully, that these Palace walls had whispering tongues that made bad-mouth secrets spread like spilt vinegar! My beautiful Mistress was not only capricious in her moods, but imprudent with her words.

But this was hardly the time for me to ponder such complexities of life in the Pavilion. Sister Xia was still waiting slyly for a response to her challenge, perhaps already knowing that she had won.

'Well, my dear Sister, shall we be permitted to see your slave-toy rise playfully for us here in the safe confines of your bedchamber?'

'He is not *my* slave-toy,' my Mistress immediately retorted. 'He was allotted to serve me by Her Grand Ladyship, so to me he is nothing more than a Junior Novice to be tutored in his duties.'

But I could see from Lady Xia's smug expression that she was unconvinced by my Mistress's protestations. They had surely come too thick and fast for there to be no measure of truth in those unsaid allegations.

An uneasy silence fell over the bedchamber again. Sister Xia was waiting.

My Mistress looked at me. But I could see that I was lost. Their Royal Ladyships were also looking at me with an eagerness that unnerved my already nervous disposition.

After a moment or two of reflection my Mistress spoke. 'Set the platter down and get on to the end of the bed. You shall massage our feet.'

Her words chilled me. 'Yes, Mistress.'

I obeyed, sliding myself awkwardly on to the bed-throne, my long legs finding it difficult to adopt a respectful posture, like a clumsy newborn fawn.

'You shall start with Royal Sister Xia.'

'Yes, Mistress.'

I shuffled myself over to where Sister Xia's feet reposed, aware of her gloating expression and glittering eyes. I heard Sister Yon giggle again, but otherwise there was silence except for the faint sound of limbs moving on silk.

Sister Xia thrust her foot out to me and I took it, beginning to massage it in the same way as I had massaged my Mistress's foot before. It seemed as if a thousand years had passed since then.

After a while Their Ladyships began to talk, ignoring my presence. Perhaps they were aware that it required time to bring on those feelings that might make me stir. And certainly I had no such feelings now, at all. I hung like a putrefied grape on a winter vine.

At least whatever tendrils of animosity had been spun between my Mistress and Lady Xia seemed put aside. Their Royal Ladyships were talking quietly amongst themselves about affairs of State. Or so I had thought, but I was concentrating upon feet, not words.

Suddenly Sister Xia remarked irritably, 'His Royal Majesty is a puny runt and a lazy one in the treatment of his beloved Wives.'

I was shocked at this, my ears burning with immediate fear. Surely such talk – even from a Royal Orchid Lady – was the height of dangerous sacrilege.

But Sister Xia was unabashed and she continued indifferently. 'I was sent word by Chief Eunuch Karif that His puny Majesty would honour me with his presence. I was dressed for him in those same exquisite jewels that he himself had given me. And I covered my body in that exotic perfume that came all the way from Paris by sailing ship.'

Indeed, I thought that even now my nostrils were filled with a scent that was unfamiliar to me. It was neither jasmine, nor lavender, nor honeysuckle nor any other that I knew. Whatever strange scent it was, it lingered on her feet and on her robe.

Royal Sister Xia was clearly aggrieved, her tone increasingly bitter as she went on. 'I waited with the patience of an angel, lying on my bed in that way he always desires me to ... my feet behind my neck in the position of the Seductive Crab, so that I should reveal both places for him to choose from, and so that he would immediately see them when he came through the door of my chamber,' she said, sniffing. 'That way he would know at once how eager was my want to host his entry into my places. But he never came ... and my legs were stiff with the waiting.'

My Mistress laughed cynically. 'A bird that has two small twittering beaks perhaps makes a sweeter song, dear Sister! And you acted as a wise crab, even though it was seductive for no purpose. His Majesty was not deserving of you.'

I listened to this in dumbfounded puzzlement. Although I could not know what manner of perversity this Seductive Crab could be, I had at least some vague image of Sister Xia lying on her back for hours with her feet behind her neck. I glanced furtively at her long legs. They certainly appeared supple and agile enough for such a strange position. That odd crease across her lower belly was as if she were accustomed to being bent almost in two, and her neck was like a pliant swan's.

But what irony, I thought! Had my ears not just witnessed the scornful talk of juggling monkeys and

146

street-contortionists? And now I should learn the antics of a Royal Lady!

It was the turn of Sister Yon to speak her mind now, and it seemed that she was no less discontented than her Sister Xia. 'I am accustomed to such disappointments, my poor dear Sister,' she said dismissively. 'I, too, was sent word by the lying idiot Karif. I prepared myself for His Majesty just as you did – although not as a crab, Sisters! My legs are altogether too short for that, but my strong thigh muscles allow me other delights to offer him!' She giggled. 'But I only wore my pretty anklets and bracelets, which he had told me so many times he found to his liking. He often said how much he enjoyed their jingling song as he rutted me like the fat boar that he truly is. I lay waiting for him as dutifully as I used to do ... even with happiness at the prospect of his visit.'

Here she frowned, adding quietly, 'But it is many moons since he last came to me. I am as dry as a barren desert there. My web grows back for lack of hosting him!'

My Mistress was silent, but I could see that she also had concealed words to say. I wondered if whatever she concealed had been the source of her dark mood.

'You will work on Royal Sister Yon now,' she ordered me gruffly, as if to use her silence to shroud those dangerous matters that were being discussed by her Sisters.

But before I could release Sister Xia's foot and slide my bottom along the bed-throne, she started to protest. 'But his hands minister so well to my weary feet, dear Sister Jiang-Li! Besides, I have seen nothing of his rising! At least do not deprive me of *that* small pleasure. I am already afflicted by disappointment from not having even seen my Emperor's puny pizzle rise. And now that I have a bull-slave before me – who is rumoured to rise at the very sight of a woman – in reality he is no better than my absent Emperor!'

My Mistress laughed, turning her head towards her. 'But, Sister dear, I told you. The slave is not a monkey. I cannot clap my hands and make him rise . . . or threaten him with the rod, particularly as he was so recently punished by the rod for the insolent rising of his own.'

Sister Xia considered this gravely. 'What should I do, then? Fondle his sac, or attach a cord to the ring and lift him with it myself? Or should I part my legs and knees like I do for His Majesty, so that an unworthy slave can view my royal portals? Meanwhile, I might wait all night, as I do with His Majesty, for something to happen.'

My Mistress was helpless with laughter. 'My dear Sister, although I commiserate with you on all accounts, I cannot give you a remedy!' she eventually managed to answer, despite her merriment. 'But let us see whether Sister Yon can trigger what you have failed to do. After all, if *she* succeeds, then *you* shall also profit from her success!'

Sister Xia shrugged. With a certain reluctance she pulled her foot away from my hands, kicking me away. 'Move, then, you sickly Novice! You are a false bull, as much as you are a false Eunuch. The Royal Physicians have tamed you well enough, it seems, after all. Whispering walls have borne false rumours in your case,' she sneered at me. 'You are no better than a gelded horse – a fine animal with lean muscle, certainly, but nonetheless a limp gelding.'

Sister Yon giggled, but there was a shyness in her demeanour now that I was squatting at her feet. I could see my Mistress watching me from beneath her long eyelashes. Her amusement was evident, but it was passively contained.

I gently placed Sister Yon's foot on the silk cushion and began with her toes. They were small, like hard-centred bean-nuggets, but her feet were not as delicate or as shapely as those of my Mistress, and nor were the soles as soft. However, I massaged them with no less devotion than if they had been my Mistress's.

Their Ladyships had meanwhile resumed their banter, even though they continued to study me intently as I worked, watching as the muscles of my arms flexed beneath the skin.

Without taking her eyes off me, Sister Xia turned her head to my Mistress. 'And did he favour you, last night, dear Sister?'

There was a moment's hesitation before my Mistress answered, as if she had been unprepared for such a direct question. 'His Majesty, you mean?'

Sister Xia gave a disdainful little laugh. 'Whom else should you think I meant, dear Sister? Surely you did not suppose I was referring to this impotent bull-slave with a limp shank?' she replied mockingly, giving me a long searching look.

Again there was a moment of silence, Sister Xia sitting there so smugly.

At last my Mistress replied, doing so with a little sigh. 'I was also sent word by Chief Eunuch Karif,' she admitted. 'I was told that His Majesty would come to my chambers well before the first birdsong. I bathed twice in the night, having to summon my Maidservant from her bed.'

She paused then, being careful to keep her eyes from my body, before continuing. 'And I had myself rubbed with eucalyptus-milk until my skin shone like my favourite silk gown – you know, Sisters, the pale-blue one embroidered with peach-gold twists?

And, by first light, when His Imperial Majesty still had not come, I was hot with anger and I tore the garment down the front with my fingernails until it hung from me in shreds.'

'Oh, you poor dear Sister!' Lady Yon exclaimed with genuine dismay. 'Surely not your most *favourite* of robes, Sister? Your anger must have been like a queen-wasp stoked in her nest!'

My Mistress nodded scornfully. 'Certainly it was, Sister. So much so that as my nails tore the silk, and so did they tear at my poor skin.'

It was now that she opened the folds of her bedchamber robe, pulling them apart to expose her breasts and the delightful plain of her belly, almost as far as the neat little place between her legs. 'You see!' she demanded of her Sisters, revealing herself to their astonished scrutiny. 'I am streaked as if the talons of an angry bird had ripped me.'

For a moment my mouth gaped stupidly. My poor Mistress was indeed streaked with several tracer-lines of livid red. They ran straight down from the tops of those so delightfully moulded orbs all the way down her belly. But fortunately the small pink roundels that formed the base of her nipple-buds were unscathed by the fury of her nails, as if perhaps they knew better than to tear at such divine satin flesh in their downward path of destruction.

Sister Xia looked at my Mistress's ravaged nakedness more out of curiosity than sympathy. 'My dear Sister! Does His Imperial Majesty know that his caged little plume-bird is in fact an angry hawk with demon-talons?' She laughed, peering at the thin red lines that so spoilt the beauty of my Mistress's skin. 'Certainly if he knew of the blackness of your moods, how justly he would choose not to come to your bedchamber, Sister!'

But my Mistress brushed off the criticism with an irritable little wave of her hand. 'My mood only turned black after he so cruelly kept me in suspense all night long. Otherwise I would have greeted him with an eager smile and a radiant heart, and he could have done with me whatever he desired.'

I was at once confused again. How could my Mistress have suffered such anguish at having been denied a visit by His Imperial Majesty? Although I had never set eyes upon the man, he was – by all accounts I had ever heard – an ugly and flaccidly rotund man of such heaviness that he needed his carrying-chair to be borne by six bearers. Moreover, only a few minutes ago, had I not, with my own ears, heard Sister Xia so shockingly describe the Divine Emperor as a puny runt, and a lazy one in the treatment of his beloved Wives? And Royal Sister Yon, whose feet and toes I now so diligently caressed, had scarcely been any more respectful towards His Divine Majesty when she had likened him to a fat boar. How strange it all seemed to me that Their Royal Ladyships should resent His Majesty's neglect! Surely they were altogether more fortunate in having been denied His Majesty's favours, and so being able to retire to a cool bed?

How much better was an empty belly than one stuffed with putrid carrion-flesh?

But it seemed that to fail in the bedchamber was, to an Orchid Lady, the same as to fail in life itself.

In the era when Her Grand Ladyship had been a young Orchid Lady it was even said that failure to arouse His Majesty's passions was so shameful that the Silk Cord of Reformed Honour was the only escape from that shame. Brother-Yellow-Crow once told me that, when he had been a Novice, one of the young Orchid Ladies had been found hanging from

151

the mulberry tree in the Garden of Tranquillity – only then absolved of her shame.

I dared now to look across at my Mistress's naked belly, seeing how its splendour was marred by those self-inflicted lines.

Oh, scarlet tears of weeping rage, I thought to myself.

Despite my own miserable slavery, my heart was nonetheless filled with such compassion for her at that moment. Even if I could not entirely understand the anger that had driven her to scourge herself in such a way, I could at least empathise with her. Perhaps she was as much a slave in this place as I was? And in her own slavery, while her body might be draped in sparkling jewels and silk-spun finery, her soul was of a caged bird that desires freedom and happiness.

And for the first time, I, the humble slave who should only ever obey, stopped my massaging work on Sister Yon's foot. What insolence! I had not been ordered to stop, but nobody reproached me yet. However, I saw that Sister Yon and Sister Xia were aghast at such brazen defiance, although my Mistress regarded me with what might have been a mixture of amused curiosity and respectful admiration.

I slid myself off the bed-throne and went to where I knew she kept a small porcelain jar of tea-tree and ky-ky berry lotion. Without a word I took the jar and went back to where she reposed, still with her robe open to show those livid lines of her despair on her delightful flesh. Royal Sisters Xia and Yon remained motionless and silent in their astonishment, only looking at me with as much contempt as if I had been a tapeworm crawling from beneath a dog's tail.

I took a liberal scoop of the lotion in my hand and leant over my Mistress, beginning at once to soothe her wounds. She allowed me to, making no sign of protest, her eyes looking up at me as if perhaps wondering whether she had misjudged me before. All the while I felt the hostility of Sister Xia's eyes, and the green envy of Sister Yon's, but now suddenly the softness of my Mistress's.

How the two Royal Ladyships must have resented her! If I had been a plaything for her – and not one for all of Their Ladyships – now I basked in my role of a good and faithful servant as I ministered to my own dear Mistress's wounds. In my nakedness I felt no shame. And even though I was so close to her exposed chest and belly, and much more of her, I was unstirred by the sight of her exposure. My gold weighted me. The barbed-dagger stares of Sister Xia and Sister Yon withered me, no longer looking at my manhood-flesh or its golden adornments with amused awe, but with sneering contempt.

But it was only my Mistress's wounds that occupied my thoughts. And these were surely the natural thoughts of a man with simple compassion for a woman, and not the thoughts of a Eunuch-slave intent only upon his mundane duty. Even so, I was careful not to let my fingers brush accidentally against the pert and unblemished roundels of her nipple-buds, which seemed so vulnerable. I should be wary of letting soothing fingers stray from the talon-streaks of my Mistress's disappointment.

Perhaps now the spirit of my own slavery had for a moment dwelt with the spirit of my Mistress's slavery.

Oh, plumed little bird of paradise in your silk-spun cage.

Yet, that day, I should not be too hasty to absolve my Mistress from her faults. Her capricious nature was as much a part of her as a flaw in any magnificent jade-stone. If she harboured resentment towards her Sisters or His Majesty, or for her own disillusionment in the Pavilion, it was clear that she would not vent her frustrations on those royal persons. There were slaves for venting anger and resentments. And, even though she regretted it in the wake of her cruel outbursts, nonetheless it was often I who fell victim to her wrath.

Looking back upon that day, in my youthful innocence and in my Novitiate status, how could I have presumed to understand such affairs of Divine Royalty? I had surely heard of such strange things from Their Ladyships' own mouths as they spoke so freely in front of me as I massaged their soft feet. Had I not heard of notions that hitherto were beyond the scope of my humble imagination? Had my ears not smarted at the matters of passion, of dangerous disloyalty, of royal rejection, of Lady Xia putting her feet behind her neck in a position that was apparently perversely known as the Seductive Crab; and had not my very own Mistress laughingly mentioned how small twittering beaks perhaps made a sweeter song?

That day my mind had much to untangle from my web of innocence and ignorance. Yet I could surely not have known then what I know today, these many years later. There was so much more to being a Royal Orchid Lady than the passive honour conferred by its title. For centuries prospective concubines had been groomed and tutored in their youth in the mysterious arts of pleasuring the Royal Dynasty, those virtues having been instilled in the girls no less than the virtues of good manners and polite conversation.

The Seven Principles, as it was called, was widely practised amongst wives and concubines of high status. At puberty or at the time a girl became old enough for respectable marriage, she would often be sent to a teacher of the Seven Principles – usually some renowned former concubine or widow. The most famous of these teachers was Lady Yan-Yan – the meaning of her name having been 'Two Elegant Swallows'. It was said that the artistry of her teachings could arouse a snoring drunk from his stupor, or make the eyes of a noble husband bulge with awe. I cannot vouch for that, since I was never once a snoring drunk, nor a noble husband, but only ever a false Eunuch.

But it was my own dear Mistress who told me of these things one day. She herself had been tutored in the art, although not by Lady Yan-Yan. However, when first I politely enquired of the Seven Principles, my Mistress was noticeably reticent. 'It is not for men to know of women's secret ways, Shani. And certainly not for a servant to enquire! What reason would he have to know of such mysteries?'

I was chastened at once, but then she laughed suddenly. 'I tease you, Shani. Yet I cannot expect you to understand. For some worthy maiden to accommodate you – what with your cruel ring – she would surely require to know much more than the Seven Principles could ever teach her ... unless she possessed a channel that was as wide as the mouth of the Great River of Abundance!'

I did not always enjoy my Mistress's wicked humour, but I had kept silent, of course, knowing that she would tell me enough to whet my appetite for more.

She had explained to me then what those Seven Principles were: tension, motion, position, lubrication, rhythm, grace and opportunity. But I had at once felt cheated. These were scarcely mysterious secrets that would ignite a lady's bedchamber, or arouse a snoring drunk from his stupor!

155

Yet these had only been words. It was her subsequent actions that defined them, having made me gawp like a staring cow.

It was in the second year of my Novitiate. One afternoon I was giving my Mistress her routine body massage, which had become an everyday chore for me, although not an undesirable one. On those occasions, how my poor mind would be engulfed in such suspended lust! She always commanded that my Apron of Good Modesty should be cast aside. And she would lie naked on her belly on her bed-throne with her face cradled in her hands. When it came for me to run my trembling fingers across the soft warm flesh of her buttocks, I cannot say how much my lust almost made me heave with the sickness of desire. Even if she could not see me, nonetheless she knew instinctively that my impetuous rod had risen like a bolt of iron, and she always delighted in that knowledge. I was astride her, kneeling tall, my hands moving towards the little knuckle at the base of her spine. The wretched gold ring of my head seemed to hang over the oiled scarps of her valley, my boom straight across the rift. How I yearned to release the spume of my forbidden lust across that divine place! My clamped spheres ached at the very prospect.

But it was what subsequently occurred that made them ache all the more. That image of her at that moment is etched so vividly on my mind, more enduringly so than those painted birds of paradise on the lacquered screens in her bedchamber. My Mistress was about to reveal secrets to me that surpassed those mundanely disappointing Principles that she had just confided in me. After all, even a rutting boar would surely comprehend the merits of tension, motion, position, rhythm and opportunity, if not grace and lubrication.

My Mistress turned over suddenly on the bed, her face teasing and sly as she regarded me. She pretended not to see how hastily I tried to conceal my boom. Her nipple-buds seemed so much like another pair of eyes staring seductively at me.

'You remember, Shani, how shocked and puzzled you were that day when I was entertaining Sister Xia and Sister Yon in my bedchamber, and when Sister Xia spoke of the Seductive Crab and how she had waited like that all night for His Majesty to come to her?'

'Yes, Mistress, I do,' I answered cautiously. With her it was always best to reply warily.

'You see how tight these muscles are here?' she demanded of me, brushing her fingers over the delicious soft-hard area between the tops of her legs.

I was only able to nod helplessly. I did not need to see them. My fingers had so often before felt the delicious little shimmering ripple there whenever I massaged her. And those fine legs of hers had always been as firm as willow saplings.

'Well, Shani, the Seven Principles have taught me how these muscles can be strengthened.' A distant look came to her eyes. 'I could sit above His Majesty's son, Prince Fid-ram-Lo, with the head of his shank held lightly between the lips of my chamber. I held him there for as long as I wanted, neither letting him enter further, nor letting him slip away . . . and I would give him rhythm and motion until he begged for me to release him from his ecstasy.'

She came back to reality, looking at me searchingly and trying to gauge my reaction. Seeing nothing but the redness of my face, she continued to enlighten me. 'There are many such things we Royal Orchid Ladies were taught in our youth, Shani. The Seductive Crab is but one of them . . . and much favoured by His

157

Majesty himself.' She paused before adding sombrely, 'That is, of course, when he was more active.'

She giggled, her eyes sparkling with mischief and merriment. 'Of course,' she said, 'we are all as helpless as netted swallows when caught by mad desire! Is that not so, Shani?'

'Indeed that is so, Mistress,' I answered as croakily as an ageing bullfrog.

Even if I were not a netted swallow, but only a ringed slave, I could surely still agree with that sentiment. My desire for my Mistress at that moment was as steamy hot as a boiling cauldron of rice.

She smiled at me in that beguiling way that always made her lips and teeth more enchanting than a thousand lilies in bloom. Her glistening nakedness was so utterly irresistible. Although she had kept her legs modestly crossed over, I could nonetheless glimpse the twin-humped rise of her vent.

'Would you not like to imagine how it would be to change places with His Majesty, just for a moment, and that he would become Shani, the ringed and clamped second-year Novice Eunuch, and that it would be *you* coming to my bedchamber as His Majesty?'

I laughed nervously. 'I could not presume such an irreverence, Mistress.'

My reply was diplomatic. Such frivolous talk was dangerous – whether for Royal Ladies or second-year Novices. Yet my intrigue was almost bursting from me. What teasing devilment was in my Mistress's mind?

But I scarcely needed to ponder this for long. She sat herself bolt upright on the bed with such abruptness that the pert mounds of her breasts had seemed almost to launch themselves at me. Her eyes were sparkling beads of mischief and intensity as she peered into my startled face. 'I asked you a question, my slave-bull! Would you not like to imagine how it would be to change places with His Majesty, just for a moment?'

She smiled at me in such a way that my heart gave a nervous flutter. 'Imagine that I am the Seductive Crab, and that you, my Royal Husband, have come into my bedchamber ... and you find me there, awaiting you!'

What could I reply? How should a humble slave dare such insolent imagination? Yet the gaze she fixed me with was so earnest that surely it would never melt without me giving her the answer she required.

'Well, must I wait until the moon drops from the Heavens before your mouth can squeak?'

'No, Mistress.'

'Squeak your reply, then!'

'It would be – I would be as if I were looking into – into paradise, Mistress.'

Her grin spread wickedly. 'Paradise?'

'Yes, Mistress.'

For a second I feared that she found my reply an insolent one. My jaw was bowed low. But her grin only broadened so that the edges of it seemed almost to reach across to her tiny ears. 'Then the boldness of your reply shall be rewarded, Shani.'

For a second she cocked her head to one side as if to look at me from another angle. Then her eyes dropped to where I was trying to sit on my unsettled flesh. She laughed. 'Why do you squat before me like a contorted Buddha straining to evacuate himself? Open your legs!'

How mortified I should have been. Yet there was the promise of reward, and the intrigue was altogether too much for a weak-willed slave to bear.

When I complied with my Mistress's order, it seemed to me that I must have sprung like an uncoiled snake, my ring flashing in the light before it quivered to its sudden rigidity. My Mistress's gleeful amusement was all too evident.

Looking down at the now resplendent head of my shank, she said in that voice of hers that was as clear as a nightingale across an evening lily-pond, 'The eye of your mushroom may never enter paradise, Shani. But at least it can behold that cruelly denied paradise from the perimeters . . . just for a moment or so.'

I could not know of her intentions, my mind hurrying itself to untangle the puzzle in her words.

'My Royal Husband, behold your paradise!' she announced mockingly. At the same time she tilted herself backwards and bent one leg back so that she could grasp her foot. 'I shall be your Seductive Crab, so that you may better behold the options of Your Majesty's pathways to paradise!'

With the utterance of those words she at once craned her head forwards. Then, lifting that same foot that she had grasped before, she twisted it round and hooked it behind her neck with almost effortless grace. My mouth dropped instantly. But, before I could even let out my breath, she quickly folded her other leg back and, in the same manner as before, she hooked it behind her neck. Both her feet lodged there neatly, her hands lightly holding them, her elbows raised up on either side of her head like wings.

Certainly I knew that my Mistress's body was as lithe as a wall-lizard's, the sinews and muscle of her limbs able to stretch as easily as tree-sap. But I had never expected that she could make her body conform to such extreme sculpture. But then I at once remembered Sister Xia, and how she had described her own abortive waiting for His Majesty that night, and how she had done so as a Seductive Crab.

So, however perverse it might have seemed to me, it was clear that my Mistress was no less practised in that strange artistry than Sister Xia had professed to be. Moreover, there was undoubtedly more to the Seven Principles than ever I had first believed.

Speechless, I could only gulp as I watched my Mistress's mocking eyes gaze back at me. Her neck was scarcely even bowed, but I could see how stressed it was to keep the grace in her contorted posture. The wing-shaped angle of her arms, the bent elbows and the way her armpits and knees seemed to thrust towards me gave her a most unnatural appearance. But it was only when she suddenly leaned right back and rolled herself slowly on to her spine that I could see how she vaguely resembled one of those desert sand-crabs. For a second or so her body rocked on the curvature of her back, before becoming motionless. The cleft of her so tautly stretched thighs faced me brazenly. In no way had this oddly submissive manoeuvre dislodged her feet from their embrace around her neck. If anything, this somehow still graceful weave of supple limbs around her torso seemed only to lock her body together all the more acutely. And, from somewhere within this crablike structure of tight, white flesh, my Mistress continued to watch me with such mischievously taunting eyes.

But it was not so much her eyes or her perversely crablike appearance that occupied my attention, but more the sudden gaping exposure of the deep gully between her legs. This so dominant chasm was almost like a rent in her, made wider by the extreme tension of her limbs and thighs, and laying open the portals of those two intimate corridors. My eyes were mesmerised by that exotic vista, and I remembered those mocking words my Mistress had once said to

Sister Xia all that time ago: 'A bird that has two small twittering beaks perhaps makes a sweeter song.'

And certainly if a sweet image could ever be worth more than the sweet sound of birdsong, it was at that moment that I considered it so. I was engulfed in it all, no less than if my head had been engulfed by that awesome chasm itself.

My Mistress grinned at me from within her woven crab. 'You may gaze upon paradise with feasting eyes, Shani – all three of them! That is your reward,' she called to me, her voice silky with both provocation and amusement.

I was still squatting at the end of the bed and I could see that she was also looking at my helplessly swollen shank. It would have taken the threat of a thousand strikes of the Bamboo Rod of Reformed Memory to have wilted me. The cursed ring and clamp hindered the elasticity of my flesh and made it sore, but it could not hinder my lust.

My Mistress spoke again, still not making any move to extricate herself from her woven crab. 'And, if you shall be more of a bull than His Majesty ever was, I shall not forbid you to let fly your passion like a silver frog leaping between a soft valley of flowering lilies.'

How I felt myself overcome with such utter desire! All consideration of danger was abandoned now. But, although I knew my Mistress was teasing me, how far would that teasing let me safely go? Should I take her words at face value?

As if to quench my doubt, my Mistress added quietly, 'But, Shani, let me see the silver frog jump first through your golden hoop before its journey to my soft lilies!'

I could not tell at first whether her words were meant in some symbolic way, or whether her instruction to jump through my hoop had been literally intended. With its natural tendency to hang down from the twist of flesh beneath the eye-slit, my ring – with its circumference four times greater than that of my mushroom-head – could be flipped back over it and so stand above it like a golden halo. It was only when I began to carry out my ministrations to myself that my Mistress admonished me curtly. 'I said for your silver frog to jump first through your golden hoop,' the Seductive Crab ordered breathlessly.

And immediately I understood, flipping back my ring.

I can laugh now, these many years later. But at the time I was so engrossed in my mission that my mind heeded nothing but the task in hand, the vista before my eyes, and how my Mistress's cunning eyes had watched me all the while. Yet afterwards, when that melancholia began to sweep across me and my sore flesh began to throb, I thought to myself that if I had been the pitiful juggling monkey, had she not been the brazenly contorted crab?

And there were other puzzlements in my mind. Whatever spurting joy had come to me, a humble slave, what joy could there have been for my Honourable Mistress? The silver-tailed frog had leapt through its golden hoop and made its wake of glistening thread across her chasm. But there was scarcely any joy for her in the accuracy of my spent spume. And, if my Mistress's soul was whimsical and complex, how much more unpredictable was her body? If she could twist it like a street-contortionist, for no other apparent reason than to see the reaction of her slave, what other things would she be capable of? And what things might she expect of me?

But at that time, for me to ponder at rational answers, it would have been to fish for the moon in a pond.

Five

The late summer shadows crept far across the Pavilion courtyard. The sun had become lazy, its dry heat and dazzling glare eclipsed now until the coming of a new spring.

But to me – now at the end of my first full cycle of seasons as a Novitiate – this new springtime seemed about as far away as the village home I would surely never see again. The nights in the dormitory were colder now. We Novices often shivered on our straw mattresses, pulling our rough linen covers close up to our chins before we could sleep. Sometimes, before slipping into that fitful sleep, my Brother Novices would talk together in hushed tones. I was usually excluded from such forbidden discourse, but nonetheless my ears listened out to hear those things that befell my Brothers during their daily toils. As I lay there silently in the darkness, I would hear how, for example, Brother Zuki had given his Mistress what she desired.

'She gave me a porcelain cone-funnel and made me fill her with warm garlic-water. And once she was full like the bladder of a goat she made me turn her over and empty her like a leaking vessel,' he had protested one evening, his whispered voice trembling. 'And that was not all, Brothers . . .'

My ears had been shocked at what he told us next. My own Honourable Mistress had never bade me do such things in her.

'She demanded that I make my fingers like an arrowed wedge,' he went on in the hushed silence of the dormitory. 'And then I had to forge a path between where I had just emptied her.'

He was a quiet boy with long slender limbs and hands, more like those of a girl than a man's, and he spoke in a tone that was full of both confusion and shame. How should this Honourable Lady have wanted to indulge in such a strange proclivity? we wondered.

And then, as if thinking we did not believe him, he added, 'You can ask Brother-Yellow-Crow and he will rebuke you for asking, but in his hushed angry voice he will tell you that the practice is known as Shooting a Comet between Two Moons.'

It was at moments like that when I felt gladdened that my own dear Mistress had clearly less onerous requirements from her attendant Novice. Before ever I had heard of such things, in my blithe innocence I assumed that such an intimate passage possessed no other purpose than as a conduit for nature's own evacuating release.

But certainly this was a fallacy. Not only, it seemed, should that intimate place permit access to alien matter, but also it must dilate its natural mouldings to host the girth of its alien visitor. Besides, I remembered, had I not myself once suffered the intrusion there of an impure wedge of wood – for whatever strange defiling and inquisitive purpose – that had rent apart my intimate flesh?

But there were yet other strange duties for my Brother Novices to perform, such as those irreverent practices known as Bracing the Pod or Bowing Before the Unjust Bull. And these were surely no less perverse than the one known as Shooting a Comet between Two Moons.

And, if my own dear Mistress had been capricious and at times cruel with her own lowly servant, it was surely preferable to being a lowly servant who must yield his trembling body to these perverse acts of Bracing the Pod or Bowing Before the Unjust Bull. And could it have been a servant's pleasurable duty to let his innocent arm become a celestial comet? And, if my Mistress was all of these things that I have sometimes accused her of, was she not, after all, a divine creature who gave me pleasure as much as I gave her pleasure over those many years that I served her? I feel sure that my Brother Novices – even that they are now ageing Eunuchs – could not have said such worthy compliments of their Mistresses, particularly those Novices who suffered such indignities for their devoted services.

When the Pavilion was seemingly at peace with itself, all these things that we Novices learnt in our dormitory at night were surely so numbing to our minds, even though we had all been taken from such far-flung places of the Empire. My own village upbringing had been a humble one; one that had not known of silver platters, or fine silks, or glittering jewels, or marble floors or jasmine and honeysuckle, but only of dirt-soil and the odour of pig-dung mixed with baking bread. But were these not more wholesome than the rich tapestry of life at the Imperial Palace? If ever I should have had occasion to tell our village elders of Bracing Pods or Bowing Bulls or celestial comets, would their wise time-wrinkled faces not have glowered back at me as if I had been a mad dog? As for those village women whom I had known before, had they not toiled happily in the fields, or thatched the roofs of their huts, or cooked the family's meals, or lovingly combed their children's hair, or made love to their menfolk to make more of those children, while never knowing of such perversities?

Yet, here in the Pavilion, the Royal Ladies knew nothing of those simple things of village women. Instead, Their Honourable Ladyships were stifled by boredom and frustrated by rejection and disappointment. When the only skill they knew became unused through their Imperial Majesty's neglect, bitterness overflowed and the only outlet for it was in the abuse of their servants. Thereafter, if Their Ladyships sought out forbidden pleasures, those narrow passages along the way surely brought as much distress to their servants as they brought pleasure to their Mistresses. And in time did I not myself learn that a passage oiled first by love or kindly devotion certainly brought more pleasure than one that was like a dry hole in the dirt. I did not need the Seven Principles or to know of the Seductive Crab to teach me that small measure of life's pathway. And as for the silk-spun cage and the perfumed mist in which the Royal Orchid Ladies lived with their multitude of servants, it was always a deceptive cage. Pleasures were often as illusive as gold-finned eels to a patient fisherman.

Moreover, a poisoned river flows as majestically as one that is as pure as a mountain spring.

In the dormitory I heard much of what my Brother Novices endured. I came to know which amongst them was made to Brace the Pod by their Mistresses, and which Novice had Bowed Before the Unjust Bull. I knew, of course, which of my Brothers wept at night, not just for want of his birthplace or his mother, but for want of less cruelty from his Mistress, or simply for fear of what might occur at next morning's Assembly of Prostration. I learnt of those petty jealousies between Their Ladyships, or those between Eunuchs or between Novices. I learnt which of those Senior Novices or Eunuchs that I should give a wide berth to – although I needed no such warning in respect of Senior Novice Ling. He seemed to haunt my shadow at every turning. I learnt which of Their Ladyships were more cruel than others, and those who were less cruel in their dealings with their servants, in particular with their Junior Novices.

From all accounts, Her Honourable Ladyship Bo-An – she of the warrior-arm who wielded the bamboo so ruthlessly – was by far the cruellest of Mistresses, and I pitied both the Junior and Senior Novices who attended her, and I even pitied her Eunuch. One day, threatened by Her Ladyship with having to prostrate himself for a flogging at morning Assembly – which would have been a matter of great shame for any Eunuch of his status – he had taken The Silk Cord of Reformed Honour to his own neck, so it was rumoured. It was only for Junior Novices to be flogged, and routinely so, since it was – in theory – only they who were in frequent need of their memories being reformed, whereas the memories of Senior Novices and full-fledged Eunuchs were already reformed.

The first-year Novice who had the misfortune of finding himself assigned by Her Grand Ladyship to her Royal Sister Bo-An was a slender and wispy young man by the name of Chin. He was in our dormitory, and it was said by my Brother Novices that he never once smiled – not that there was ever much reason for Novices to smile. But in his case everything about him seemed tainted by the Bad Luck of the Grey Dragon. Morning Assembly to him

169

was always so full of uncertainty, and it was seldom that his hindquarters were free of the scars of Her Ladyship's attention. Indeed, it was not only the bamboo rod that assaulted him with such regularity but it was as much the black bull's pizzle that was stiffened by goat-hair and sawdust. For him to Bow Before the Unjust Bull was, it seemed, one of Her Ladyship's particular proclivities.

One night I overheard talk between two of my Brothers. From what they were discussing it seemed that Her Ladyship Bo-An would have preferred Novice Chin to Brace the Pod for her. Yet, by virtue of his Bad Luck of the Grey Dragon, his own meagre flesh was apparently inadequate for that perverse bracing. Therefore, as an alternative she made him Bow Before the Unjust Bull. Whether this had exacerbated her bitter temperament, I cannot say, except that I recall that poor Novice Chin was in a state of almost perpetual soreness from one day to the next. The bamboo rod was a wretched enough punishment for a Novice's rump to bear, but how much more punished it must have been to be rutted afterwards by Her Ladyship's thunderous thighs and her false pizzle.

The Garden of Tranquillity had now shed its resplendent colours and its bright blooms, that diversity of rich fragrances having mellowed into a single composite fragrance that was one of autumn-ripe decay. And were not sweet fragrances the very essence of life in the Pavilion of the Divine Orchid Ladies? Wherever Their Honourable Ladyships travelled in their shimmering silks, they left a glorious perfumed mist in their wake. The corridors and the halls and their drapes and furnishings smelt always of jasmine or lavender. And in the exotic cosiness of my Mistress's bedchamber my nostrils were always filled with its scent of magic and intrigue, and rosewater and honeysuckle, and much more besides. And the Eunuchs who served their Honourable Mistresses so devotedly smelt always of fresh sandalwood and coriander, as if those fragrances had come from the very pores of their Eunuch skins. And every Novice would be wise to ensure that after his morning bathing there should never be a trace of any natural bodily secretion upon him afterwards, and that he should remain smelling 'with reverent freshness and giving no offence' to Their Ladyships throughout his busy day.

During summer this was no easy feat. Although the corridors and halls of the Pavilion remained relatively cool in comparison to the sometimes sweltering heat outside, we Novices often felt as if we were working in a furnace, and our naked torsos glistened with running sweat. The worst of our chores, and by far the most energetic and exhausting, was the daily cleaning and polishing of the marble-tiled floors.

Brother-Yellow-Crow told us that to toil at this task was as much a benefit to us as it was to the marble tiles themselves. 'Hard work and brisk movement shall make your muscles as strong as willow branches, and your oozing pores shall drain out the jelly of fatness in your leaking sweat,' he was in the habit of saying.

And I could believe him, all the more so whenever I was near the point of exhaustion. By that time those many marble tiles I had polished would seem like a vast shining ocean stretching into the distance, and my sweat would truly run from me with the jelly of fatness that Their Ladyships so despised in their servants.

On the hottest of days, Brother-Yellow-Crow would take pity on us, but only once the floor-shining duty had been completed. He would summon the Maidservants to attend to us, and they would come rushing with buckets of freshly drawn well-water. Divested of our aprons, we would stand meekly in the courtyard with arms upstretched, while the Maidservants sponged us down, taking care to wipe thoroughly in those places where stale sweat can fester unpleasantly.

'Never must you smell like a dog drying itself in the sun after wading in a foul river,' Brother-Yellow-Crow would often warn us.

For my Brother Novices this sponging ritual was certainly a most welcome respite from their harsh toiling on the marble floor, and they luxuriated in the icy water sluicing down their hot torsos. I, on the other hand, although enjoying the iciness of the water, was more sensitive than my Brothers to the hand that sponged my body. Even though I was usually too weary for my manhood-flesh to react to such tender contact, this was not always so. I might, after all, feel a stirring if the Maidservant were to sponge against my shank or my sac, which task was no less than she was supposed to perform. And then I would be concerned that my impetuous rising might be noticed by Brother-Yellow-Crow Kanchu, or even by Senior Novice Ling – since it was often he who would be supervising us. His eyes always followed me everywhere, seeking out any imperfection in my demeanour or in my work. Should he have found any cause for complaint, he would surely report me, such was his malevolent attitude towards me.

It was no less indelicate for me during those many routine shaving rituals, which occurred every fourth sunrise. After his daily inspection, Brother-Yellow-Crow would select those of us to be shaven. We would assemble in the long gloomy corridor outside that much hated Chamber of Body Preparation. It was here that I had been fitted with my golden adornments. And it was here that our heads, faces and chests and all those intimate recesses of our bodies would be scraped to glistening baldness by the Maidservants. Yet, whereas my Brother Novices seemed oblivious to the soft and agile hands that worked upon their bodies, and to those gentle and youthful eyes that looked down upon them, I was more prone to manly sensitivity.

This was all the more so when it happened that Maidservant Li-Mei – she of the Beautiful Plum Blossom – found herself in attendance upon me. It was quite often she who sponged me down in the courtyard on those sweltering days. And in the Chamber of Body Preparation, it would sometimes be she who held the shaving-urn or wielded the razor on my body.

When she looked at me so coyly with those large soft eyes and with the faintest trace of a smile on her lips, I was always enchanted by her. And if my ringed head had not stirred from its repose, it would only have been because Senior Novice Ling or Brother-Yellow-Crow were watching me with close scrutiny. And on such occasions it was even more difficult for me if my eyes had dwelt for too long on the way Li-Mei's pert mounds pressed so tautly against the cotton fabric of her smock. I could always see so clearly the imprint of her hardened bud. And immediately I would be reminded – and no doubt would she have been – of that first night under the stars when she and I had stood in the Garden of Tranquillity together and when she had made me fly my bolt like silver lightning across the cool air.

Since that night we had met there several times, although our meetings had usually been fleeting ones.

173

It was never easy to outwit the Eunuch whose duty it was to patrol the halls and corridors at night. Our clandestine encounters would surely have come to an untimely end if he had caught us. We talked in whispers and held each other in trembling embrace, our ears constantly attuned to the quietness of the night and listening out for any telltale sign of our discovery. If we were bold, and if the shadows enveloped us sufficiently into the dark fabric of night, we would quickly discard our servant-garments. Then as I pressed up into her belly, how I thrilled to the feel of her small frame and its delightful contours pressing against me.

On those nights when we were less bold, I would lift her servant-dress and she would lift my apron. Then, knowing my desperation, she would release me as before. And even though my passion would be vented thus, hers was vented in her furious kisses of my breast and perhaps in the way her suckle-buds were like hardened beans against my skin. We were always breathless with our whispered words of passion and in our outpouring of lonely love. Always aware of what little time we had together, we would promise each other so much, but our words often tumbled meaninglessly, oblivious to those innocent promises.

What future could there be for love between slaves?

Better to take a solitary ripened plum now, rather than await a dozen to ripen later.

Only for us, her ripened plum could never take the golden-headed shaft that so desired to breach its soft fruitiness. I could never be truly hers, nor could she ever be mine. We were only for our Mistress. My purpose for her was different to Li-Mei's. But, if Li-Mei – knowing how the Palace walls had whispering tongues – were envious of those things that bad-mouthed tongues had whispered to her, she gave no sign of it. On the other hand I was envious of Li-Mei's habit of sharing her mattress with fellow Maidservant Huan-Yue – the lonely creature of a damaged heart. I shamefully admit my envy now, but I also endeavoured to give no outward sign of it. Certainly on occasion I might have questioned Li-Mei about that strange relationship. But she dismissed it as being nothing of any greater significance than 'two young nesting birds whose plumes brush against each other in their mutual confinement and loneliness'. But, after all, should I not have wanted to know more of how Maidservant Huan-Yue lay with her and touched her? Whereas my golden constriction would forever deny me breaching Li-Mei's fruity plum, had she not herself told me how Huan-Yue had often breached her there?

I remember once how Li-Mei had grinned so wickedly at me in the moonlight when I confronted her with my poisonous question. I remember, too, the magic of her laughing whisper in my ear. 'Then, my bull-man, you shall feel me in that same place and by the same gentle means as she does.'

And with that she had taken my hand and brushed it against the soft-hard portals between her twinned humps so that immediately my gentle finger came naturally to rest in that divine breach. The soft moist warmth of it sent a pulse of ecstasy up my arm.

'Explore me there, my trembling bull-man, and then I shall tell you if your manly finger makes my velvet flutter like a moth, and whether I shall flutter more by you ... or if Huan-Yue makes me flutter more!'

Certainly the challenge was irresistible, even though it made my envy prick my pride all the more. I held her close against me, our mutual nakedness in the cool air making our skins tingle deliciously, her buds harder than ever against my breast.

When I parted those tiny lips I felt her shudder, the loose folds so willing as they settled again around the hilt of my finger in a soft clinging embrace. It was such smooth virgin territory to me. Whatever resistance might have existed before melted away in the oily warmth of that precious labyrinth.

She gasped, and I delighted in her gasp, going deeper, feeling around that narrow place of velvet thrills. Even though this humble village boy had once or twice ventured before to touch a girl in that forbidden but so inviting terrain, I had never once journeyed to the end of the rainbow. But Li-Mei of the Beautiful Plum Blossom had known before of other more skilful explorations – ones that had made her velvet flutter. And had I not been like a fumbling baboon that knew not the button of a woman's ecstasy?

'To travel far is not always the best journey, my sweet bull-man,' she muttered urgently, almost giggling in my ear.

And then she guided me, making me withdraw slightly to the wider flush of her entrance, and up to where a small forked cleft of twirled tissue came to my fingertip.

'It is here, my eager bull-man. Press lightly at the top, no more than if your finger were the soft nuzzling nose of a rabbit, rather than the snout of a hungry boar. Yes. Good! Like so, my sweet man. Circle me gently there, as if you were orbiting a fragile soap-bubble that must never burst.'

And I complied meekly, knowing now her own desperation. As I circled that tiny bubble, it pressed eagerly into my finger, as if fusing her soft tissue with it. And her loins seemed to come alive, so that through the nerve-ends of my fingertip I felt the pulsing force come from her very core.

'Oh, Shani, if – if only we could be . . .'

But she did not finish, only sighing, and it was a wistful sigh that seemed almost loud enough to disturb the fragrant stillness of the night air. That tiny fluttering of her velvet and that little gasp that came just at the end were perhaps as much her acknowledgement of ecstasy as it was a silent cry for freedom.

So it was not the demons we stirred that night, but the restless spirits of our souls.

One night I was lying on my mattress, huddled up under the thin cover. It was cold and silent all around me. My Brother Novices and I had been worked hard that day by Brother-Yellow-Crow and we were glad to rest our weary bodies now. The darkness enveloped us, concealing so many miserable thoughts. If we dreamt, our dreams were surely of faraway places we had known before, or perhaps of fantasies that would never become reality.

I heard the sound of padding feet and I saw two oil-lamps approaching in the gloom. They, and the shadowy figures behind them, came nearer to where my mattress was. For a moment I could see the light reflected in the eyes of several of my unsleeping Brothers. Other of my dormitory companions stirred in their uneasy sleep, not wanting to awake. After all, oil-lamps that come in the night seldom bring bright omens with them.

'Get up!' a voice that I knew commanded gruffly, a foot kicking at me. 'Hurry yourself, and go and bathe.'

'Go and bathe?' I heard myself mumble petulantly. Surely it was the middle of the night? Even slaves must rest, but it seemed that Senior Novice Ling had no respect for that notion.

He looked down at me, his face like a malevolent ghost's in the lamplight. 'Your Mistress requires you to attend her,' he said, by way of surly explanation. There was an edge to his voice that was either one of contempt or envy, but I could not decipher which. 'Do not delay in going to her,' he added ominously, kicking me again.

There was never any point in questioning Senior Novice Ling. If ever he deigned to make a reply, it would always come as the spat venom of a snake. I rose from my mattress with the reluctance of a cosy field-mouse prodded from its warm burrow. How cold it was as I reached for where my Apron of Good Modesty lay neatly folded.

'You have no need of that,' Senior Novice Ling hissed. 'Follow me as you are.'

I saw then that the figure behind Senior Novice Ling was that of Maidservant Huan-Yue. She stood there in silent disdain, holding her lamp high enough for her to look down upon my worried face. What servant duties were keeping her from her mattress? I wondered. But at least they were keeping her from Li-Mei's.

'Our Mistress desires that you be oiled after you have bathed, and I am to assist you.' Maidservant Huan-Yue spoke to me in a sneering voice, glancing down at my gleaming nakedness as though it offended her.

But it was not how she looked at me that concerned me. It was her words. What perverse things were these that had interrupted my fitful slumbers? And what strange desires my Mistress had. If she had suddenly become a bird of the night, it was surely another of her unpredictable guises. And, if the

178

Pavilion around her was swathed in its night-robe of silent shadows, why was she awake and summoning me from my weary mattress?

But I had no further time to ponder. The cold air chilled my body as I hurried to keep up with Senior Novice Ling, the marble floor so icy beneath my bare feet. Maidservant Huan-Yue followed behind as we went to the servants' bathing-pool. Here, some of the lanterns had been lit, but they cast a grim and lonely light and made the surface of the water glitter like a mirror of ice.

The prospect of bathing in such uninviting coldness was no more desirable than it was to be in such hostile company as that of Senior Novice Ling and Maidservant Huan-Yue. Their eyes regarded me with the soulless malevolence of two waiting vultures.

'Make haste, you golden-ringed worm,' he sneered. 'My mattress and my night-covers are long overdue for my weary body, which has tired of my Mistress's desires. I have attended her with such devotion all day, and now at night she still makes demands on me. Fetch this! Fetch that! Brush my hair! Pour my lotus-tea! And now I am charged to bring her her pretty plaything – the one that can stand with its rod and spurt its putrid seed,' he scoffed.

I did not reply. Even though I could have taken his puny arm and twisted it to breaking point, I was but a yet more humble slave than he, and lacking his seniority. By now he should have been honoured with wearing the saffron robes of a fully fledged Eunuch, but, even if he no longer bore the scars of the bamboo rod, he still wore the cloak of his shame, no less than he still wore his Novice's Apron of Good Modesty. Her Grand Ladyship had not yet seen fit to reinstate him.

'Get into the water, and wash yourself diligently with soap . . . and heed well that place where that vile sac and freak's horn sprout like poisonous fungus from between your legs.'

But it was not his words that stung me as much as the shock of immersing myself in the ice-cold water. I gasped aloud, much to his apparent delight, and no doubt to the delight of Maidservant Huan-Yue. To have to bathe in the cool of a winter morning was already unpleasant enough, but how much more unpleasant was it to bathe in the cold hours of a winter's night. I shivered, forcing myself to lather the soap on my skin. All the while my unwanted companions watched me with such utter contempt.

'I have not all night to wait on you, pretty slave-boy. Get out! She will wipe you with drying cloths.'

As I stepped out of the stone pool I was numb all over with cold, my chest heaving for my lungs to catch breath.

Senior Novice Ling laughed suddenly, peering between my legs. 'So! The proud golden-ringed bull is certainly the wretched limp worm now,' he jeered. 'You are like a shrivelled pepper-pod! I hope that our dear Mistress shall not be offended by such a feeble pizzle – or her mood shall become that of a Black Moon.'

Maidservant Huan-Yue stifled a laugh, looking at me scornfully as I stood there dripping and shivering. It must have been true what Ling had said. It certainly felt as though my entire body had withered from the cold. The thought of my Mistress looking at me with distaste on her pretty features, and then falling into a mood of the Black Moon was no consolation to me, either.

Ling motioned for Huan-Yue to begin drying me, and she did so roughly and without regard for any sensitive part of my body, her disdainful expression

180

never diminishing for a second. I stood there in my wet nakedness, trying to control my shivering ague. But at least I was awake now. And it was as well to be wakeful and alert in the presence of my Mistress, even in the midst of night.

As Huan-Yue rubbed me down, my mind needed a distraction from such humiliation. I began to think about the reason for my Mistress's nocturnal summons. I massaged her in the day and did those small chores she bade me do in her bedchamber. She would watch my movements all the while, and always with the daylight streaming so brightly through her window. Why now should she require me in the darkness of lonely night? Whatever servant duties I performed for her, surely I could do them better in the daytime. At night the oil-lanterns cast such flickering shadows in the Pavilion, making the corridors and hallways hospitable only to wandering ghostly spirits or scuttling rats.

I tried to think back on the day, searching my memory for any imperfection in my duties. But I could think of none. If ever there were any reason for her displeasure it was her habit to let me know thereof immediately, and not to keep herself from her sleep in order to chastise me for my faults. Besides, the bamboo rod only ever reformed memories during morning Prostration and, as far as I knew, never at night. But she did keep a small brush-whip, and on occasions I had known its sting.

Senior Novice Ling was standing to one side with his arms folded and his chin arrogantly set, as if he had presumed the status of Chief Eunuch Karif. He glowered at me, his insipid body ghostly and sinister in the dim light. 'The Honourable Mistress bids me to ensure that I shall bring you to her smelling as sweet as the dew of spring grass, and not with odour of stale sleep upon you,' Ling observed with such mocking spitefulness. 'Those were the words that came from her honeyed mouth, my golden-ringed worm. And our dear Mistress speaks always so wisely – even if the barbs of her tongue are so razor-sharp.'

Maidservant Huan-Yue sniggered again, Ling's wit and sarcasm evidently so appealing to her. She was still rubbing me vigorously from behind, and now suddenly she reached between my legs, pushing the wadding of cloth under me and roughly dragging upwards with it through the valley of my rump. So forceful was she that my balance was compromised, this having caused some measure of amusement to Senior Novice Ling.

Once he had recovered his composure, he gruffly ordered me to spread my feet more and raise my arms higher. 'Her Ladyship's pampered and golden-ringed worm is to have his sleek body made to shine like the marble floor he polishes each day!' he snarled mockingly, waving his hand at Maidservant Huan-Yue for her to end her drying task.

Bending down he picked up a large earthenware jar. Uncorking it he came back to where she was waiting beside me with the palms of her hands cupped in readiness. He poured some oil liberally into them, and at once she began to work it into my torso. She commenced with my chest and belly before moving behind me to rub the oil down my back and across my buttocks and down my legs, working briskly with her small hands all the while. I stood there as rigid as a marble statue, except that now I was a statue that gleamed slickly with a layer of oil. Whatever oil it was, it smelt of lavender and figs with just a trace of eucalyptus, but it made my skin tingle with freshness, despite the cold. My senses had come alive, and I felt that first small seepage of anticipation. If my body were being prepared in oil and being made to smell so fragrantly, surely my Mistress had a purpose for having commanded it so. Perhaps the night would be worth my cruel awakening, after all.

Every so often Ling poured more oil into Huan-Yue's cupped hands, his movements ever so reluctant and as if the task were beneath him. She moved round to my front again. Her eyes looked up into mine with such loathing. Or was it malicious gloating? How I wished I could say something to her, but I knew instinctively that I should not. All I could do was to avert my gaze and hold myself rigidly with whatever dignity I still could muster.

Senior Novice Ling made a sneering sound. 'Do not forget his proud bull-flesh with its golden trinkets, Huan-Yue,' he said to her as if I were absent. 'Our dear Mistress shall not want it dry like a withered prune or with its pepper-pod still shrivelled from the cold! Warm him and oil him there . . . and make him swell and become her bull-man again!' He laughed sardonically, and so did Huan-Yue, and not with any humour. Theirs was the cackling of cunning jackals.

The Maidservant said nothing, letting him fill her cupped hands again. She squatted down suddenly in front of me, before glancing up at me, her lips twisted into a malicious grin. I looked away, knowing what was to come. But it came shockingly, nonetheless. First there was the warm greasy wetness of the oil and then her hands pulling and clutching at my bulk, drawing me down and manipulating me with such irreverence. Her fingers were like the claws of busy crabs as they grappled me with their oiliness, sometimes clasping like pincers at my trunk or dragging all the way down to my ring, and not with any tenderness. Then she would seize the top of my sac and, like the gold clamp that already circled me there, she

183

would make her claws form a band around me and then slither down to my twinned spheres below, stretching me as if the elongation of my flesh were her sole purpose.

'Oh, celestial Heavens, take me back to my poor mother, that she might soothe my troubled brow and wake me from my black dream,' I cried silently to myself in my miserable humiliation.

I trembled as I stood there, no longer from the cold, but perhaps from anger and discomfort at these rough attentions at the hand of another slave. I thought that, if I were not in a black dream, would I not, after all, have been better to have suffered my fate in the Room of Glorious Transformation?

Certainly I was no more the shrivelled pepper-pod, but my flesh had been worried to expand, rather than to do so by kindly arousal. I remembered then the irony of how those crab-claws clutching at me were at other times the gentle skilful fingers that made my Beautiful Plum Blossom's velvet flutter. And had I not myself been like a fumbling baboon that knew not the button of a woman's ecstasy?

I remember, too, how, just before Senior Novice Ling had led me away, Maidservant Huan-Yue had suddenly looked at me in ever such a secretive and gloating manner. I knew in that instant that she was going to my Li-Mei's mattress, and Huan-Yue wanted me to know it.

The gloomy corridor was so silent that the sound of Senior Novice Ling rapping his knuckles on the ornate doors seemed unnaturally loud – perhaps loud enough to awaken those whispering spirits of the entire Pavilion.

From beyond the doors I heard the faintest sound of my Mistress's command to enter. Senior Novice

Ling made another of his sneering noises as he turned to me, peering contemptuously at me in my nakedness. I had not even been made to wear my apron. My only cloak was the glistening oil, and it was certainly not any cloak of modesty.

He put his mouth to my ear. 'I am glad to go to my mattress at last . . . and glad that Her Ladyship's freak can attend to her now with whatever putrid tasks she bids him do,' he hissed, adding finally, as if it were his parting insult, 'In the midst of night, surely only a she-devil spurns sleep, and so wickedly desires that her slime-drenched worm comes slithering to her bed.'

It was surely a most blistering insult, and shocking in as much as it was intended no less irreverently towards our Royal Mistress as it was intended for me. At that moment I realised he hated her as much as he hated me. Whatever devotion he once possessed towards her had withered away and become but a thin veneer, no more than enough to sustain his wretched survival here.

Turning away with a final flash of contempt in his eyes, he pushed the door open.

I at once went inside, and the sight and fragrant magic of her chamber overwhelmed my senses immediately. For a moment I hesitated in my trance of awe, looking stupidly about me. A dozen different scents came to my nostrils all at once. There were huge hanging lanterns at the corners of her bed-throne and each of them was shrouded in a coloured veil of silk, so that the flickering light given off was of turquoise-blue or pale pink or soft amber. Apart from a few charcoal heating-urns, several tall vases had been placed all around the chamber. These seemed to burn incense, making a cosy scented haze hang in the warm air.

'You may depart, Ling,' my Mistress told him coldly.

'Yes, Mistress.' He bowed low, keeping his deceitful eyes downcast now, lest she might sense the disloyalty that lurked in them.

I, too, hastened to bow, my mind having been so dangerously distracted. I heard the doors close softly behind Senior Novice Ling, and now I was alone with my Mistress in her exotic bedchamber. The cosy warmth of it enveloped the very core of my being.

'Approach my bed-throne,' she ordered, smiling, her eyes taking in my gleaming nakedness.

I muttered a polite acknowledgement, stepping closer, my bare feet happy at the soft warmth of the rug beneath them. She lay in her habitual repose, propped up against a plush mound of cushions, and she was wearing the silk bedchamber-robe with the billowing sleeves. The garment was loosely drawn across her, the gold-braided cord not tied. Her feet rested as usual on a small cushion, and I could see that her toes were twitching.

She looked at me with amusement, and perhaps with something else. Her eyes were everywhere upon me. 'I see that my servants have oiled you well, Shani! Or have they dipped you headfirst into a vat of pressed olives? Your torso has a lustre that is like burnished copper. Even your shaven head glows like a beacon.'

'Yes, Mistress.'

'Turn yourself.'

This I did and I heard her sigh mockingly.

'Your cheeks are glorious moons of white gold that shine in the heavens! The Maidservant has put a sheen upon them that could light up my bedchamber. Even the valley between them is like an oily river.'

'Yes, Mistress.'

'Turn yourself back to me, and take your hands from where they clasp together so stupidly in front of you. As if you needed to be like a coy little mouse in my presence, rather than a bronzed bull!'

'Yes, Mistress. I am sorry, Mistress.'

'Is that all you can squeak to me today, "Yes, Mistress, no Mistress"?' she mimicked me. 'It is not the company of a chirping mouse – even one as bronzed and handsome as you – that I seek in the lonely hours of night, Shani, but that of a bull who can speak like a man.'

'No, Mistress, I mean I – I would speak gladly to you . . . if you would guide me in what manner of things I should speak about.'

She tipped back that pretty head of hers and laughed. 'What should we talk of in the night, Shani? Tell me, I pray you.'

I was at once caught like a moth in her web. Indeed, what things could a slave talk to his Mistress about in the dead of night, when sleep was surely worth more than idle conversation? So flustered was my mind and empty of any answer that I could only look at her dumbly, and with crestfallen desperation.

She laughed again, but now her eyes narrowed slyly. 'If you are struck like a silent mute, at least you must have something to offer your lonely Mistress instead of clever words. Or what purpose would you have for coming to my bedchamber?'

I swallowed, hoping she would not see the jerk of my throat. 'I – I do not know what service you require of me, Mistress. I was not told. Shall I massage your feet for you . . . or – or I could massage your back in the way you like me to?'

A cloud of irritation passed across my Mistress's face. 'Should I have ordered you to be bathed and oiled only so that I should summon you to massage my feet?'

A cloud of confusion enveloped my brain. 'No, Mistress, but – but I am glad you summoned me. Whatever service I can render, I am honoured to perform it, and – and I would do so diligently.'

Her brightness returned at my words. She condescended to smile regally and with patronising grace. A slave should never forget his servile status. There would always be that distance between us, even on those rare and intimate occasions that my raw flesh was a fly-wing's thickness away from hers.

'Come here, Shani, and sit beside me.' She patted the bedcovers. 'I shall think of some service for you to perform.'

I saw how close to her that she wanted me to sit. Hitherto I had always positioned myself at her feet. At least that would be where I would start my duties from. But now she wanted me at a place that was level with her knees.

'But, Mistress, I am wet with greasy oil. I shall surely stain your bed-silks.'

She laughed at my naivety. 'Then, if you do, I shall have you change my bed-silk for another. Or perhaps I shall sleep all the better for having the sweet lavender stain upon it. And, if not, perhaps I shall have your greased cheeks made burning dry by the bamboo rod!'

She giggled again, watching me with such mischievous eyes. 'Come, my golden-ringed bull-slave. Sit your oiled rump here beside me . . . and make haste to obey me.'

I needed no further prompting. Getting myself quickly on to the edge of the bed-throne, I slid myself over to her without any particular grace in that stilted movement. Not knowing what I was to do for her, nor what posture I should adopt, I sat there stiffly, my knees drawn up in modest screening of myself.

Again my nostrils were so luxuriously invaded by that rich honeysuckle fragrance of hers – one that I knew so well by now.

She lay languidly on her heaped cushions, still in that amused composure that invited such dangerous things, her eyes watching my every ungainly movement. I knew better than to ask any question of her. She would tell me when it pleased her to. Yet I could almost hear her churning thoughts and the mischief there that made her eyes glitter like black diamonds.

With a sudden unexpected movement she leant forwards, reaching out with her hand and running her fingers gently over the muscle of my breast. 'Hmmm. Your chest-buttons are like two cherry-stones carved on to gleaming marble buttresses, Shani.'

I held my breath, feeling the pounding of my heart. The shock of her warm touch sent a shiver of both delight and fearful intrigue down my spine. I held myself rigidly, letting her fingertips explore me. First they crossed the width of my breasts and then they slid very slowly down the hard plain of my belly, feeling along the ribbed contours as she went.

I felt the rapid stirring of my flesh. How could I not? And this was, in any case, my Mistress's intention. Her eyes told me as much.

'Open your legs, my rampant bull-man. Why try to conceal your impertinent rising? The head already strains for its big hoop to peep above the precipice like a golden halo. Let your rod spring boldly forth!'

I obeyed, parting my legs to release my brazen stance. If it were impertinent, she clearly revelled in it. And, even if she did not, I was powerless to contain it. Her hand was resting momentarily on the lower pit of my belly, her fingers now glistening with oil as much as my skin was.

Her voice became suddenly distant, as if she were reminiscing. 'Many full seasons have gone by since the day I tumbled from between my mother's legs, but tonight I celebrate that time of my coming. Did you know that, Shani?'

'No, Mistress,' I breathed, only wanting to hear things of the present.

She went on casually, her hand still on my belly, and looking all over my body so that there was not one fly-wing space of it that escaped her scrutiny. 'For many years I did not know that I was destined to become a Royal Concubine. Neither could I have known then what emptiness and loneliness would curse my life, Shani.'

'No, Mistress. I am sorry. I can also understand loneliness.'

For a second her eyes had another faraway look in them, and her ears had seemed not to hear my own declaration of loneliness. Now did I not share with my Mistress a common affliction, and one that might perhaps unite our souls in mutual sadness? But I was a slave, and she my Royal Mistress. What was my own humble loneliness compared to hers?

Her distant look vanished as quickly as it had come. Now she was alert again, my bold rising once more the focus of her attention. Her eyes were wide and intense as she looked at my brazenness – a brazenness that so clearly fascinated her. Moreover, it seemed to do so all the more by virtue of the oily sheen that covered me everywhere, including my thrusting shank.

As if to answer the question I dared not ask, she said in a very seductive tone, 'I like to see the way your body glistens in the light, Shani, and how the lanterns cast such shadowing contrasts across the undulations beneath your skin and the way the texture of it becomes like gleaming silk.'

She paused, glancing up at the lantern that was draped in a diaphanous veil of turquoise-blue. 'See how the glow from that lamp has softened the sun-coppered colouring of your muscled arms and shoulders. Yet the glow from the lantern behind you makes your chest and belly shine like rich amber, and the oiling of your whole body has made all those manly contours stand out in their rich contrast, one from another.'

I looked down at myself. Certainly there was truth in what she said. The glossy sheen of oil made my skin almost reflective. It could have been a membrane shroud left clinging to my flesh after I had slithered from my mother's womb.

'I am in torment for new pleasures, Shani. And if my own flesh shall be so often denied pleasure, then surely my eyes can be allowed to gaze upon the beauty of another's flesh?'

I was unsure whether my Mistress wanted me to reply, but I kept silent. If the beauty of my body could provide that pleasure for her, my heart must certainly be gladdened by the pleasure she derived – even if *my* beauty was unworthy next to *hers*.

She continued, still stroking my lower belly. 'And if I must behold beauty at night, because I cannot sleep and because I have royal duties during my tedious day, then surely I must make that vision of beauty as bold and as exalted as I can. Do you not think so, Shani?'

It was not for me to think. But, if the beauty she saw in me could be enhanced only by greasy oiling, I would most surely have preferred it otherwise. The cheeks of my rump felt more like heavy blubber on her bed-silks than they did spherical accoutrements of beauty to be exalted. And sometimes oily drips would run down my glowing forehead and into my eyes. I was uncomfortable in my oily shroud.

Yet I replied enthusiastically. 'Indeed, Mistress. Your wisdom and understanding of beauty is – is enthralling to me. I hope that my humble body shall always give you pleasure, whether you have me oiled or otherwise.'

She smiled appreciatively, looking at my boom and at how much it had retained its rigidity. So many idle words had not made it wilt by even a mouse's whisker.

'I find that oiled flesh is so much more exciting to the touch,' she continued conversationally, not ready yet to do those things to me I knew she would do. 'And does it not also make your body come alive, as if the texture of your skin needs to be polished like a silver urn to make your inner-self sparkle? A slave who has the dryness of the desert about him shall surely be a sickly one. And the sweat of toiling is not always sufficient to make a slave glow with good health.'

Rather than thinking of silver urns, I thought more of those marble floor-tiles on which I expended so much of my own toiling sweat.

'Yes, Mistress. I have no wish to be a sickly slave for you. I will make myself sparkle for you ... in whatever way you command me to.'

She grinned at me slyly, her face as radiant as ever I had seen it. 'You shall certainly sparkle for me, Shani. And for you, my golden bull-man, there will be no dryness from within. You shall ferment your passion for me like a cauldron of boiling oil and unleash it like a volcano ... but only when I command you to.'

She was teasing now, her grin spreading to her ears.

Her hand dropped suddenly lower, her fingertips caressing me softly just above the base of my trunk.

192

Then, with one finger lodged into the angled join that formed the pivot between root and trunk, she traced a half-moon across the solid girth of my protrusion, first one way, then the other, repeating it several times, her gaze never wavering.

'Shani, you may only be a poor slave and a humble Novice Eunuch in this lonely Pavilion, but in the swell of your passion you become a bull amongst men ... a beautiful bull who is yet greater than the greatest of emperors, and untamed by rings and clamps.'

I considered her flattering words for only a moment before replying. 'Mistress, I am made in whatever way that I tumbled – just as you did in all your beauty – from a mother's womb.' I said this, feeling that perhaps I had slithered rather more than tumbled from the womb. 'But it is you, my dear Mistress, whom I must thank for having kept my own birthright, otherwise I would surely have been rendered half a man, and one not worthy of my mother and my father's blood and seed.'

As an afterthought I added, 'Nor worthy of you ... and I should not then have been able to be a cauldron of boiling oil to ferment my passion for you.'

It was not that I intended such eloquent words, nor did I wish to engage in any, but I knew that my Mistress was in need of more than just the brazenness of my thrusting span and the beauty she saw in my gleaming body. I knew that she craved not only my forbidden flesh, as I did hers, but she also craved company. Perhaps I did, too – even if hers was capable of such capricious dangers. My rod might at this moment appeal to her craving, but by dawn it might be another rod to satisfy her daylight whims, and one to bring only pain to my servant rump.

Expect not to find an orchid in the mouth of a hungry vixen.

She said nothing for a while, but her fingers moved slowly and very softly like spiders' legs along the swollen veins of my shank. At that moment certainly I could not have uttered another wisely eloquent word. Whatever pulsing energy was needed to make fine words spout from my lips was surely now diverted to my pulsing loins. I could only manage little gasping breaths, looking down at her beautifully sculpted hand as it travelled my gleaming flesh so sensually.

But that same sensuality caused my span to make tiny convulsions as if somehow it had become deranged by those spiders' legs walking upon it, therefore needing to rid itself of so delicious a torment.

My Mistress laughed, brushing me again all the way along my shaft, and as far as the head, but going no further and avoiding my hoop. 'Do you dare jerk away from me, like the tail of a skittish kitten that declines to be stroked?'

'I cannot help myself, Mistress, I assure you. I do not make it bounce from you willingly. Quite the contrary, Mistress. I would wish to have you stroke me so, all night long . . . if that were your desire.'

She smiled, her small white teeth gleaming as much as my oily skin. 'Perhaps it is the clamp the Royal Physicians put around your sac that makes you jump, as if it strangles the nerve-ends of your potency.' She ventured this opinion as if it were a serious one. But then she laughed suddenly. 'So be careful, Shani, that you shall not jump like a demented grasshopper through your own hoop!'

I smiled dutifully. 'Yes, Mistress. I shall try not to do that, Mistress, unless it is to make my silver thread jump and fly . . . at your command, of course, Mistress.'

Her pert little nose twitched, as if perhaps as a warning that I should refrain from more frivolous retorts. Then she said rather coldly, 'At my command . . . certainly. You speak wise words, my slave.'

I swallowed my tongue, looking crestfallen. But she pretended not to notice. In any case she was reaching out at me again, and I could see that her intention was to tame my involuntary spasm.

This time her finger and thumb came at me from underneath, before clasping loosely around the base of my shank. But still I bucked from her.

'I tell a washer-woman's lie, Shani!' She laughed gleefully. 'You are not the tail of a skittish kitten, but the tail of a slippery eel!'

And now it was my duty to laugh, although it caused a bouncing swing, rather than the spasm of a slippery eel.

She became serious, lowering her hand. The playful banter between slave and Royal Mistress was evidently at an end. Her eyes were feasting on my span, and also upon the huge gold hoop at its extremity, her mind contemplating silent mischief.

Eventually she spoke and with slyness in her voice, as if her mischief were about to be unleashed. 'I can see that I shall need to tether it . . . and make it have polite manners for its Mistress. Like any dancing street-bear, a wild beast requires taming before it can play for the crowds.'

I had no concept of her meaning, not at first. Perhaps the boiling cauldron in my loins had steamed my befuddled brain. I said nothing, but I did not have long to wait to see what would happen.

The ends of the gold-braided cord of her bedchamber-robe had been lying loosely on either side of her. She pulled one end from behind her, removing the cord completely. Otherwise she stayed in her reclining position, with the cushions against her back.

When she spoke again, her voice was stern, even though her eyes twinkled with her mischief-making. 'Get up and kneel astride my legs.'

It was a posture I knew well, and I obeyed quickly, placing one knee on each side of hers. She did not like me to sit back on my feet in a relaxed poise. If I did so, she would say scornfully, 'You resemble an indolent frog that basks on a lily-leaf. Hold yourself upright, and make your leg muscles strain to keep a graceful posture.'

And therefore I would adopt this bracing stance, raising myself so that I would be standing upright on my knees, having to maintain that steady balance until such time as she allowed me to relax. In the Pavilion of the Divine Orchid Ladies did we Novices not always learn the virtues of gracefulness? Whether it was during the ritual of morning Prostration with our rumps tensed and raised so debasingly, or whether it was in the performance of our tasks in Their Ladyships' bedchambers, there was no apparent difference. Whatever 'grace' there was, I should perhaps rejoice in the knowledge that Their Ladyships found pleasure in it. The fact that a Novice was a perpetually humbled creature did not entitle him to be ungraceful or ever to be unpleasing to Their Ladyships.

My Mistress looked at me now with her head cocked slightly to one side, her eyes like wicked slits of black twinkling diamonds. 'Raise yourself higher. I do not want a slovenly frog as my companion,' she said testily. 'Have I not told you before?'

For a moment I wondered at which aspect of my raised posture I needed to raise more. Was I not already raised up, and proudly so? But tonight it seemed she required an ever more acute standing than usual, even though I was already aching in my upright rigidity.

Nonetheless I murmured, 'Yes Mistress.'

And, at once puffing out my chest more, I pulled in my belly-button, at the same time straining my legs to make myself grow taller. This must have been what she wanted because I saw her chin nod condescendingly.

I towered over her, my boom spanning straight along the valley between her legs, although the thrusting angle of my shank made it point more up towards her forehead than at her belly. Besides, when my elevation was as proud as it was now, there was always a natural tendency for it to curve upwards in a gentle sweep.

My Mistress sometimes called it her Naked Emperor with the Gracefully Arched Spine, or He Who Bends Backwards with the Golden Halo.

But on this occasion there were clearly no such frivolous notions in her mind. For a second I wondered whether a capricious cloud of the Black Moon had suddenly crossed her features. She was looking at me intently again – almost critically. But, if there were something that might have suddenly displeased her, I had no notion of what it could be. All I could do was hold myself so acutely upright over her and let her scrutinise me. If she found some imperfection she would doubtless tell me of it.

But the moment passed, and she smiled up at me, almost tenderly now. Except that there was still that mischievous glitter in her eyes. Suddenly she bent forwards, her tentative fingers slowly reaching out to me. It could have been a game to see whether her touch alone could induce my involuntary spasm.

When finally she ventured to brush me lightly underneath, I again jerked upwards and away from her touch. She laughed with such girlish delight, her fascination at my improper convulsion so clearly evident. My rod was nothing now but an amusing toy!

This time she approached me from one side, brushing her fingertips along the swollen vein. Again there was that same convulsing jerk, and again she laughed, quickly withdrawing her fingers as if afraid that this same twitching ailment might have been contagious.

'Oh, Shani, my dancing bear, I must stop your dance and tame you now. Your ring demands me to capture it.'

I noticed that she held one end of the gold-braided cord of her bedchamber-robe in her hand. She reached out to where my ringed boom thrust out above her, and very nimbly she inserted the end of the cord and pulled it through.

'There now,' she declared gleefully, tugging the cord until it was taut. 'You are not only my slave but so too is your bull-flesh!'

Then, as if experimentally, she pulled down on my thrust, making it bow lower and point directly towards the V of her legs.

'So now my Naked Emperor with the Gracefully Arched Spine is made to bow down. Yet still he defies me and tries to curve upwards in that same impetuous sweep.' She laughed with playful delight. 'And how strongly does he resist the cord. But my oily eel is captured at last!'

Her smile faded abruptly, her pretty face at once serious with some new purpose in her mind. Her eyes flashed up at me, blazing in mischievous intensity. With her free hand she slowly drew back the silk folds of her garment so that the divine fullness of her naked body was revealed.

Even though she had so often let me gaze upon her nakedness before, every time I did so it was as if I were gazing for the very first time upon the splendour of it all. She was like one of those exotic birds of paradise that were so lovingly depicted on those lacquered screens around her chamber. Each bird was painted as if by an artist blessed with Heaven's Vision. You could look upon the craftsmanship and gaze upon each richly plumed bird for a lifetime, but even then you would not have had your fill of their magnificence.

And how should a humble slave dare to marvel each time at such perfection? And where should he begin? *When the platter of gluttony confronts a dragon, he should take care that the flame he spits shall not burn his feasting eyes.*

As always, my darting gaze sped at first to the brazen flush of her femininity. There was so much there of velvety intrigue that it made me gulp stupidly, my greedy eyes always wanting to dwell upon those delicious portals. Her skin on either side and above was as satin-smooth as the finest sheet of vellum, and as unblemished as the surface of fresh goat's milk in a jug. Her Maidservants shaved her daily there and bathed her in limejuice before a steaming poultice made of kirikangina pulp and wild honey was then applied.

How should a man – and one as humble as I – be permitted to dwell upon the precincts of such enchantment, and feel the spell rising within him? But over those many years was I not granted this privilege, even if I were never once to glide a path of ecstasy beyond those lush portals? The long breach in the smooth vellum was as if some heavenly angel had cut a fine swath from top to bottom, those delicate folds parted as if the velour was of soft curds. I knew by sight every soft little twirl and twist of them, and the way the puckered lips were arranged neatly at the sides, just peeping out as if teasingly so.

Oh, Divine Sculptor, how skilfully you moulded that forbidden beauty, but is it to mock lusting eyes?

I wanted to linger there, but now my Mistress denied me that opportunity. She was exerting pressure on my leash, pulling my ring and making me come nearer. And, if I faltered, she would jerk irritably at it, making me come quicker. My uncertain feet and knees had to scramble ungraciously on the silken bedcovers to find a new place to anchor myself on either side of her legs. But this was not her intention. Still she tugged at me, drawing me further up along her body, so that quickly I had to find a new position for my knees.

She giggled at my confusion and at the indignity of my ungainly attempts to comply with her tugging movements at my ring. I clambered further up until eventually I was astride her slender torso.

'Why do you fumble like a big insect that is frightened to mount its mate, Shani? Stand tall on your knees and lift yourself so that your sac shall hang freely and not slither like a fat slug along my belly!'

I looked down at her, seeing that undulating plain that I had so inadvertently travelled. I had not even been aware of my trailing pouch against her flesh. I had been concentrating more on keeping the inner sides of my legs – which were so thickly coated with oil – away from her thighs and her silk gown.

I could say nothing, nor did I know what she wanted of me. But I quickly rose up on my haunches as before, the muscles of my legs tensed again and with that same trembling ague to them. I glanced down. Delightful as it was, the plain of her belly was not all that came to my fascinated gaze. It was more the delightful vista of her mounds, and the way they perched so gracefully on her ribcage. I thought how they seemed almost precarious in their balance, as if at any moment they might be in danger of slipping down on either side of her.

They could have been two exquisite fruits, so firm but yet so ripe in the pertness of their moulding. And, whenever she moved, there was a tiny quivering to them that only enhanced their glory. And at their peaks, the neat roundels were ever so slightly puckered, but their raised buds were like two tiny smooth stalks, seeming as if only recently plucked from their mother branch.

Like the tiller of a boat she guided my shank by her cord and my tether-ring, drawing me further up until my boom hung centrally across the valley between her delicious mounds. I hung there in my brazenness above her, but she kept my flesh at a respectful distance from hers, not bending me to her yet, as if those satin peaks should remain unconquered.

She looked up at me, evidently pleased with what she saw, because she let out a tiny laugh that made her mounds quiver. 'Oh, Shani, my iron bull, how your boom delights at what is below!'

For a moment the cord went slack, releasing the tension so that I rose in my sudden freedom. But I was not to be free. Her fingers wanted precision in their control, and they plucked at my ring, seizing it and not tenderly so. The cord still hung from it, but it was her hand that guided me. Again she tugged sharply at me so that I had to move my knees even further up against her sides to retain my balance.

I saw the quickening of her breath, her ribcage and her pert mounds rising and falling in shallow bursts beneath me. Her eyes were focused only upon my captured head. This she swung over to one side and forced it down to nudge at the bud of her mound. Again a little laugh erupted from her. 'Your eye-vent

201

is to be the tiny mouth of a slippery eel, Shani. I hope it has no teeth, because I want its lips to suckle at my bud!'

While she still held the ring tightly, keeping my head against her bud, her other hand came into play. Gently, the fingers of that hand closed upon the smooth satin of my head. Then, pinching open that tiny breach, she pulled it directly on to her risen bud and made my parted lips close over it.

'There now!' she declared gleefully. 'Your eel-mouth shall succour me in its fragile embrace . . . and, even if it shall take no milk from me, perhaps it will make yours boil with eager fury in your loins.'

And that I could not deny.

Her fingers held me there for a while. Then eventually she let go of me so that I bounded up again. The soft lips of a slippery eel had evidently tasted all that she desired them to. Her gold-braided cord was still threaded loosely through the ring, but now she slipped it out. For a moment or two she continued to scrutinise my boom as it hung there over her, but her glittering eyes from time to time darted up to look upon my oiled torso towering over her.

'Oh, Shani, my Golden God. Yet it is not only your golden adornments that shine in the light. The lustre of your chest and belly make my eyes shine with desire.'

For a second there was a sudden wistfulness in her voice, as if she knew the futility of her words. But then her eager intensity returned and she smiled again, whispering seductively to me. 'I know what your lips yearn for, my golden bull-man!'

My mind was momentarily confused. There were so many lips of passion that I knew not which of them she meant.

'They desire to kiss my own velvet lips,' she went on teasingly, touching my belly and running her fingers over it. 'And then, would your slave tongue not desire to venture into places that are forbidden to it?'

My lips knew not what to reply, but she was looking at me with such intensity. Should I now bend myself down to that so regal and beautiful face and then kiss her mouth? Would it not be sacrilege for a lowly slave to kiss a Divine Orchid Lady? Yet how could I not comply with an order my Mistress had given me?

I bent over her, lowering my face to hers. But instantly her hand came against my chest and she pushed me back. 'Oh, foolish slave!' She laughed. 'Would you not better desire to kiss me where you shall most bring pleasure to me?'

'Yes, Mistress,' I mumbled stupidly, wondering where that should be.

'Well then, I shall permit the wet passion of your lips and the eagerness of your tongue to suckle at my secret place . . . a place that is forbidden. But it is a place less forbidden to you than my royal mouth, Shani! My lips there would be as cold as ice and lacking kindly passion, because they have only ever known a harsh prince's kiss upon them before . . . and only when his lust for me made him spew his faithless passion as he rutted in my secret place.'

She said this with sneering contempt. So, it was not that I was an unworthy slave, but only one who should be denied the pressing of his lips against those that a faithless prince had once so harshly kissed. Yet I was to be permitted to kiss the secret place – one through which he had vented his royal seed!

Perhaps I understood, but still I did not move. My heart was racing now.

'Turn yourself.'

I hesitated, not knowing how I should comply.

'*Turn* yourself, Shani,' she repeated irritably. 'Turn your rump the other way and kneel over me so that your lips are above mine and so that your golden sac can touch my nose. Are you an eager bull ... or a feeble puppy who knows nothing of how passion is made?'

Seizing my ring suddenly, she swung it to the side so that at once my knees had to clamber in such ungainly manner over her. Letting go of me for that instant so that I could adopt this turnabout posture, she reached between my legs and seized me again, pulling me back towards her until I was positioned how she wanted me.

Now the sweet face of a smiling orchid lay beneath my hanging pouch, but it was the gossamer petals of her ripened bud that I looked down upon so lustfully. Although my gaze had often dwelt upon them before, they had always remained partially wrapped in their cocoon of velvet, emerging only to peep coquettishly over the crimson parapet of her breach. Yet now there was invitation in them, and they gaped brazenly, peeled back in their eagerness.

Oh, beautiful Heaven, your earthly flower is now unfurled in its splendour.

I marvelled at the delicate neatness, at the tiny crumpling of the little folds, at the pale rose-blush of the tissue, and at the moist softness that glistened from within.

'Kiss me now, my bull-man,' she breathed huskily. 'Explore me there so that your lips shall become the suckers of a gentle limpet ... and that your soft tongue shall lap me like a newborn lamb's.'

I bent over her, the sweet musk of her fragrance rushing to my nostrils. My mind was empty of all thought, except of how I should become the newborn lamb and make the passion she desired of me. What tingling of ecstasy came to my lips! And how did that rich softness of hers make me tremble! And when my feverish tongue parted those delightful folds, venturing into that magical domain, I became a slave of passion, floating in a warm mist of euphoria.

Although I was not a prince, I felt a king. And did I now not know the button of a woman's ecstasy?

A little quiver rippled across her body and she sighed blissfully. Then, even as my busy tongue found its mark, elsewhere I felt her mouth reach up and come upon my sac. She nibbled there with such gentleness, my tender orbs for once content in their swollen embrace of cruel gold – and now also of kindly lips.

In my floating mist there was no notion of time. The lush mystery of this new domain overwhelmed my every sense.

'Open me with your fingers,' she commanded breathlessly, her mouth for a moment breaking off from its busy nibbling of my sac.

I obeyed hesitantly, my fingers fumbling at those delicious lobes.

'Wider!'

And again I obeyed, more confidently now. Holding that wondrous chasm open, I gazed into her glorious cushioned depths, seeing the soft pink intricacy of those gossamer folds of tissue. There was warmth there, and such exquisite intrigue, and fruitfulness. And, when it came, it came almost as a shock. Released furtively from that mysterious labyrinth, her honey-sap gathered there, its silver threads nestling now between the gaping furls of her bloom and glistening in the lamplight.

'Oh, my Mistress!' I gasped.

What regal composure she had, even in the shedding of her sap! Not for her the impetuous silver streak of a slave that bursts its spurting joy so furiously in the night. Her spume of passion was almost benign in comparison, content to yield its fruitfulness in such gentle gossamer charms.

That night I was the pure instrument of my Mistress's pleasure, and mine was in the making of it. Certainly my lamb's tongue took delight in its soft lapping, and the buds of my mouth melted with such divine infusion, yet did not my loins ache for their impetuous release?

I returned later to my cold mattress with unreleased passion. For the rest of that night I could not sleep and I lay there in my oily shroud, thinking of her, and thinking of Li-Mei.

He who rides the tiger's back can never easily alight.

Six

Time was slow at passing in the Pavilion of the Divine Orchid Ladies, yet on occasions it bounded forwards in leaps of a mountain-goat.

I was at the end of my second Novitiate year when Her Grand Ladyship died. I recall how much wailing and gnashing of teeth there was, but it was not out of affection for her, because there was none. It was simply a matter of custom and protocol, and we Novices – no less than Their Royal Ladyships and our Brother Eunuchs – needed to show our false sorrow.

In death she was as grotesque as she had been in life, her haggard face caked in mortician's *maquillage*. When we dutifully undertook our vigil in the Great Hall where she lay in State, by the third night the deathly smell was no longer masked by lavender and honeysuckle.

Brother-Yellow-Crow told me that she would be succeeded as Grand Lady by one of her two Senior Sisters – those grim Ladies who had always sat so quietly at her side. This was the custom, he had said.

But for once my Tutor was wrong.

Whatever Wandering Spirits of Bad Omen had stalked the corridors of the Pavilion, it was evident that mere custom and practice had been usurped by

207

higher powers. Not even Their Royal Ladyships could have had any forewarning of what was to come. Whether it had been some royal whim on the part of His Majesty, or a result of some underhand dealings by a few Court Ministers with greedy eyes and sticky hands, nobody could say. But the new Grand Lady came as a shock to all of us who dwelt in those royal precincts.

Her Grand Ladyship Bo-An – she of the warrior-arms and vicious hands – began her reign of terror with a rod of iron that was no less cruel than the rod of bamboo she wielded so skilfully. It was said that she had once been the favourite of His Imperial Majesty, and even though she was now a Faded Orchid she had nonetheless retained His Majesty's veneration and respect. Moreover, she had retained her wealth and all those many splendid gifts he had given her. Therefore she had been so well equipped to pander to greedy eyes and sticky hands.

My Mistress had been dismayed by the news of her Royal Sister Bo-An's so exalted appointment, just as no doubt most of her other Royal Sisters had been. Yet there was a clique of them who seemed now to have bright faces of smug contentment – like plotting hens that have let the vixen into the coop. Brother-Yellow-Crow had been unusually grim faced, but perhaps not as much as we Novices were – particularly the new intake of Junior Novices who were in so much need of having their memories reformed.

Her Grand Ladyship no longer delegated the bamboo rod to any of her beloved Sisters, and now it was not only she who presided over the morning Assembly of Prostration, but it was also she who reformed those erring memories, and always viciously so.

Those morning Assemblies were surely now to be endured all the more fearfully. They were longer, too, such that, by the time Her Grand Ladyship departed with her Senior Sisters and her retinue of Eunuchs, we Novices – those of us left unscathed by her bamboo rod – ached from head to toe, particularly as we were all the more inclined to 'keep a good grace in the manner of our prostration'. From time to time even second- and third-year Novices had their memories reformed by her. Her Grand Ladyship clearly enjoyed her walk behind us. Her eye was always critical as she stalked our ranks like a sly wolf. Whenever she stopped behind the unfortunate Novice of her choosing that morning, he knew at once the inevitability of his fate. The Great Hall had never before echoed to such distressing cries of agony as it did now.

In one sense this was a guilty blessing for me, because my dear Mistress never again made any complaint against me. If she had cause to have my memory reformed, she would do so in the privacy of her chambers. She kept a small brush-whip of spindly thongs for that purpose, and on rare occasions she brushed my rump with it. But she seldom did so more than lightly, such that any marks were scarcely visible by the next morning's Assembly.

She disapproved of Her Grand Ladyship's new reign of cruelty. To my Mistress it was a matter of sound reason to punish lazy, slovenly or sullen-faced servants, but only insofar as to redeem errant memories, but never for cruelty's sake. That would have affronted my Mistress's sense of good virtue and benevolent justice. Consequently I never again suffered the bamboo rod at morning Assembly – at least never upon my thrusting rump.

There was, however, one occasion that my Mistress could not have saved me from, even had she been forewarned of Her Grand Ladyship's wicked intentions. It was during one morning Assembly, and my nose was pressed to the marble, my spine arched as if fit to break, every muscle and sinew of my body and limbs so acutely tensed. Her Grand Ladyship had halted behind me and I was at once seized by icy fear, at any moment expecting that first stinging blow.

But it seemed that Friendly Fortune shone down on me that day. Her Grand Ladyship had been in one of her more playful moods, and a wicked cackle came from her lips – one that could surely have instantly frozen the pond in the Garden of Tranquillity. However, instead of that numbing strike, I felt something even more shocking. The split-bamboo nudged speculatively between my legs, as if seeking out what it knew was hanging there. And then my so helplessly suspended flesh felt the tails jounce teasingly against it.

Oh, my mother, was I truly born of you to suffer such mortification?

Yet it seemed that I had been. Her Grand Ladyship rummaged there with such painful irreverence, knowing how the spindly tails must sorely worry my clamped sac. At first she only tapped me experimentally from one side and then the other, neither too gently nor too harshly, but enough to set a pendulous motion. Once the momentum had gathered pace, she would interrupt each returning swing with a sudden menacing flick of the rod. And then she would laugh gleefully.

All the while I managed to keep the grace in my prostration, albeit with difficulty, and flinching each time. Had I moved from my debasing posture it would have been an act of insolence, but the cruel jiggling made me want to weep with humiliation. Yet for once, it seemed, I had given pleasure to Her Grand Ladyship.

Much later my Mistress confided in me – but not without some amusement – that Her Grand Ladyship had seemed to tremble in taking her wicked enjoyment, and that her expression had been one of pure rapture. Moreover, for the remainder of that day, according to my Mistress's testimony, Her Grand Ladyship had been unusually well disposed towards her beloved Sisters, even displaying to them a gracious and generous temperament that they had never seen in her before.

Afterwards, my Mistress, seeing how I had remained dangerously sullen and lacking appreciation of her humour, chided me with mocking sarcasm. 'Oh, Shani, my golden bull-man whose ripened seed-pod stretches to the ground like the unpicked fruit of an overladen branch, was it not better to be tickled by Her Grand Ladyship's playful rod rather than have it flay the skin off your rump?' She laughed again, making dimples in her cheeks. Then she added, pretending to become serious, 'Having explored such hallowed precincts, her rod is surely now anointed with fresh purpose, Shani. The bamboo is no longer just for reforming memories, but for knocking forbidden fruit from its branch!'

Of course she was right, but at the time I was still smarting from the indignity of my ordeal, and I was not much disposed to sharing my Mistress's humour. Yet, in truth, despite her light-hearted teasing of me, she remained wary and nervous of Her Grand Ladyship Bo-An, as did everyone else in the Pavilion. It was as if a gloomy shadow of uncertainty had descended over the place, casting a yet more sinister twilight over that silk-spun cage. Indeed, my Mistress was ever more cautious now, summoning me only in the dead of night to her chambers, and therefore at a time when Her Grand Ladyship was certainly asleep in hers.

At morning Assembly my Mistress adopted a quiet indifference to the proceedings, never glancing my way. Her seniority as a Royal Sister was only that of Third Divinity, and as there had been no influx of virgin Orchid Ladies for more than a year, her position in the Court remained unchanged. She could not afford to fall foul of Her Grand Ladyship – she who undoubtedly had the Emperor's ear and all the power that went with her exalted status. And, if my Mistress were my protector, was my own position therefore not any less precarious than hers?

Yet perhaps it was our mutual insecurity that brought us closer. I continued to serve her in those routine prosaic duties that Novices performed for their Mistresses. From time to time I might suffer a lashing from her tongue – or even from her small brush-whip – for some trivial misdemeanour. Yet, once I was alone with her during our special nights she was kinder to me than ever she had been before. Her cycles of capriciousness were diminished, although not entirely extinguished. She might on occasion still erupt like a cracker thrown on to a smouldering fire, but that impetuous streak of cruelty seldom reared its dragon's head.

It was only once that I had cause for serious grievance against her, and that had been on that sordid occasion when she 'lent me' to her beloved Sister Lin-Yao.

It was rumoured that Sister Lin-Yao had been cruelly rejected by His Majesty's eldest son, His Highness Prince Fid-ram-Ong, in favour of an Orchid Lady younger than herself. So distraught had Her Ladyship Lin-Yao been at her rejection that my Mistress had commiserated with her. After all, had she herself not known of princely faithlessness? However, the extent of her commiseration had been to offer me to her wronged Sister as a token consolation.

On that peaceful night of my loaning, it was then that I experienced the impure ordeal of Bowing Before the Unjust Bull. Even now I shudder at the thought, the image still etched so vividly on my troubled mind. If the Bamboo Rod of Reformed Memory had been a cruel instrument of torture, how much worse was the stiffened bull's pizzle to endure? Not only did its wretched shaft tear an unnatural expansion into the pathway of virgin flesh, even with the goosefat and jasmine oil, it breached the very core of my loins and sullied the private domain of my soul.

It was therefore an episode that I did not thank my Mistress for.

However, to give her rightful credit, she did confess her contrition to me. This she did sometime after my ordeal, while she was applying tea-tree lotion and ky-ky berry juice to my poorly flesh. I was lying face-down on her silk bedcovers at the time, with my feet wide apart and she kneeling daintily between my legs. Whatever soreness I was suffering was perhaps compensated by the softness of her hands as they worked the lotion into my damaged rift. I could even forgive her those occasional teasing chuckles, and also when sometimes her hand strayed beneath me to fondle playfully at my undamaged flesh. Nevertheless, no matter how soothing her ministrations or how playful her intentions, I retained my resentment of her loaning of me – as if I were a mere chattel without heart or soul. Therefore, I was petulant and sullen, not rising to my Mistress's attempts to shift my sullenness.

But although she professed honest regret for having lent me like a chattel, she excused herself all the same. She considered that I was exaggerating my distress, and she slapped my rump once in sudden exasperation, sighing irritably. 'You swish your tail like an angry old mare who shuns the stallion's sheath!' she scoffed. 'You've not been spiked by the devil's horn, Shani, but only playfully rutted by my beloved Sister.'

I was scarcely consoled at her wisdom. I might just as well have been spiked by the devil's horn, but my Mistress was most indignant by my unreasonableness, even though she herself had been surprised at her beloved Sister.

'I thought she would desire real bull-flesh rather than the leather of a dead bull,' she sniffed dismissively, perplexed at the notion.

It seemed such a strange remark to me at the time, and one that heaped confusion upon my mind. Had not my real bull-flesh been grotesquely ringed and clamped for no other purpose than to prevent me entering upon those royal and private precincts of Their Ladyships? Therefore, I puzzled, how should Sister Lin-Yao have availed herself of the pleasures of my real bull-flesh, if that had been her true desire? She could have used me playfully, in much the same way that my Mistress did, and have me do those pleasurable things I habitually did for her. No doubt that had been what my Mistress had expected of her Sister. Yet it seemed that Sister Lin-Yao was more ambitious in her predilections, orientating herself towards a dominant and active role, rather than a submissive one. My endowment alone was an insufficient catalyst to ferment her lustful enjoyment. That much at least I could divine from my experience, even though such knowledge had been so painfully acquired. Having suffered the wicked leather and Sister Lin-Yao's ample thighs crashing into me, I was surely better off being the slave of my dear Mistress.

Much later, however, I was to learn from Brother-Yellow-Crow that there were other reasons for my loan to Sister Lin-Yao, rather than it having been purely an act of benevolent friendship on the part of my clever Mistress. It transpired that Her Grand Ladyship Bo-An was well disposed towards Sister Lin-Yao, and more so than she was towards my Mistress. And she was certainly in need of cultivating diplomatic friendships with those of her Sisters who were better connected with Her Grand Ladyship.

How deceptive were those silk-spun corridors of power!

And when tigers sleep soundly their fangs are no less sharp.

As for myself, I was as much a miserable pawn as a miserable plaything.

But there were always black dragons lurking in the long shadows, even though spring had come with its warm brightness. A still docile sun filtered through the grilled windows of the halls and corridors, and the Pavilion was once again filled with such sweet fragrances. But, if ever our Novice spirits were to rise and hover like early butterflies in the lush gardens, there was always something to cast those spirits down again.

Oh, sweet warmth of springtime, does not your morning dew still lie wet upon the ground and make a chill mist hang ghostly there?

I had entered my third Novitiate year and thus my Apron of Good Modesty was now proudly draped at the sides with two white tassels to denote that meagre seniority. Not that there was any reason for rejoicing, but there were at least some small consolations. No longer did we have to toil at so many sweating tasks. My poor knees and my aching back and muscles were saved now from the grinding work of cleansing and polishing those endless oceans of marble tiles. This was now the work of Junior Novices. I at least rejoiced in that, but pitied them guiltily.

Senior Novice Ling had finally been awarded his fully fledged Eunuch status, and now it was a familiar sight to see him strut with such arrogance in his saffron-yellow robe. Moreover, he was like a slimy pond-leech clinging to the trailing robes of his elder Eunuchs and even Her Grand Ladyship's. Now that he had ceased to be my Mistress's Senior Novice, that honour was now exclusively mine. Yet Eunuch Ling's resentment of me still festered in him like maggots in an open sore. No less apparent was his bitterness towards my Mistress. Even though many seasons had passed – and his scars had certainly healed by then – the flaying he had received all that while ago still made him seethe with anger.

What irony, I thought! Before her exalted appointment, had it not been Her Grand Ladyship Bo-An who had administered his punishment with such cruel ferocity? Yet, Eunuch Ling wore the sickly honeyed mask of fawning devotion to Her Grand Ladyship now, while aiming his barbed arrows of fury not towards her – but towards my Mistress and I.

When I complained of this to my Mistress, she only shrugged dismissively. 'You cannot blame a dog with fleas for scratching its sores.'

Nonetheless, it was always wise to tread cautiously where snakes lurk, and there were many of them in the Pavilion of the Divine Orchid Ladies.

Yet I should be wise to tread cautiously in other respects. My youthful passions were a fermenting turmoil that steamed my brain. And if my heart ached it was because it was pulled one way and then the other, until sometimes I wondered if it should be rent in two. As much as I was devoted to my Mistress, I also had as much affection for Li-Mei – she of the Beautiful Plum Blossom whose gentle fingers had so often tended me.

Now that the spring evenings were warm again, she and I would often meet in the Garden of Tranquillity. This quiet place of starlit memories had emerged now from its grey mantle of winter. The vegetation flourished again, alive to the buzz of insects, and the rich scent of virgin blooms rekindled the heat of our passion. And, if the springtime sap delighted in its moist freedom, my own yearned for relief from its winter confinement, even if during those summonses to my Mistress's chambers I was often made to fly my sap. But with Li-Mei it was different. Disobedient passion between slaves was on a more noble plain of ecstasy. Yet I loathed my golden accoutrements of slavery, even if they had grown into my flesh as though I had been born with them.

My beautiful Li-Mei understood this, far better than I understood her relationship with her companion Maidservant Huan-Yue. At least during those long winter months the two girls had been able to snuggle together like young nesting birds on Li-Mei's cosy mattress in the Maidservants' dormitory, whereas I had shivered alone in mine. And, when I padded in my bare feet at night along those freezing marble corridors to my Mistress's chambers, it was always with the knowledge that I was going there to satisfy her pleasures, rather than for her to satisfy mine.

After so long, on that first clear spring evening it was like heaven again in the Garden of Tranquillity. A huge hanging moon made our naked bodies shine with a pale luminescence so that we might have been ghostly spirits of the night, rather than disobedient slaves of passion. Li-Mei knew my urgency, but we always had such little time. It was not only the stars that had watchful eyes.

She smiled up at me and my heart melted. My eager jib seemed to spear the velvet fabric of the night, the golden halo glinting as if in wicked expectation of things to come.

Then she glanced down with a little sigh. 'Oh, my Shani, if only – if only I should have the wide mouth of a bullfrog, I would take your bull-shaft – and its cruel ring – altogether into me,' she whispered, touching me so that I jerked upwards with that involuntary little spasm.

But my Beautiful Plum Blossom had the sweet lips of a dainty mouth and not those of an ugly bullfrog. Certainly it would have been sacrilege even to contemplate their unnatural stretching for so unworthy a purpose, even if the notion of it made my sap rise all the more.

She held me, and tightly so, perhaps in awe at such steely girth and resplendent thrust. Then she slowly knelt down in front of me, not releasing her hold. I heard her gasp in the silence. Then those sweet lips came boldly to me, kissing me there and then opening around me until they covered the satin head entirely. I was locked into her tenuous embrace, pushing eagerly against it until the evil ring was lodged right up against the soft corners of her lips – lips that were such a teasing frontier to the moist warmth beyond.

Her hand let go of me, but only for a moment to fondle gently at my sac. All the while her mouth held me there and, when I looked down, it seemed to me that my hideous ring was as much a part of her soft lips as it was a part of my own poor flesh.

Oh, friendly moon, cast your magic spell upon us miserable slaves and let us dance like butterflies in graceful harmony.

Without releasing me from her lips, she took me again in her hand and began to glide her fingers along my swollen shaft, this so tender motion making a glorious friction against my tautened sheath.

'Ah, Li-Mei,' was all I could mutter, speaking more to the moon than to her.

I felt then the suckling vacuum at my eye-vent. Her teeth secured the rim of my head, oblivious to the ring below it, and the rhythm of her fingers made the sap rise from deep in my loins.

'Ah . . . ah, my Mistress!'

These breathless words tumbled unthinkingly from my stupid lips. In my feverish abandon had I not called out my Mistress's name? But, if I had done so, my Beautiful Plum Blossom seemed either not to hear, or else she simply disregarded my hurtful confusion.

Oh, woeful folly, how cruel is your unintended guilt, come as it is by so many conflicting emotions heaped upon me!

Yet how could I forgive myself? But at that moment of ecstasy I had ceased to be the dumb goat, only becoming a raging bull. All thoughts and thoughtlessness were overwhelmed in the rush of my passion.

And, as it came, the suddenness of it caught my Beautiful Plum Blossom like a fragile river-lily swept back in a swirling torrent. So long imprisoned by winter's abstinence, now I erupted in my joyous freedom. That bolt came neither as a leaping frog nor as a streak of silver lightning, but more as the thundering report of a cannon. Her slender swan-neck seemed to jerk backwards at the force, her lips at once blown open and as big and round as the hanging moon above us. Her bulging eyes were so wide in astonishment.

For a second or so her face was turned upwards at me, frozen there in the wake of its astonishment. Threads of my silver spume glistened on her lips, on her small white teeth, on the pink of her tongue and in the moist cavity of her silent mouth.

Then, as if awakening from her stupor, she smiled suddenly, her eyes sparkling up at me in the moonlight. For several moments she remained kneeling there, her small tongue exploring around her wetted mouth and lips, but not with any haste. Finally, she consumed my spent passion, doing so as if appearing to savour this new richness. Yet from her expression I could not tell whether she found it as the nectar of gods or the phlegm of jackals.

Eventually she grinned mischievously. 'I know you now, my sweet Shani,' she declared in that husky whisper of hers. 'I can smell and taste the creamy fruitiness and every fibre of your body. Your seed is forevermore a part of me! Even if it can never spurt into my velvet burrow, it shall trickle down and feed my soul.'

Warm spring gave way to blazing summer. The halls and corridors were again a welcome sanctuary from the heat outside. The morning sun rose quickly to become a fierce ball of fire that singed the silk blue edges of the sky and sapped the minds and bodies of toiling slaves.

After dusk we Senior Novices went to our mattresses and slept uncovered. After those many seasons, and now that we were in our third Novitiate year, my Novice siblings had softened their resentment towards me. Even if I were still the Devil's Freak Amongst Goats, I was nonetheless one of their fraternal flock. Apart from my escape from the Room of Glorious Transformation had I not toiled and suffered as much as they? Some of them even pitied me, and most ignored my frequent nocturnal absences from the dormitory. After all, my siblings at least could sleep soundly after their toiling of the day, whereas I still had duties to perform during those hours of darkness. Moreover, in the mornings my Brothers could rise refreshed from their slumbers, whereas I would often stumble from my mattress with my eyelids heavy like lead. Perhaps, rather than fraternal empathy, it was pity that might have faded my Brothers' resentment.

But like a passing rain-cloud there was always a coldness in its wake.

Once the oil-lamps had been dimmed, whatever subdued conversation there might have been at first, soon trailed off into silence and then for a while I would only have the whispering spirits for company. How then should I sleep, never knowing when I might be summoned? There was always so much the night could bring from the eerie shadows.

It was my Mistress's habit to send Senior Eunuch Shek whenever she desired my nocturnal attendance. He would usually find me awake, as if I had been expecting it. Without a word he would kick my foot and I would rise and dress in my apron. Then I would follow silently behind him as we padded to our Mistress's chambers.

Yet, if I were a unicorn, how should I slay the passions of two lionesses with only one horn?

Although it was not always so, quite often during the evening my beautiful Li-Mei, being one of my Mistress's Maidservants, could predict her particular disposition, and so be forewarned as to the likelihood of my being summoned to the Mistress's chambers that night. Therefore, whenever Li-Mei had wind of this, she would remain in her dormitory and perhaps

221

console her disappointment by sharing her mattress with Huan-Yue. But inevitably there were several dangerous evenings when Li-Mei and I would be together in the Garden of Tranquillity without knowing that I would later be summoned to attend my Mistress.

On those evenings, once our passions had been vented, like thieves in the night we would scuttle silently back to our dormitories, scarcely daring to breathe for fear of detection. And when I was safely lying on my mattress I would perhaps be on the point of closing my weary, yet contented eyes when Senior Eunuch Shek would kick me harshly to wakefulness.

It was on one such fateful occasion that I came to my Mistress still in the drowsy wake of my vented passion and with my eyelids drooping for want of sleep.

Oh, Unjust Spirit of Misfortune, shall you now expose my unworthy deceitfulness?

My Mistress peered at me from her silk cosy bed, seeing at once my slothful lethargy. When I manoeuvred myself clumsily to kneel at her feet, she immediately rebuked me, the dark ink of suspicion already clouding the twinkle in her eyes. 'Tonight you are like a limp poppy dying in the cold of winter, Shani. Is my golden bull-man unwell? Or has he toiled so much during the day on his Mistress's errands that now he flops around her chamber, uncaring that his poor Mistress needs his spear to shine with the lustre of his passion?'

How could I reply to such a question? Truth must surely not embellish my answer. And certainly I felt as cold and limp as that winter poppy. Scarcely had an hourglass trickled more than a few grains of sand into its sump since mine had been shot of its seed.

I massaged her feet, but lacking my usual eagerness. Try as I might, I could not coax myself to stir even a fly-wing's length, my passion no less stubborn than a dying mule's. At first my Mistress's patience was confined to teasing remarks and her soft caressing of my knees. She even opened her bed-robe earlier than was her usual custom, as if expecting that this glorious view of her exposure would certainly be enough to stir my reluctant flesh. But it did not, and now her teasing became stinging insults, such that whatever chance I might have had to redeem myself was now snuffed out like a candle-flame.

'You are surely afflicted by some weakening fever, my unworthy bull! Should I perhaps put a cord through your dangling ring and raise you up like the slack boom of a ship's mast? Or should I blow into the eye of your flute until my breath expands your empty bag?' she scoffed relentlessly.

I was mortified, but helpless in my affliction. Yet it was one that could surely be so quickly abated, if only I could have had a few grains more of sand to replenish that untimely hourglass. But whatever remained of my Mistress's patience turned to anger, and even stark suspicion.

Yet I cannot say that it was ever her suspicion or any complaint against me that contrived to bring about my downfall – and also that of my beautiful Li-Mei. It could simply have been that she and I had been observed earlier that evening when we scurried back to our dormitories from the Garden of Tranquillity. But, whichever scheming nighthawk's eyes had spied us, it was already too late.

The Black Dragons of Evil Destiny were now loosed upon us.

At first my natural suspicions fell upon Eunuch Ling – he with such bitter grudge against me. Yet there were so many whispering shadows and restless souls in the Pavilion. And there was not only resentment towards me, but also towards my precious Li-Mei, and even towards my Mistress herself. Certainly there were some of her Royal Sisters who had cause for resentment. And as for Li-Mei, was there not her friend, Huan-Yue, with whom she so often shared her own cosy mattress and where my beautiful Li-Mei soothed away the loneliness of her friend's tortured soul? Yet perhaps my logic here was flawed. Huan-Yue might certainly wish to destroy me – her unworthy rival of Li-Mei's affections. But surely the girl would realise that in destroying me she must also destroy our Beautiful Plum Blossom?

But there were so many tortured paths and so many dark souls, so how should I ever know which one had thrown us into the scorpions' pit?

Her Grand Ladyship's face was a mask of pure malice, one that made my knees weak. She sat upon her throne, her two Senior Sisters beside her. Chief Eunuch Karif stood there grimly, his arms folded. The silent ranks of prostrated Novices were assembled behind where Li-Mei and I stood so pitifully in our conspicuousness, facing Her Grand Ladyship.

The Bamboo Rod of Reformed Memory was no less conspicuous. It lay across Her Grand Ladyship Bo-An's lap as if it might almost have been an object of veneration to her. How I wanted then to reverse that hourglass of black destiny.

Li-Mei's sweet face was like that of a white ghost, but she stood proudly in her courage, whereas I was faint with fear and shame. I dared not look over at where my Mistress was seated on her cushion. How I should have wilted in my shameful disloyalty! I could not even dare to observe the expression of hurtful disdain that undoubtedly blighted the beauty of her features. Would she ever feel a kindly thought towards me again, loyalty having been the greatest virtue? My treachery was certainly worse than that of a rabid dog who bites its Mistress.

The Great Hall rang to the echoes of Her Grand Ladyship's venom, which was like a red tide engulfing me. I could not say how long her ranting lasted, but by the end I was a quivering wreck. My Novice brethren kept their noses hard against the cold marble, but grateful that for today, at least, their thrusting rumps were safe from Her Grand Ladyship's wrath.

I scarcely heard the words that she spouted. Suffice to know the insults and the dreadful meaning of them. Some words I recall clearly enough, and my heart sank at the dawning of what I knew to be our fate.

'You shall be cast out, you disobedient cockroaches, and you shall be ground into the dust, and your lowly skins shall be flayed until the red pulp of your flesh and the whites of your bones are exposed. And afterwards, if you are not already dead and with your skins hanging from you like sodden rags, you shall sweat away your lives in . . .'

'Please, Your Grand Ladyship, it was I to blame, and not Li-Mei,' I managed to beg, but Her Grand Ladyship silenced me with a thunderous roar. Brother-Yellow-Crow glanced at me with pity.

Her Grand Ladyship was finding it hard to catch her breath and her face was puce with rage. When eventually she composed herself sufficiently to speak again, her words came clearly and they chilled my body to the core.

After she had given her pronouncement, the Great Hall was as silent as the grave.

* * *

The cell was pitch black and the smell of it was rancid. The floor was warm dirt that clung to my sweating skin as I lay there in the silence. I was gasping for water. The putrid bucket that had been left there was empty. Yet it was not knowing what had happened to Li-Mei that was my greatest torment. I had no idea, nor had I any notion of how long I had been there. It might have been two days or three. I could hear nothing, except for a strange and frightening booming and groaning sound that seemed to come from beyond the cell walls, and even from the very bowels of the earth. I had no notion of what it could be, only that it sounded like some demonic machine that made the stone walls shudder with dread. Occasionally I could also hear other sounds of groaning and even wailing. At times they seemed close by, and at others more distant, so that it was altogether a hellish cacophony, as if despairing souls were being tormented by demons.

All I knew for certain was that Li-Mei and I had been dragged from the Pavilion by the Warrior-guards. Then with sacks over our heads we had been frogmarched to a place outside the Palace walls before being chained and thrown into these fetid cells. Whether she was still in one of them I had no idea, and certainly I had never once caught the slightest sound of her frightened voice. There was only ever that eerie cacophony of noise from all around, not just from the infernal machine but also the cries and wailing of men devoid of hope.

After what had seemed an eternity the cell door opened and I quickly hid my eyes from the glaring light. From where I crouched I could make out two Warrior-guards standing there beyond the doorway. One of the men carried a long whip of many tails. So this, I thought grimly, was the time when my flesh

226

was to be flayed from my bones. Not now the humble bamboo rod, but a weapon far more cruel.

I peered out into the passageway, vainly hoping for some sign of poor Li-Mei. From what I could see now it was clear that the place we had been brought to was a large sprawling prison. Everywhere there was such squalor and wretchedness, and the stink of jackals came pungently from the cellblock. I could see a grim courtyard with some sort of timber frame in the centre, and the surrounding walls of drab grey stone seemed to reach to the sky.

I wondered if Li-Mei were already dead, and at once a vision of her sweet tender face came dancing before my eyes. But I had no time for such contemplation.

'Get up!' the Warrior-guard growled.

'Where is Li-Mei, the – the young Maidservant?' I stammered groggily, my lips cracked with dryness.

'Silence, slave prisoner! Get up and come out before I kick you out and beat your head.'

I stumbled from the cell, still shielding my eyes with my hand and trying to look around me. I stood as erect as I could in my nakedness, but the two chains that ran from my neck to my ankles restricted me, and I had to bend my knees to stand.

There was another figure behind the Warrior-guards and he was waiting there with menacing patience. I blinked to see him more clearly, and I realised that he was an official of some rank, even though his dress was shoddy for someone of high status.

When confronted by the dragon in his lair, hold your head boldly, lest he see your fear.

When the official spoke, his voice had the devil's guttural edge to it. 'So you are the Novice Eunuch who has dared to tweak the withered nipples of Her

Grand Ladyship?' he laughed wickedly, peering at me with evident curiosity. 'And I am told that you are a false Eunuch and a magnificent specimen that has been spared the shearing of his sac, and for no other purpose than to give pleasure to the bored eyes of those poorly deprived Royal Orchid Ladies.'

He stooped lower to see between my legs, and then he let out a crude guffaw of laughter that made the other two men join in with his merriment. 'His manhood is truly of – of mighty proportions.' He pointed at me mockingly, scarcely able to speak for his mirth. 'But he is like an overladen vine that sags to the ground, and see how those Palace Eunuchs have ringed and clamped him so that he is like a freak bull adorned with gold!'

I could only stand there in my dejection, mustering whatever was left of my fragile dignity. The two Warrior-guards were as much consumed with laughter as he, yet I could also detect greed in their eyes. Gold was the devil's metal, after all, and it was there to tempt out the viper's head of wickedness.

If the official had noticed the guards' interest, he gave no indication of it. But his mocking torment had purpose now, as if he were warning them as much as he might be warning me. 'This freak should be wise not to dangle his gold-ringed manhood before the eyes of other prisoners for, while they might be hungry for his gold, their empty bellies are also hungry for food,' he warned, before pausing and grinning slyly at me. 'And like rats they might come upon him in the night and gnaw his fleshy meat from him!'

I felt a jolt of fear, which was so clearly his intention.

He became serious, turning to the guards. 'See to it that the freak is issued with a loincloth to hide his freak's branch of abundance. The other prisoners shall not be told of his strange affliction . . . and there shall be no mention of gold,' he commanded sharply, and I could see by the faces of the guards that he would be obeyed.

This puzzled me, but nonetheless I felt a flood of relief. Why the official should be concerned for me, I had no idea. Did he want the gold for himself and, if so, by what means would he take it? I could therefore not be entirely reassured in my momentary relief, and there were other fears to confront me now.

He addressed me sourly. 'You are to be permitted your life, slave prisoner. This has been decreed. But you will serve for two full seasons at the Water Treadmills.'

Although I had no concept of what this was, I realised instantly that it must be the source of the demonic booming noise, which had become much louder now that I had emerged from my cell. But he had not finished with his pronouncements yet.

'You shall wear the Harness of Tight Constriction, so that it will squeeze the putrid sweat from your pores. And, if you survive the Treadmill, you will be taken to the stone quarries and work there until you drop . . . or until Her Grand Ladyship instructs me to return you in whatever state your wretched body might be.'

So, now at least, I had hope! It was not intended for me to die in this hellish place. Yet, I could not know it then, but in those next few seasons how often would I think that death would have been preferable to life.

For a moment I looked at the official, summoning my courage. 'Master,' I addressed him, feigning polite subservience. 'Tell me, I beg you, what news is there of the Maidservant Li-Mei? Is she here and – and what is her punishment?'

A black cloud of thunder crossed his features. For a second he did not reply. Then he smiled menacingly. 'If you shall ever once ask of her again, a dozen of these shall rip the skin from your back.'

He nodded at the Warrior-guard with the whip, and out of the corner of my eye I saw the leather tails swing back and then, reversing abruptly, they flew at me, lashing down upon my shoulders with such viciousness that it forced the breath from my lungs.

At night, when the darkness was as black as the devil's cloak, I could hear the scurrying of rats, or perhaps the scurrying of my wretched fellow prisoners. Many of them indeed resembled emaciated rodents, divested of all humanity. And I would make myself into a clenched ball, so fearful was I of that dreadful threat. If those human rats did not actually gnaw at my flesh, they gnawed at my mind and sapped my spirit.

Each morning before dawn we were taken from the long airless cell, and I would feel almost glad to be out, even though I knew what sweating rigours the day had in store. We were herded down the steep flight of steps into the huge chamber that housed the Water Treadmill. It was like entering hell itself. The creaking and groaning of timber and the clanking of iron and chain were unremitting. It assaulted our ears, and far below in the deep well-shaft there was that constant low echoing boom as the chain-buckets heaved up their streaming loads as the huge tread-wheel turned.

My dreadful harness was made of thick leather straps that hung vertically from my shoulders and wound horizontally around my torso, such that my chest felt as if it were being compressed in a vice. The strapping was buckled at the back so that I alone could not have loosened it, and it chafed my skin and made my sweat run like steamy rivers. There were two large rings at the shoulders, so that, when I mounted the stepping plank of the tread-wheel, two chains could be fastened to them. In this way, if we missed our footing on the stepping-planks or dropped from exhaustion or the failing of our hearts, the harness and chains would save us from plummeting down the well-shaft.

Yet I cannot say that there was any benevolent purpose in this consideration. It was simply that dead prisoners in His Imperial Majesty's well would interrupt the pumping of his water, and therefore the irrigation of his many fields and gardens to the north of the city.

And for those many seasons did I not make them lush and green? From dawn to dusk I toiled on that infernal wheel, with only brief respites to quench my gasping thirst. At the end of each day my legs were like heavy trunks of lead, my body as weary as a dying man's.

Oh, Mother, have I not trudged a million steps and watered an empire of vegetation?

At dusk, however, there was always food. And I was puzzled at first. I soon realised that my wooden bowl was always laden with meat, whereas the bowls of my hapless and emaciated fellow prisoners contained only a slimy gruel and mouldy bread or fat. I said nothing, only guiltily taking care to eat quickly and furtively – and keeping my loincloth tight about me.

One night, however, the mystery was solved. The Warrior-guard who carried the whip-of-tails leered down at me, whispering as he thrust the bowl at me, 'How fortune shines on you, Golden-Freak, that I am paid so well to keep you alive ... or else by now I should have fed your skinny corpse to the jackals!'

231

I felt then a sudden joy.

Dear Mistress! Can it truly be you who protects me, even now in my misery ... and even that I have wronged you so?

When at last I was returned to the Pavilion my heart was torn so many ways. Memories came rushing back so thick and fast and, when first I caught sight again of the red-gold roofs of the Palace, tears stung my eyes. Overhead, the new summer sky was as blue as ever it had been so long ago in my far-off village. The sun was now a friendly sun; and all beneath it glittered.

Yet, an old bull saved from the slaughterhouse shall return to the bosom of his herd, no longer as a proud beast but as a humble lamb.

Certainly I trod those first steps up to the Pavilion with humility, and not least with anxiety. Had Her Grand Ladyship's anger been fully vented? And would my Mistress find forgiveness in her heart? And would there be news of Li-Mei? And how should I enquire, if it meant punishment to do so? All these things and much more did I wonder as I entered the ornate doors of the Pavilion. Nearly a full cycle of seasons had passed, and there were so many changes in those silk-spun corridors and hallways.

Of course, I knew that it must have been my dear Mistress who had bribed the sticky-fingered prison official to keep me alive – firstly in the hellish Imperial Water Treadmill, and then later in the terrible stone-quarry. In that dreadful place, where a haze of grey dust hung permanently in the air, I had broken a mountain of stone with an iron hammer that made my hands blister and my ears ring to the metallic cacophony all around me. My fellow prisoners dropped like flies in the fierce sun or in the cold winter air, and those who did not had skeletal bodies and hollow eyes, dulled with despair. I at least had hope, and it was this and my extra rations and fresh limes that kept my soul and body together. I could grit my teeth whenever the whip-of-tails lashed my back, and I would think of my Mistress and wonder whether she was thinking of me at that moment.

It was even a joy to wear my Apron of Good Modesty again, and more so to bathe in the servants' wash-pool. The grime and stone-dust had turned the copper lustre of my skin to a dull grey pallor, and, when the Maidservants shaved me all over and pampered me with soapy sponges and fragrant oil, how I rejoiced at such delightful cleanliness and freedom, the lustre of my flesh once more restored.

There were many new faces, as well as many old. My dormitory brethren of the past were all fully fledged Eunuchs now and they wore their saffron-yellow robes with haughty pride. My new dormitory companions were all third-year Novices. I could only dimly recall them, and they were wary of me, though some of them harboured a measure of secret respect for me, and even awe. My lean-muscled frame and bulging limbs made me a giant amongst these puny Novices. Nonetheless, I who had worn the prisoner's cloak of shame was best to avoid – a leper to shun for fear of contagion.

As for the Eunuchs and my peers, was I not as much a Devil's Freak Amongst Goats as ever I had been before?

When Her Grand Ladyship Bo-An eventually summoned me to her chambers, I entered there with much trepidation. Yet for a brief moment I was struck dumb by such richness of décor and such fine silk furnishings. Her chambers were truly a palace within a palace – much more than my own dear

Mistress's – and I gaped stupidly before I quickly bowed low.

She was seated on a small velvet-cushioned throne. Chief Eunuch Karif was by her side and he glared at me sternly. Several other Eunuchs and Novices were in attendance and there was a constant coming and going as they did her bidding. Affairs of State were clearly an onerous burden.

'So, Senior Novice Shani,' Her Grand Ladyship greeted me pleasantly enough in a crisp but cold voice, her black twinkling eyes consuming me all the while. 'I see that His Majesty's watermill and his stone-quarry have made you grow with iron muscle, although your loins are like those of a rangy wolf!'

She laughed in that evil way of hers that always sent a cold shiver down my backbone, but I was relieved that there was no sign anywhere of the Bamboo Rod of Reformed Memory.

'When your Mistress sees you again she will marvel at how you are twice the bull you were before! Perhaps she will forgive you your disloyalty and disobedience now.'

I gulped at her mocking tone, my mouth dry. 'Yes, Your Grand Ladyship,' I replied timidly, wondering indeed when I might see my Mistress again and whether or not she might greet me warmly.

Her Grand Ladyship studied me with interest for a while before speaking again. 'You have your Royal Mistress to thank for persuading me that you were worthy of my mercy ... otherwise your scattered bones would be outside the City gates and bleached white from the sun.'

'Yes, Your Grand Ladyship.'

Her eyes narrowed. 'However, it is not her decision, but mine, that you be examined by the Imperial Physicians.'

The Imperial Physicians? Was she concerned that my health had suffered during my imprisonment?

She went on with a tone that had a menacing edge to it. 'You were spared the Room of Glorious Transformation and your manly flesh was ringed and clamped so that you might remain here in the Pavilion. This was in defiance of the law, and only because the Imperial Physicians staunched the putrid seed of your manhood so that it could never more spout its lustfulness into a woman's burrow.'

She paused for a moment, watching me darkly. 'Yet, it is rumoured that you spouted your seed nonetheless . . . and that you did so with Maidservant Li-Mei.' Her voice rose at the end and I trembled, not knowing what to reply.

But she did not demand my answer. Thus, I was spared giving her a true account that would have surely condemned me. She only went on as if the subject had tired her suddenly. 'Take him for the examination. And, if the Physicians find that their remedy was unsound, he shall be sent to the Room of Glorious Transformation.'

My heart shuddered at these words.

Oh, Mother, have I not already endured so much: the bamboo rod, the whip, the tread-wheel and the stone-quarry; and a broken heart. Yet now I must perhaps face again that terrible cut that I had thought to have escaped.

I remembered the Imperial Physicians from before. They were those same three grim-faced and surly old men whose eyes were not so much filled with venerable wisdom as with sinister purpose. They watched me as I lay on the cold stone slab in the Chamber of Body Preparation.

Brother-Yellow-Crow had whispered to me that I should not be afraid, but I was. I could recall all too vividly that dreadful silent place at the end of the Garden of Tranquillity that I had secretly visited all that time ago. The Room of Glorious Transformation with its cross-shaped ceremonial trestles might at this very moment be awaiting me. And, if so, would my life-blood gush from my severed flesh, and would my echoing screams mingle with the spirit cries of long-dead Novices?

Chief Eunuch Karif gestured at the Physicians to begin, and as one they stepped forward, peering down at me, their lips twisted with disdainful curiosity. I was not bound to the slab but my legs were held open by two Eunuchs, one of whom was Eunuch Ling.

Oh, by what gloating malice were his features set!

'The band around his sac is tightly circled and his seed-stones are no less strangled than when first he was clamped,' one of the Physicians remarked in a casual tone, reaching down and lifting me with a suddenness that made me flinch.

The two other Physicians nodded in apparent agreement, and one of them mused, 'If we had clamped a Billy-goat in that way, the animal would surely have been as dry as a barren spring.'

'And as limp as a soggy marrow,' the third Physician interrupted. He turned accusingly towards Chief Eunuch Karif.

'I cannot believe that this Novice was able to couple with one of the Maidservants, let alone spurt his seed! How should that be? We are certain that we have made the slave barren by his clamping. And, even if that were not so, the ring would deny him entry to the girl. Furthermore, he would first need to make his pizzle stiffen to a steely rod, and we doubt he can manage more than a piffling measure of rigidity and then only for a few miserable seconds.'

The other Physicians nodded solemnly, but the hand that held me turned me to one side so that they should scrutinise me closer.

'I only know what I was informed of,' Chief Eunuch Karif replied with an audible sniff. He was not one to have his word challenged or his authority undermined, but he wanted no disagreement with those who were of higher rank than himself.

At that moment there was a sound of rustling silk robes. I opened my eyes and glanced down across my chest to observe who was entering.

Oh, unwelcome image that greets fearful eyes! A black-hearted dragon is best heard in the night than encountered in the day.

Her Grand Ladyship Bo-An stood there. Behind her, even though I scarcely recognised her now, was Maidservant Huan-Yue. She was standing there respectfully, holding up the long train of Her Grand Ladyship's dress.

The Physicians bowed low, as did Karif and all the Eunuchs. Even the Physician who held me bowed, but he did so without releasing his hold of me.

'How do you find the condition of this Novice?' Her Grand Ladyship enquired imperiously. 'Shall he be safe to be permitted to reside in the Pavilion or must I presume that your doctoring of his flesh was an ineffective remedy from the beginning?'

I could tell that the Physicians were at once uneasy, their faces shifty and eyes darting to each other as if for reassurance. The man I thought to be the Senior Physician – he who held me so irreverently – replied to Her Grand Ladyship in guarded tones.

'Your Ladyship, if it pleases you, we find his clamp is tightly set, so that the fermenting of his seed is suppressed. Whatever flow there might be, it is certainly no more than a meagre trickle, kept at bay by this gold band that circles his seed-stones.'

Here he tugged at me in a twisting motion as if to demonstrate to Her Grand Ladyship the proof of his worthy diagnosis and the pitiful redundancy of my masculinity.

'If Your Royal Ladyship would care to observe, you will see how the clamp is set low down around the drop of his sac and just above the spheres.'

I saw that Her Grand Ladyship's face was the very picture of haughty disdain. Nevertheless she condescended to come nearer and bent forwards over me so that her silk-edged shadow seemed to loom above me like the wings of some evil bird of prey, and her eyes were glittering beads of wickedness as she observed me.

The Physician who held me stepped politely aside but nonetheless kept his grip on me, holding me out for her inspection. 'Madam, you will see how his spheres are drawn so tightly in by the band, such that there can be no freedom for them to spin a natural sap. They are fused together in their uselessness, Your Grand Ladyship!'

And as if to emphasise his point he tugged at me, making me gasp aloud with pain. The Physician added with attempted levity, 'Despite the bulk of his flesh, Your Grand Ladyship, he is as impotent as a withered prune, and whatever pitiful residues of masculinity he still retains they are no more than the drips from a sieve set down in front of a huge river dam!'

He cleared his throat, seeing that Her Grand Ladyship showed no sign of amusement. He went on hurriedly. 'These are our findings, Your Grand Ladyship. It is our opinion that this Novice could not have done those rumoured things. The restrictions we put upon him make him barren and limp. Even if that were not so, the ring would spoil the entry of his shaft into any woman,' he said with an air of pompous finality.

Her Grand Ladyship's face was etched now with sly malice, but she continued to study my flesh with interest, as if there were mysteries to it that she could not properly fathom. Eventually she spoke again, her voice sounding innocuous enough, but to those who knew her there was such danger lurking there. 'But I have heard several accounts that suggest he can rise boldly to become a rod of iron that would not disgrace His Majesty's favourite stallion!' she challenged. 'What say you to that?'

Now the Physicians were clearly alarmed at such searching questions. I realised then that they could not lose face. Their reputations and status were at risk. Relief swept over me like cool rainwater. If their clamping work had been in vain, how shall they now admit to failure? Hubris built on falsity is no less stubborn than rightful pride.

But Her Grand Ladyship was sly. She knew more than she was revealing, but her motive was unclear to me. I knew only that she was playing with these Royal Physicians, and perhaps she was also playing with me. A tense silence fell over the chamber. For one terrible moment I wondered whether she might question Chief Eunuch Karif, or even my Tutor-master, Brother-Yellow-Crow Kanchu, or even the hateful Eunuch Ling, but she did not. If she had, how should I have been undone. My Mistress's secret and my own would surely have been exposed.

The Senior Physician cleared his throat nervously again. 'Well, Your Grand Ladyship, we believe any such accounts to have been greatly exaggerated. He could no more rise like a stallion than a puppy-dog's tail could be made into a hunting spear! If he can rise at all, it will be nothing stronger than a mouse's whisker.'

He gave a polite little laugh. Then he bowed obsequiously and withdrew with the air of a courtier who had nothing more to say.

Her Grand Ladyship slowly straightened herself, the merest trace of a wicked grin lifting the corners of her lips. She turned then to Maidservant Huan-Yue. 'Come forward, girl,' Her Grand Ladyship commanded, beckoning her impatiently.

I saw then how terrified Huan-Yue was, but there was also a sadness about her that softened my heart. Gone was that defiant hostility of old. Her eyes were dull, as if the spark of life had left her, and she stepped timidly forwards.

'Stand there between the Novice's knees and remove your smock,' Her Grand Ladyship ordered, pointing. Her words were said with such icy calm and in a tone of such mundane normality that at first everyone in the chamber was like a frozen statue.

'Remove your smock, girl, I commanded.' Her Grand Ladyship's voice, although still with quiet patience, seemed to disturb the silent air.

I saw Huan-Yue gulp, and then very quickly she lifted her smock over her head and dropped it to the ground. She stood there in her nakedness before me now, her arms at her sides and attempting no concealment of her femininity. Her chin was raised up and she did not look down at me.

Her Grand Ladyship came to my side, her face smiling mischievously. 'Behold this girl, Shani! Is she not a pretty specimen?'

'Yes, Your Ladyship,' I mumbled from the slab, glancing up at the girl, my mind hurrying to make sense of Her Grand Ladyship's game.

Then she reached out suddenly with that sturdy hand of hers and grasped one of Huan-Yue's breasts, squeezing it tightly so that the pink-brown nipple seemed as if fit to burst.

'Are not her breasts as ripe as young peaches, and is she not as finely made as any girl could be?'

'Yes, Your Grand Ladyship,' I quickly agreed, seeing Huan-Yue's pitiful look of humbled resignation.

Her Grand Ladyship turned to the poor girl, letting go of her breast. 'Take his flesh in your hands, and knead it as if it were baking dough until it becomes not soft but hard.'

Huan-Yue barely hesitated. She was, after all, conditioned to obey without question, just as any slave was. But, if she knew the purpose of Her Grand Ladyship's perverse command, she gave no sign of it. Bending forwards slightly she reached out and took me in both hands and began to manipulate my flesh with her fingers, doing so with robust motions. Indeed it was no less than how I remembered my poor dear mother had once prepared baking dough. I moaned at this discomfort, but I could not pull away. Eunuch Ling and his startled companion held my legs tightly.

Her Grand Ladyship gave a sudden cry of delight. 'Ah! So now we shall see whether there is any truth in the rumours. If you wise Physicians are correct in your opinions, we shall surely know it soon enough!' Then she snapped at me. 'Open your eyes wide, Novice, so that you shall clearly see the pretty girl who handles you ... and so the vision of her bare body shall excite you!'

I obeyed instantly, but my eyes saw nothing that stirred me to excitement. The vision of her bare quivering breasts – one of them still bearing the pink impression of Her Ladyship's fingers – above my gaping loins was without the slightest hardening effect. All I could think of was how the girl's breasts had once pushed cosily up against my beautiful Li-Mei. And the fingers that kneaded me only softened my flesh all the more, as if it were being pounded to a wretched pulp. How much did I want to lie on my mattress and let cool air soothe my unhappy soreness.

After several minutes, during which time I writhed and groaned pathetically, Her Grand Ladyship suddenly barked out with amusement and feigned surprise, 'So, now at last we have the proof! The rumours were unfounded. Our Royal Physicians were wise in their remedy. This Novice remains like flaccid dough. He cannot rise for a pretty servant-girl who fondles his pizzle so earnestly! He is a limp bull – a freak that is as emasculated as any Eunuch who has been honoured in the Room of Glorious Transformation! Senior Novice Shani may remain in the Pavilion and his paltry flesh will have no need to be cut from him. His gold adornments have been sufficient to strangle his manly seed of passion.'

There seemed to be relief now, all round: from the Physicians, from Chief Eunuch Karif and from Brother-Yellow-Crow; and not least from poor Huan-Yue and particularly myself.

Yet, my ordeal was not quite over that day. In the Pavilion of the Divine Orchid Ladies there were always so many demons to leap out unexpectedly.

Her Grand Ladyship's eyes had narrowed now to cunning slits and when she next spoke her words came chillingly. 'However,' she began slowly, as if about to pronounce some grave matter of state. 'We must be certain that there cannot be any abuse of the

242

laws that govern us here. And, although this Novice was punished for his crime of disobedience – that of fraternising with a Maidservant in a forbidden place and late at night – we shall take additional measures to ensure he will not ever dare disobey again.'

She paused, revelling in the tension. She looked first at the Physicians and then at Chief Eunuch Karif, before speaking again. 'It has been decreed that Senior Novice Shani will henceforth wear a bell. In this way we shall know his whereabouts.' She looked down at where I still lay on the cold stone slab, which was now moist with my sweat. 'The bell shall be a weighty one and it shall be forged by a chain to the ring of your pizzle.'

When I came to my Mistress's new bedchambers, I did not know the true reason for her having moved to these more modest quarters, but I was shocked at the plainness and bland modesty of the furnishings. Only a few lacquered screens and tapestries remained, but it was night when I entered there and the lamps were dimmed, such that I could not see everything. Besides, were my nerves not stretched taut to breaking point? My only thoughts were how I should find my Mistress, whose loyalty I had so shamefully betrayed.

I stood before her bed-throne. Just as was her custom, she lay there reclining against the silk cushions. She was dressed in her same robe. Even in the dim light I could see that she was as beautiful as ever. Yet there was a sadness in her face that tugged at the strings of my heart.

'I see you, Shani.' Her voice was ever so quiet but it came as clearly as the song of a nightingale across a lily-pond.

'I see you, too, my Mistress.'

243

'Let me see more of you. I can only see how your muscles are swollen from the cruel prison work, but I cannot see if you are still my golden bull-man. Take off your Apron of Good Modesty.'

I shifted uneasily from one foot to the other, knowing how ugly the perverse bell was that hung so heavily from me. Whenever I moved it tended to swing, making an unpleasant hollow jangling noise.

'I am ashamed, Mistress,' I said flatly, not obeying. 'This vile bell is like a testament to my treacherous disloyalty . . . and I am not worthy of your forgiveness, even though I beg it from you.'

'Take off your apron,' she commanded gently.

I obeyed now, but my eyes were downcast. I stood there, knowing that she was looking at my defiled nakedness.

For a while she said nothing, but eventually she smiled. 'My poor Shani! How Her Grand Ladyship mocks you! Yet she cannot rob you of the splendour of your manhood.' She giggled suddenly. 'Why, I do believe that the weighty bell has even stretched you out! You are more of a golden bull-man than ever!'

She was silent, her smile gone, but her humour was never much to my liking. 'Come here, Shani, and sit upon my bed-silks so that we can talk. You have much to tell me. But we shall not talk of your disobedience. I forgive you that.'

I went awkwardly to her, the wretched bell jangling plaintively from its chain. She patted the bedcovers where she wanted me to sit. Holding the bell so humiliatingly in one hand, I hitched myself up beside her.

I looked into her eyes, and she into mine. A mist of tears came to both of us. She leant forwards and clasped me close to her. Her robe came open now and I felt that divine softness of her breasts as they

244

pressed against me. Already the stirring that was forbidden me surged through my loins. In an instant I was as majestic as a mast of iron.

My Mistress laughed, looking down at me and taking the bell in her hand as if it were some object of lustful intrigue. 'Despite Her Grand Ladyship, tonight I shall ring your bell and make you fly like a streak of silver lightning. And this time, my golden bull-man, you shall place your soft head against my velvet lips while I hold them open for you.'

I wept then with joy, and later I sped my passion through those velvet portals of the night. And my Mistress rang my wicked bell.

Before comes the raging torrent, how calmly runs the whispering stream.

It was like so that year. The summer was at its height when the Yellow-Pox Plague devastated the Imperial City. It devoured its helpless souls with a vengeance. The smoke from the pyres of burning corpses and torched houses obscured the horizon for many weeks. The Palace gates were sealed, as if vainly trying to keep the deadly vapours at bay. But, whatever sanctuary was offered by those high compound walls, it was little better than a cruel illusion. The virulent pox devoured royal flesh as easily as it did the flesh of humble peasants.

To begin with it was the Warrior-guards at their posts who succumbed, leaving the Palace vulnerable to the desperate milling hordes beyond the walls and gates. The Pavilion windows were closed and shuttered, the atmosphere within gloomy and foreboding. But it was not long before the first shocking signs of the disease struck.

One of the early victims was Chief Eunuch Karif. I had noticed one morning how sallow was his complexion, and there were yellow blemishes on his neck and forehead that almost matched the colour of his saffron robe. On the second day his skin had erupted into ugly pustules that burst with a foul odour. And, even though the alarmed Physicians had quickly quarantined him in his quarters, it was not soon enough. By the fourth day other Eunuchs had developed the same deadly symptoms and, once those were visited upon their victims, death was seldom far away. The stench of human effluent pervaded everywhere, and death stalked the halls and corridors with random efficiency. The afflicted sometimes dropped without apparent warning and lay where they fell, shivering and groaning in their macabre embrace with death.

After Chief Eunuch Karif died, then so did Eunuch Ling and Senior Eunuch Shek, and there were many others of my brethren. Then some of the Divine Orchid Ladies themselves became ill. Amongst those to perish were my Mistress's dear friends, Royal Sisters Xia, Yon and Lin-Yao. And there were many of the young Maidservants who succumbed. Although I saw nothing of her, Maidservant Huan-Yue – she who had so often shared the mattress of my beautiful Li-Mei – was one of them. I could surely bear her no ill-feeling now. Perhaps she had wept no less than I had when the Warrior-guards had taken Li-Mei from the Pavilion, but now that Huan-Yue was taken from there, who should weep for her?

The Yellow-Pox was indiscriminate in its wretched harvest, and the whispering spirits of the night were drowned out by the groans of the dying. Strong incense – so pungent that it stung the nose – burnt constantly, but still the sinister body-collectors in their brown cloaks came early in the morning like rustling phantoms to perform their grisly task.

It was I alone now who as a servant went to my Mistress's chambers. There she remained reclusively and I attended to her undemanding needs. Only at night would I return to my dormitory, and, with death all around me, I could only ever sleep fitfully. Each new morning would find fresh victims. My Novice brethren were dying like withered moths, and I was fearful of my own life.

Her Grand Ladyship Bo-An died in the day of the new moon. I saw her as they carried her body from her sumptuous chambers. In death her royal status gave her no favours. Her face was bloated, her skin ravaged by pustules that seeped with a noxious yellow-green fluid.

Oh, wicked Lady! How shall your cruelty issue from you now? No longer from your vicious bamboo rod, but from the suppurating pus of your flesh.

But it was that same evening that I noticed with horror those faint yellow blemishes that had appeared on my Mistress's neck.

I tended to her with such care and devotion that my past sinful disloyalty was surely now atoned. I mopped her brow and laid cooling herb poultices on her blistering sores – even on that once silk-soft budded place where my lips had met hers so delightfully before and where my eye-vent had rested before the spume of my passion had erupted.

She tossed and turned in her bedsheets and mumbled incoherently, but as the fever broke she gradually spoke more lucidly, saying things to me that warmed my heart and brought her closer to me. Once, I even leant over her and kissed her gently on the forehead and she smiled up affectionately.

Days passed but eventually she was able to rise from her bed-throne and I was overjoyed. I bathed her gently in her wash-pool. This was a duty normally performed by Maidservants, but she desired me to do it now. Her sores were almost healed and her beauty had returned gradually, even though the scars on her skin would never entirely fade away. We laughed together as I sponged her breasts and between her legs. Although her body was still as weak as a newborn foal's, there was still a spark of mischievous passion in her soul. And, when she bade me drop my Apron of Good Modesty so that she could fondle me while I tended her, I knew at once that she would soon be herself again.

'Shani, my golden bull-man! Although you are weighed down by such a cruelly heavy bell, still you can stand for me like a Naked Emperor with a Gracefully Arched Spine!'

How gleefully she laughed, and then she made me fly my spume at the gleaming soapy valley between her breasts.

Even though she had lost so much of her wealth – and on my account – she was least alive, her passion intact. Moreover, she had retained so much of other things that her Royal Sisters had never acquired.

And as for me, if the Grey Dragons of Misfortune had so often been unleashed upon me before, now they licked their wounds in their dark lair.

It was only much later that I learnt of how much my dear Mistress had sacrificed. Apart from having to give up her fine quarters with the windows overlooking the gardens and all those many exotic embroidered tapestries, beautifully lacquered screens and hanging drapes of silks, it seemed that she had given up most of her jewels to save me. Her Grand Ladyship Bo-An had taken all of the most precious of them, including my Mistress's most treasured sapphire and emerald butterfly hair-clasps. All had been gifts that she had once been given by His Imperial Majesty – or by his faithless son, Prince Fid-ram-Lo. The jewels had been kept in that pretty silver casket with gold beading that I knew so well.

It was Brother-Yellow-Crow who told me of these things in a hushed voice. Now he was Chief Eunuch and, with the new Grand Ladyship's permission, he had made me a fully fledged Eunuch.

One evening he came to my spartan chamber, and without a word he put a small silk-wrapped bundle into my hand. I was overjoyed and so was my Mistress when I was able to present her with her favourite sapphire and emerald hair-clasps. Brother-Yellow-Crow had managed to take them from the deceased Bo-An's belongings before they were returned to the Court Ministers.

The Pavilion of the Divine Orchid Ladies was never to be the same again, and we rejoiced in that celestial blessing. The new Grand Lady was a placid and kindly soul and the Bamboo Rod of Reformed Memory was seldom used thereafter at morning Assemblies. There were many new and shy young Orchid Ladies who came to the Pavilion to make up the numbers of those Royal Sisters who had succumbed to the Yellow-Pox, and there were many new Novices and Maidservants. Once more the halls and corridors had come alive to that silk-spun bustle, and the sweet fragrances of honeysuckle, jasmine and lavender filled our nostrils.

After one season of wearing it, the weighty bell was struck from my ring. Her Grand Ladyship had ordered it so, and I was grateful to her, even though my Mistress had been strangely indifferent. My punishment was finally at an end, although my gold adornments were otherwise to remain until the spirit left my body.

Oh, what friendly providence had come from that wretched plague!

Yet, still I had no word on the fate of my poor Li-Mei, and although I had twice dared to ask Brother-Yellow-Crow his face had become a grim mask of feigned indifference, and he forbade me from enquiring again. I could not summon the courage to ask my Mistress, nor did I wish to offend her.

Now that I am old and my hair is permitted to grow again, it is grey. Since those turbulent times of the Yellow-Pox, the years have passed uneventfully and I shall not complain.

My beloved Mistress has taught me so much. I have learnt the skill of writing and reading; and of making potions of herbs; and of knowing what seeds to plant in spring so that they shall sprout in summer; and of painting on fine silk screens and of weaving bold tapestries. The sand of a thousand hourglasses must have run softly down for all that time I sat at my Mistress's side. Sometimes we were silent, only exchanging affectionate smiles, but more often we laughed together and at other times we enjoyed between us what sweet vestiges of intimacy my once cruel clamp and ring still allowed.

When my Mistress became ill and I could see that she was dying, just as she knew it herself, she instructed me to bring her silver casket. With weak fumbling hands she unlocked it and handed me a small folded parchment letter. 'Shani, my dearest friend. Do not reproach me, I beg you. Nor be angry, for I was wrong to keep this from you all this while.' Her breathing was laboured and her face, although still with its residue of beauty, was pallid and drawn.

I took and read the letter, which I knew had been written on the parchment by some paid village scribe. At once I knew that the words were from Li-Mei and I was consumed by emotion, but I could not define the essence of it. How should I be angry with my dying Mistress, who had sacrificed so much? Yet here before me now were the sweet words of Li-Mei, and they came up at me as if she herself were speaking them.

My dearest Shani. I shall never know if you might ever read my words or by what means you could. I can only pray that in time this message might come safely to you on the wings of celestial angels. I pray too that you were saved the wicked cruelty of that place they took us to, and that by some Divine Fortune you were spared those horrors. As for myself I have at least survived. At first they hung me from a frame in that grim courtyard outside the cells they put us in, and then they flogged me. But the pain was more from knowing your incarceration and from not knowing what wickedness they would do to you. I was taken then to a village called Kahnja, which is on the Great River far to the North. I toiled there in shame for many years, but now I am redeemed from my disobedience and the place is my home now. There is tranquillity here, and fields that are made green by the flooding river in spring. My scars are not healed even after these few years, but a kind man has given me a roof and . . . oh, my dear Shani, be neither sad nor angry . . . but he has given me love and comfort, and I have found a quiet happiness. I pray that you might have, too. I shall remember you always with such abundance of affection.

Li-Mei.

My heart was heavy with so many things. I put down the parchment with shaking hand and looked then at my Mistress, but her eyes were already glazed. Mine were blinded by tears, yet did I not glimpse the misty veil of her spirit rising from her so peaceful body?

nexus

The leading publisher of fetish and adult fiction

TELL US WHAT YOU THINK!

Readers' ideas and opinions matter to us. Take a few minutes to fill in the questionnaire below and you'll be entered into a prize draw to win a year's worth of Nexus books (36 titles)

Terms and conditions apply – see end of questionnaire.

1. Sex: Are you male ☐ female ☐ a couple ☐?

2. Age: Under 21 ☐ 21–30 ☐ 31–40 ☐ 41–50 ☐ 51–60 ☐ over 60 ☐

3. Where do you buy your Nexus books from?

☐ A chain book shop. If so, which one(s)?

_____

☐ An independent book shop. If so, which one(s)?

_____

☐ A used book shop/charity shop

☐ Online book store. If so, which one(s)?

_____

4. How did you find out about Nexus books?

☐ Browsing in a book shop

☐ A review in a magazine

☐ Online

☐ Recommendation

☐ Other _____

5. In terms of settings, which do you prefer? (Tick as many as you like)

☐ Down to earth and as realistic as possible

☐ Historical settings. If so, which period do you prefer?

_____

☐ Fantasy settings – barbarian worlds

- ☐ Completely escapist/surreal fantasy
- ☐ Institutional or secret academy
- ☐ Futuristic/sci fi
- ☐ Escapist but still believable
- ☐ Any settings you dislike?

_____

- ☐ Where would you like to see an adult novel set?

_____

6. In terms of storylines, would you prefer:

- ☐ Simple stories that concentrate on adult interests?
- ☐ More plot and character-driven stories with less explicit adult activity?
- ☐ We value your ideas, so give us your opinion of this book:

_____

_____

_____

7. In terms of your adult interests, what do you like to read about? (Tick as many as you like)

- ☐ Traditional corporal punishment (CP)
- ☐ Modern corporal punishment
- ☐ Spanking
- ☐ Restraint/bondage
- ☐ Rope bondage
- ☐ Latex/rubber
- ☐ Leather
- ☐ Female domination and male submission
- ☐ Female domination and female submission
- ☐ Male domination and female submission
- ☐ Willing captivity
- ☐ Uniforms
- ☐ Lingerie/underwear/hosiery/footwear (boots and high heels)
- ☐ Sex rituals
- ☐ Vanilla sex
- ☐ Swinging
- ☐ Cross-dressing/TV

☐ Enforced feminisation
☐ Others – tell us what you don't see enough of in adult fiction:

_____
_____
_____

8. Would you prefer books with a more specialised approach to your interests, i.e. a novel specifically about uniforms? If so, which subject(s) would you like to read a Nexus novel about?

_____
_____
_____

9. Would you like to read true stories in Nexus books? For instance, the true story of a submissive woman, or a male slave? Tell us which true revelations you would most like to read about:

_____
_____
_____

10. What do you like best about Nexus books?

_____
_____

11. What do you like least about Nexus books?

_____
_____

12. Which are your favourite titles?

_____
_____

13. Who are your favourite authors?

_____
_____

14. **Which covers do you prefer? Those featuring:**
    (tick as many as you like)

☐ Fetish outfits
☐ More nudity
☐ Two models
☐ Unusual models or settings
☐ Classic erotic photography
☐ More contemporary images and poses
☐ A blank/non-erotic cover
☐ What would your ideal cover look like?

_____

15. **Describe your ideal Nexus novel in the space provided:**

_____
_____
_____
_____

16. **Which celebrity would feature in one of your Nexus-style fantasies?**
    We'll post the best suggestions on our website – anonymously!

_____

THANKS FOR YOUR TIME

Now simply write the title of this book in the space below and cut out the
questionnaire pages. Post to: Nexus, Marketing Dept., Thames Wharf Studios,
Rainville Rd, London W6 9HA

Book title: _____

TERMS AND CONDITIONS

To be published in August 2006

CARNAL POSSESSION
Yvonne Strickland

Glamour model and writer of erotica, Joanna took the old house for peace and quiet. But her occupation attracts the lustful attentions of a perverse local coven, whose interests and practices are not entirely at odds with Joanna's strong but hidden sexual urges. Soon, under their influence, her bizarre fetish-fantasies become a reality of strict bondage and sexual power games.

£6.99   ISBN 0352 34062 2

BIDDING TO SIN
Rosita Varón

Just when everyone is depending on her to win a vital contract, Melanie Brooks, a talented manager of Bermont and Cuthbertson's creative design team suddenly finds herself pitched into a tumultuous sexual adventure that makes her head spin and her backside sting. Her normal cool competence seems a thing of the past as the problems escalate out of control and she becomes immersed in an explicit world that threatens to sabotage her team's future.

£6.99   ISBN 0 352 34063 0

THE DOMINO ENIGMA
Cyrian Amberlake

At Estwych Josephine had learned the value of obedience. She had tasted iron and leather; she had been abased and degraded and exalted to eternity. Her training had hardly begun.

Summoned by the double blank to a life of subjection at the hands of the unknown masters, Josephine must learn to surrender completely. To surrender her body – and her soul.

In this sequel to *The Domino Tattoo,* Josephine Morrow undergoes the hardest trials she has ever known – and survives the greatest rewards.

£6.99   ISBN 0 352 34064 9

If you would like more information about Nexus titles, please visit our website at www.nexus-books.co.uk, or send a large stamped addressed envelope to:
  Nexus, Thames Wharf Studios,
  Rainville Road, London W6 9HA

nexus

This information is correct at time of printing. For up-to-date information, please visit our website at www.nexus-books.co.uk

All books are priced at £6.99 unless another price is given.

- - - - - - ✂ -

Please send me the books I have ticked above.

Name ....

Address ....

....

....

.... Post code ....

Send to: **Virgin Books Cash Sales, Thames Wharf Studios, Rainville Road, London W6 9HA**

US customers: for prices and details of how to order books for delivery by mail, call 888-330-8477.

Please enclose a cheque or postal order, made payable to **Nexus Books Ltd**, to the value of the books you have ordered plus postage and packing costs as follows:

UK and BFPO – £1.00 for the first book, 50p for each subsequent book.

Overseas (including Republic of Ireland) – £2.00 for the first book, £1.00 for each subsequent book.

If you would prefer to pay by VISA, ACCESS/MASTERCARD, AMEX, DINERS CLUB or SWITCH, please write your card number and expiry date here:

....

Please allow up to 28 days for delivery.

Signature ....

Our privacy policy

We will not disclose information you supply us to any other parties. We will not disclose any information which identifies you personally to any person without your express consent.

From time to time we may send out information about Nexus books and special offers. Please tick here if you do *not* wish to receive Nexus information. ☐

- - - - - - ✂ -